HE HELD HER ARM TIGHTLY, WITH URGENCY

"I hate this business that's between us," Cleve said, searching her eyes as though he might find concurrence.

"Cleve..."

Before she could say more, his mouth descended on hers, taking it certainly, but tenderly. Diana stood frozen with surprise as his arms wrapped around her. The caress of his lips and his familiar masculine aroma instantly breached her defenses. Diana accepted his kiss without thinking, but when he whispered his desire for her, she came to her senses.

She pushed him away. "No, Cleve, I can't. Don't you understand?" she implored, tears brimming in her eyes.

"I know how you feel about that girl, but..." He grasped her shoulder, but she pushed his hand away.

"Don't make it any harder than it is, please." Without another word Diana turned and ran.

1.35

ABOUT THE AUTHOR

Janice Kaiser is no stranger to exotic lands. This California author has traveled through Asia, Africa, Europe and the South Pacific, and has chosen vibrant Honduras for the setting of her third Superromance—a real sizzler. When she's not hard at work writing (two more Superromances are coming out soon!), Janice's children, Matthew and Sybil, and husband, Ronn, help keep her hours filled.

Books by Janice Kaiser

HARLEQUIN SUPERROMANCE
187–HARMONY
209–LOTUS MOON

These books may be available at your local bookseller.

Don't miss any of our special offers. Write to us at the following address for information on our newest releases.

Harlequin Reader Service
901 Fuhrmann Blvd., P.O. Box 1397, Buffalo, NY 14240
Canadian address: P.O. Box 603,
Fort Erie, Ont. L2A 9Z9

Janice Kaiser

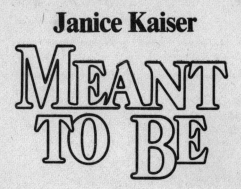

MEANT TO BE

Harlequin Books

TORONTO • NEW YORK • LONDON
AMSTERDAM • PARIS • SYDNEY • HAMBURG
STOCKHOLM • ATHENS • TOKYO • MILAN

Published August 1986

First printing June 1986

ISBN 0-373-70224-8

Printed in Canada

For my first hero, my father.

PROLOGUE

THE GRAY-HAIRED WOMAN looked up from her needle-point when the man sitting opposite her fell silent. He was staring into the fire crackling nearby, his expression wistful and dreamy. She watched him for a moment, thinking how handsome he was and how, in his uniform, he reminded her of her own husband when they first met nearly thirty years before. Cleve Emerson, her nephew by marriage, was now forty, but from the perspective of her years he seemed a young man nonetheless.

Sensing his aunt's eyes on him, Cleve turned and smiled at the woman. There was apology on his face for having let the conversation lag.

"Judging by your expression," she said, returning to her needlework, "you were back in Honduras, probably on one of those operations you aren't supposed to talk about."

He laughed softly. "Are you referring to the soldiering or the women?"

Sarah Emerson shot her nephew an admonishing look. "Certainly not the women. I really can't imagine that those peasant girls have much attraction for you. No, Cleve, that was the nostalgia of a soldier on your face. I've seen it too often on Paul to be fooled."

The man turned back to the fire, silenced by his aunt's insight and wisdom.

"Surely there aren't any women there worthy of your attention . . . serious attention, I mean."

"No, you're right. Not serious attention."

She saw the muscles of Cleve's jaw tense as he stared into the fire. "Do you ever regret what happened with Carolyn? Do you ever miss her, Cleve?"

His soft brown eyes registered surprise, then respect as he returned her gaze. "As a matter of fact she went through my mind just then. I think there's always regret over a marriage gone bad." Cleve Emerson leaned forward and picked up the glass of bourbon on the coffee table between them. He drained most of the liquid. "But I don't miss her—it's been eight years. We were never really happy, Sarah. She wasn't cut out to be an army wife. She hated my career, my life. And . . . there was no love lost, especially at the end."

She studied her nephew; he looked so much like her husband. The hair and trim mustache was the blondish chestnut brown of the Emersons, the jaw strong and square, the frame large, angular, muscular. Cleve had his mother's eyes, though. The Emersons had blue eyes, coldly handsome pale eyes. Not at all like Cleve's. Sarah had always thought of him as being different than the others because of the softness of his brown eyes, but deep down he was his father's son. His temperament was one-hundred-percent Emerson. No denying that. If his spirit was any different, it didn't show.

"I know that Carolyn herself means nothing to you now, but don't you ever hunger for a relationship with a woman who understands your career? I mean, how can you be satisfied with liaisons with nameless girls in whatever corner of the world you find yourself in?"

Cleve smiled indulgently, and Sarah realized she had overstepped her bounds. She dismissed him with a wave of her hand. "No, I won't lecture you. Don't worry."

The man unconsciously tipped his glass, draining a final drop or two of the bourbon into his mouth.

Sarah Emerson rose to her feet and, taking the glass from Cleve's hand, went to refill it. "I do wish you'd stay for Thanksgiving, though," she said from across the room. "You haven't taken a full leave in years, and it's only a few days away. What can be so pressing in Honduras that you have to go back just two days out of the hospital?"

"I shouldn't have left to begin with. If that quack in Panama hadn't panicked and misdiagnosed me, I never would have left Central America."

"I don't care what you say. Walter Reed is one of the best hospitals in the world, and they were right to have sent you here for tests."

She had returned and was handing Cleve his drink when they both heard a door slam. "That must be Paul," she said, turning toward the kitchen. "I didn't even hear his car."

A moment later a tall distinguished man entered the room. He wore the uniform of a major general in the army. He had already removed his hat and was unbuckling the belt of his topcoat when his wife approached.

"Well, well. How's the patient?" he asked Cleve as he kissed Sarah on the cheek and handed her his hat and coat.

"I'm fine. Not a thing wrong with me," Cleve said, rising to his feet. The men shook hands heartily as Sarah stepped into the entry hall. Paul and Sarah had been all the family Cleve had had in years. He had been a boy when his father had died in Korea, and barely out of school when his mother had passed away. The man he now embraced with gruff affection was the only father he had known.

The men sat down by the fire, and Paul accepted the drink his wife handed him. "What are your plans, Cleve?"

"I'll be leaving for Panama tomorrow from Andrews, then on to Honduras."

"Too bad. I was hoping you'd stay for a while."

The men touched glasses in a silent toast. "Just as well that I get back. The longer I stay the harder it would be to leave."

Paul Emerson studied his nephew's face. "So what are you doing your last night stateside?"

"Matter of fact, I was planning on going to a party."

"Oh? One of the clubs?"

"No, Jack Dawson invited me to an open house his firm is having tonight. I called to see if he was free for dinner, and since he was tied up with this party, he invited me to come by." Cleve drew on his bourbon. "I figured what the hell, it'd be good to see Jack again."

Paul Emerson's face was wrinkled in contemplation. "Dawson, Dawson..."

"Jack and I were together at the Point. He left the army after twelve years for a career in consulting."

"Oh yes, of course. Jack Dawson. Does a lot of work with defense contractors—feasibility studies for weapons systems, that sort of thing."

"Yeah. That's Jack. Congress sometimes looks to him for second opinions when they don't trust your Pentagon experts. Now that he's on the outside, his word seems to carry a lot of weight."

A glance at his uncle told Cleve that the usual speech was formulating in the older man's mind on how the military was losing too many of its good young officers. He stood up, hoping to divert the general's attention. "I probably should be leaving soon," he said as he wandered toward the front window.

"I'll call a cab for you now, then. If you're going downtown I'd suggest you get a start. There's snow in the air. I could smell it."

"CARE FOR ANOTHER DRINK, sir?"

Cleve Emerson swirled the ice cubes in his glass, drank the last of the bourbon-tainted water, then handed it to the girl. Just as he did she was knocked toward him by someone pushing their way through the crowded room. Her full breasts pressed against the front of his uniform, and Cleve glanced down the gap in her dress.

The girl's bright red lips curled coquettishly, and she looked up at him through heavy, dark lashes. Cleve's hand, holding the empty cocktail glass, was between them, just beneath her chin, and when she was slow in pulling away, he lightly ran the tip of his little finger across the skin in the opening of her dress. She seemed to like the gesture because the expression on her face was brazenly inviting.

"I think there's something I'd like even more than another drink," he said in a low, husky voice.

The girl arched one eyebrow. "Such as?"

"Such as getting to know you a little better." He glanced down the front of her dress again.

She gave a little laugh, then took Cleve's glass. "It'll be bourbon then?"

"Bourbon now, maybe dinner and dancing later."

She shot the officer a look, then searched his eyes. When the girl decided that he was in fact making a serious proposition, she turned abruptly and headed toward the bar. Cleve let his eyes drift down the curvaceous lines of the woman, which were amply revealed in the tight nylon dress.

She stopped fifteen feet away to take another drink order and offered Cleve a profile view of her body. He admired her for a moment, deciding the girl's breasts were exquisite. Their mere existence tantalized him, and when she turned her head and looked at him, half smiling, half challenging, he suspected that he would sample her feminine charms before the night was through.

After a moment the waitress disappeared into the crowd and Cleve contemplated his good fortune. Except for the nurses in the hospital in Panama and Washington, he had not been close enough to touch a *norte-americana* for more than a year. The amply endowed, fair-skinned woman he had just flirted with had a much more potent effect on him than she otherwise might, because she was the first in such a long time.

Cleve waited impatiently for the girl to return with his drink, letting his eyes meander around the room. Most of the people were young professionals in their late twenties to early forties. It was the usual Washington crowd; earnest, rather full of self-importance, playing their status and prestige games. The women wore suits just as the men, affected the same expressions and had totally repressed their sexuality.

Snatching a stuffed mushroom off a passing hors d'oeuvre tray and popping it into his mouth, Cleve realized that in his own way he was feeling as smug as any of the others. But there was a difference. His objective at the moment was a little more basic, and he couldn't care less about politics, networking or rubbing shoulders.

Finally he spotted the girl making her way back toward him. Cleve noticed for the first time consciously that she was a blonde. Her hair was cut short in a fashionable style that didn't appeal to him, but that sort of thing hardly mattered. She was available.

He decided that she was in her early twenties, substantially younger than he, but not so much as to make him uncomfortable. Women over nineteen blurred in his mind into a single, homogeneous group. And the passing years seemed to make the routine come more easily to him.

The girl stopped to deliver another drink and Cleve again admired her body, realizing how much he wanted this anonymous female. They had not exchanged more than a dozen words, but he could almost envision the scenario that would be played out between them.

She started toward him again, her eyes unwilling to meet his, her expression blasé. She expected him to work a little for it—that was apparent. Cleve's eyes were locked on hers. He was like a serpent, deadly certain of its prey.

"Bourbon?" she stated matter-of-factly, and extended the drink.

When Cleve didn't immediately take the proffered glass, her eyes finally engaged his.

"Well?" he said, as his hand slipped around the glass and the fingers that held it.

"Well, what?" the girl replied uncomfortably, extracting her hand.

"I was hoping you'd be my guest for dinner," he said simply. "I find this party and these people terribly boring."

The waitress studied Cleve. She wasn't smiling now. After a moment, though, his practiced charm got through to her. She lowered her eyes, but didn't comment. He knew he had her.

"Well?"

"I've gotta work."

"The party will be over in an hour or so."

"I have to clean up after."

"I can wait."

She squinted through her heavy lashes. "Where you from...Mr. Emerson?" she asked as she read the nameplate on the breast of his uniform. "You married?" she added hastily.

"I'm not married, but I should warn you about something." He gave her his best disarming smile. "As an officer and a gentleman I have to tell you that I just got back to the States. I've been in the jungle for more than a year, and it's been that long since I've even seen a creature half as beautiful as you."

The girl's lips twitched into a smile. The little laugh that bubbled up was one of amusement. "I never quite heard it that way before."

"It's true...Lynette," Cleve said, noticing the girl's name tag. "Honestly."

She looked him up and down, obviously impressed with his athletic good looks in the uniform and his handsome, enticing face. "So maybe you're a wild man..."

"That's a risk you'll have to take."

"I'm not supposed to. I could lose my job."

"We'll be discreet."

Lynette looked around her. The room was so crowded and noisy they were in virtual isolation. Cleve could see time was on his side; she couldn't stand there all evening talking to him, and it was apparent she didn't want to walk away without resolving the matter. Still, she was resisting more than he had anticipated.

"Look, Lynette," he said, leaning forward and whispering in her ear, "if you're as much a sucker for champagne and good French food as I am, there's no way you can say no." Cleve took in the aroma of her strong, cheap perfume, and it doubly aroused him. He tried to calm himself, knowing being overeager would unnerve her.

"Well, all right . . . Mr. . . . ."

"Cleve."

She smiled. "All right, Cleve, for dinner then."

"Wonderful. I'll wait downstairs in the lobby after the party."

Lynette gave Cleve a provocative look and turned on her heel. "Okay."

As the young waitress disappeared, Cleve heaved a silent sigh. *God is good to the virtuous,* he thought, and sipped his drink.

"Cleve Emerson, you sonofagun, here you are!"

Cleve swung around to the voice. "Jack! Good to see you!"

The men greeted each other warmly, shaking hands.

Jack Dawson was a nice-looking man, the same age as Cleve. His blow-dried hair was long in comparison with Cleve's and was starting to gray at the temples. His dark horn-rimmed glasses gave him a scholarly, intelligent look, quite different from the image of him Cleve carried in his mind from their Vietnam days.

He smiled at his friend and drew on his bourbon. Cleve took in Jack's dark three-piece suit, the expensive Italian shoes and gold watch in one languorous glance. "Jeez, Dawson, you've become a Washington dandy."

The other man laughed and slapped his friend on the arm. "Look who's talking! When you going to get out of the hero business and join the real world?"

"Hell, I'm good for one more war—or at least a police action."

"What are you up to in Honduras?"

"Just what you'd imagine."

Jack nodded. "Well, nobody really cares what you Rangers do down there, as long as no one gets killed and you keep a low profile."

Cleve grinned. "Yeah, that's what I keep hearing."

"Seriously, what's keeping you in?" Jack glanced at the silver lieutenant-colonel insignia on Cleve Emerson's shoulder. "You that hungry for a star?"

"Good Lord, Jack, I'm not a bird colonel yet."

The other dismissed the comment with a wave of his hand. "That's just a formality, Cleve. Frankly, I'm surprised you haven't gotten it already."

"Matter of fact, Paul told me he heard I'm up for promotion this time."

"Hey, good for you, Cleve. Congratulations!"

"The list's not out yet, so congratulations are premature."

They lapsed into silence, and Cleve glanced around the crowded suite of offices that represented Jack Dawson's new life. He saw a nostalgic, almost affectionate expression on his friend's face. "Nice place you've got here, Jack."

"Listen, pal, whenever you're ready there's a place for you here. We can always use an extra Rhodes scholar."

Cleve smiled and took a long drink. "Anything for an old army buddy, eh?"

Jack frowned. "Hey, wise guy, I'm dead serious."

Cleve could see he was. "Thanks, Jack. I'll keep it in mind."

"It's not a bad life. Believe me."

The comment reminded him of his conversation with his aunt that evening and her questions about Carolyn. Cleve and she had been friends with Jack and his wife when they were all young marrieds in the army. "By the way, how's Pammy?"

"Just terrific!" Jack enthused. "She's here tonight. Obviously you haven't seen her, you'd have noticed." The man chuckled. "Number three's in the oven. She's out to here," he said, holding his hands out in front of his stomach.

Cleve laughed. "Well, congratulations to *you*. Hell, three kids. I haven't even seen the second one yet."

"It's your own damn fault. Sybil's two years old, and you've had a standing invitation to visit...."

"Yeah, I know, but I don't have to tell you how it is. I would like to see Pammy, though. Where is she?"

The men looked around the room, craning their necks.

"She might be in one of the other rooms. I'll go find her, Cleve. Pam knew you were going to be here. She's anxious to see you, too." He turned away.

Cleve watched his friend work his way through the crowd. He smiled at the thought of Pam Dawson. She and Jack had been the attendants at his wedding. Cleve realized that it was that connection with Carolyn that made the prospect of seeing Pam bittersweet, but he wanted to see her anyway.

Being the wife of his best friend, Pam was Cleve's connection with respectability, with the life he himself had once had with Carolyn. He was especially happy for the Dawsons now that Jack was a civilian—the army could be hell on a marriage. That was the thing about it he disliked most. The army deprived him of the sort of relationship he would like, but which was damned hard to find. As he drank his bourbon he wondered how much longer he could make do with the Lynettes of the world.

Cleve was languishing in his self-deprecation, his emotional courage bolstered by the bourbon fog that had

enveloped his brain, when her face leaped out at him. She
was immersed in conversation, just another being in the
alien crowd of humanity surrounding him, but her careful, studied beauty jolted him nonetheless, like a church
bell in the frozen night.

Cleve Emerson consciously closed his sagging mouth,
blinking through the smoke at the incredible female vision standing not twenty feet from him. There was a
narrow corridor in the sea of bodies between them
through which he was able to observe her from head to
toe. She was tall, willowy. Her dark hair was parted in the
middle and pulled back into a close, elegant chignon.
Pearl stud earrings adorned each delicate earlobe, and
her wide mouth added sensuality, softening her classical
beauty.

The woman's turquoise eyes were as intelligent as they
were beautiful and Cleve watched her expressive face with
fascination, noting the ironic quiver of her lip just before she laughed and the lilt of her eyebrow as she listened. When she smiled, she smiled completely, her face
at once joyful and demure. Cleve grinned with her, an
unseen and uninvited participant in the little tête-à-tête
across the room.

He knew at once there was magic in the woman, a
mystique that transcended her obvious beauty. She was
markedly more feminine than the other women in the
room, though she, too, wore a suit. What was it that set
her apart? Was it the provocative plunge of the deep vee
of her cream silk blouse that accentuated, rather than
hid, her sexuality? If so, there was nothing obvious about
her statement. The brown gabardine of the tailored jacket
and slim skirt were elegant in their simplicity. Was it her
statuesque figure, her almost regal demeanor? No. Cleve
decided her warmth and engaging manner touched him

even more than her sophistication—a quality in women he usually associated with icy aloofness. Whatever it was about her, it was intangible, a masterful composition of feminine qualities that touched his inner being.

"Goddamn," he muttered under his breath as he continued to behold her. And then almost as though she had heard him, she raised her eyes and engaged his, a touch of surprise on her face at discovering the visual eavesdropper.

Cleve felt as though that gap in the crowd had been made by divine intervention, a sort of parting of the sea, enabling him to discover the incredibly fascinating creature at the other end. He was ready to walk down that human corridor, a latter-day Moses in uniform, when his name was hurled at him from behind. The elegant female across the room, perhaps intrigued by the officer's candid observation of her, had been returning his scrutiny and only now turned away, their communion finally broken.

Cleve felt a tugging at his elbow as his name assaulted him again, and he turned to the smiling face and rosy cheeks of Pam Dawson.

"Pammy!" he exclaimed, and he bent down and took the pregnant woman into his arms, kissing her on the cheek.

"Cleve, it's so good to see you! I can't believe it!"

"How long has it been?"

"Much too long. You look just terrific," she said, beaming.

Cleve smiled broadly and Pam Dawson reached up and ran her finger along his mustache, giggling like a schoolgirl. "Where'd you get this?"

"Had it for years, Pam."

"You see! It's been much too long."

"Hell," Cleve replied, gesturing toward the woman's protruding stomach. "I haven't even seen the second one."

Pam turned to her husband, who had been watching them in silence. "When shall we have him over? How's dinner tomorrow night?"

"I'm afraid the good colonel will be back in Central America by then, Pam. Cleve is leaving in the morning."

"Oh, shoot!" she said in exasperation, and turned to the officer.

Cleve had been only half aware of the little interchange between husband and wife. He was looking again at the woman across the room, who seemed once more oblivious to his existence, making him wonder if their fragile communion had only been the prodigy of his fertile imagination. He engaged the pouting woman at his side again.

"Cleve, are you really going so soon?"

"Afraid so, Pammy."

"Why did you wait till now to call?"

"Eh . . . I was in the hospital. This wasn't leave."

"Yes, Jack told me about that." She gave her husband a forlorn look.

"Listen," Jack said to his wife, "you talk to Cleve, I'll get you something to drink. Want some club soda?"

"Okay. Just a little though."

"How about you, Cleve?" Jack asked. "Can I get you more Scotch?"

"Bourbon," he replied, and extended his glass. A look passed between the men. Both knew Cleve was the only person in *this* crowd drinking bourbon.

"So," Cleve said to Pam as he gently pulled her around to a position where he could see the elegant brunet over her shoulder, "tell me about your little girl."

During Pam Dawson's monologue that followed, Cleve caught the brunet's eye twice more, but, unlike the first time, the resulting contact was so fleeting no one other than he with his well-traveled eye might have seen it. His plotting mind was deeply into an analysis of the delicate web of mutual interest and its portent when Pam stopped in midsentence and looked at his inattentive face.

Caught in the act, he smiled apologetically.

"Is she a blonde or a redhead?"

Cleve leaned down and kissed Pam on the cheek. "Sorry, doll, I've been in the boonies for more than a year."

"At least you're consistent, Cleve." She laughed good-naturedly.

"Since you're so understanding . . . there's a gorgeous brunet in a brown suit with her hair up, about seven or eight meters directly behind you. When I give the word, would you turn around and tell me if you know her?"

"Sure, Mr. Bond," she chided. "Blink your left eye when the coast is clear."

Cleve chuckled. "You're a good sport, Pam." He saw that the woman had turned to another person who had joined her group, and he nodded to Pam. "Okay, have a look."

She casually looked back, then, after a moment, turned to Cleve again. "Sorry, never have seen her before in my life."

"Nice work, lady," he said in mock derision.

"What's the matter, tired of the *señoritas*?"

"In a word, yes."

"Not enough variety?"

"Well . . ." he replied, his mouth twisting into a grin, "I'll admit to several of them."

Pam laughed, and Cleve again caught the eye of the mysterious creature on the far shore.

"So, what are you going to do, Cleve, abduct the poor girl and take her back to Honduras with you?"

"Don't I wish."

Pam shook her head. "It's your own damn fault. If you'd settle down instead of—"

"Hey, Pammy, you related to my Aunt Sarah by any chance?" He winked, and she was duly chastened.

There was laughter across the room, and Cleve looked over and saw a broad, happy smile on the face of the brunet. In spite of his protracted admiration of her, she didn't look his way, and he felt a pang of resentment.

"She really pushed your button, didn't she, Cleve?"

"Yeah. Sad, isn't it?"

"Maybe she'd like a pen pal from Central America," Pam teased.

"You're all heart, lady."

She turned around and looked at the woman again. "Maybe the direct approach would work. She might be a sucker for a uniform."

"Well, I think some subtlety is called for, but you're right about one thing—I won't get anywhere from here." Cleve took his eyes off the willowy brunet long enough to clasp Pam's hands and kiss her on the cheek. "Listen, doll, you have a nice baby, hear?"

She smiled and nodded.

"Oh, and thanks for the advice." He turned to walk across the room just as Jack squeezed past some people and took Cleve by the arm.

"Cleve, I want you to meet somebody. This is my partner, Alan Duckett."

Cleve turned to greet a shorter, plumper version of Jack Dawson.

"Alan, this is Cleve Emerson. We were at the Point together."

Cleve took the man's hand and glanced at Pam, who was about to break into laughter. "I've been telling Cleve he ought to get into consulting..." he heard Jack saying, and realized there was no gracious escape. He sadly stole a glance in the direction of the woman and saw that she was starting to move through the crowd with her companions.

Damn, he pronounced to himself, and tried not to look as crestfallen as he felt. He looked at Jack Dawson's empty hands and realized that his friend had even forgotten the bourbon.

A moment later, the full-breasted cocktail waitress slid by and gave Cleve a knowing smile, which he returned. He pretended to be listening to Jack and Alan Duckett with rapt attention, but he was in fact trying to console himself with thoughts of the waitress, whose name he'd already forgotten.

Once Cleve had extricated himself from Jack and his partner, he wandered the suite of offices looking for the sophisticated brunet, but she had disappeared. He cursed his bad fortune and drank more bourbon in a futile effort to drown his disappointment. He never got to the point of deciding what he would have said or done with her had he found her, but he would have liked to test her mettle—and in the process his own.

When the party started winding down, Cleve sighed with relief, whispered a few words of reinforcement to the waitress, bid Jack and Pam farewell, then made his way downstairs to the lobby to wait.

He was surprised to find that snow was falling, though Paul had told him it would, and he contented himself with thoughts of the amply endowed blonde once he'd plied her with champagne. He was picturing a modest little studio apartment with one faucet dripping in the kitchen and another in the bath when a group of people exited the elevator with indifferent, noisy laughter.

Cleve turned his whiskey-numbed attention to them and was struck once again by the crystalline beauty of the woman who had entranced him earlier. She hardly paid him notice, walking past him in a full-length fox coat, her arm linked through that of a faceless twit like all the others he had seen upstairs.

There were two men and another woman in the group, all talking rather loudly, as though the party had followed them into the outside world. They stopped at the doors, and one man and the other woman made their farewells. "Good night, Diana, Tom," he heard them say as they left.

Diana! The name jolted his foggy mind just as her face had earlier. Her back was to him now, her head nearly hidden by the fullness of her collar, which she held against her cheeks and ears. *Diana,* he screamed into the turbulence of his thoughts.

The couple was talking softly, their voices, but not their words, audible to him. They seemed to be discussing arrangements for getting home. Finally the man stepped toward the door. "I'll pull up right in front. Watch for my car," he said, and stepped into the night.

They were momentarily alone in the drafty, cold lobby, she staring out the glass wall at the falling snow, he watching her, his mind reeling, cursing his bourbon as he never had before. Words repeatedly formed on his lips, only to be lost in his alcoholic haze.

In twenty-four hours he would be thousands of miles away, separated physically as well as spiritually from this unknown and obsessing creature. Strangely, his villa at the air base in Honduras, his bed, the familiar face of his housekeeper were more real than this woman a few yards from him. She was no more real than a dream. His world was verdant Honduras with its pungent smells: beans cooking and tortillas, and jet fuel wafting in his window at night.

Cleve was feeling frustration because of his helplessness when he finally noticed the reflection of the woman's face in the black glass before her. She had been watching him silently, secretly, during the confused ramble of his thinking, just as he had watched her at the party. When he engaged her reflection, she abruptly turned away. Had she watched him out of curiosity, out of fear, admiration?

He wanted to ask her, to respond to her oblique overture, but before he had gathered himself a car glided to a stop at the curb and the woman, Diana, stepped silently into the snowy night.

CHAPTER ONE

DIANA HILLYER WATCHED the fly make a lazy circle over the table, then light on the far edge. After remaining immobile for a time, it casually rubbed its hind legs together, made a desultory journey across the oilcloth, then flew off, buzzing around her head. She took an impatient swipe at the insect, then gave the two men in the doorway a sideward glance. She knew they had been watching her.

Diana had grown more worried than impatient during the past half hour. Something must have gone wrong. Raul and the girl, Elena, should have been there long ago. What's worse, the men who had been standing around staring at her had developed more than idle curiosity. She felt her vulnerability growing by the minute.

The short waiter in the dirty white jacket who had been serving her sauntered by Diana's table, picked up the empty Coke bottle, drained the last drops into her glass and pointed at the bottle. *"¿Más, señora?"* he asked in an emphatic voice, as though the volume would make his meaning clear to her.

Diana shook her head. *"No, gracias."* She hesitated. *"Cuenta, por favor."*

The waiter smiled at her awkward pronunciation, but acknowledged the request for the bill with a nod. The blank spot in the top row of his teeth disappeared with his fading smile. Taking the empty bottle, he went back into the kitchen.

Out of the corner of her eye she saw that one of the men who had been watching her was approaching her table. She didn't look up until he was standing opposite her. There was a grin on his face.

"Buenos días, señorita," he said with exaggerated politeness.

Diana nodded hesitantly, but her failure to greet him had no deterring effect. With a rather bold motion he pulled a chair out, spun it around and straddled it, facing her.

She turned anxiously toward the kitchen, but no one was in sight. Only rapid palaver in Spanish, unintelligible to her, echoed from the noisy room. She faced her interlocutor again.

"Bonita," he said, pronouncing the word with care. "Pretty," he added in English.

She eyed him warily. He was in his late thirties or early forties, rather dark complexioned with wavy black hair. He squinted at Diana through the smoke drifting into his face from the cigarette perched between two extended fingers.

"You speak *Inglés*?" he asked, tapping the ashes onto the concrete floor.

"Yes, I do," she replied harshly. Her face hardened with her words, finding courage in the opportunity to express indignation at the man's intrusion. "I didn't invite you to sit at my table."

The man's reaction was ambiguous, and Diana was uncertain whether he understood her. She turned toward the kitchen, but the waiter was not to be seen.

"I speak *Inglés*," he said matter-of-factly.

"Why don't you leave then?"

He seemed unmoved by her question, and Diana decided he either didn't understand her or was incredibly arrogant. "Where es your husband?" he pronounced with difficulty.

"My friends are coming soon."

"Maybe . . . friends not come?"

It was an obvious ploy, but the question flickered through her mind whether he might know something, because she had begun to wonder if Raul and the girl had left without her. "No," she said with assurance. "They're coming."

The man was staring at the front of Diana's shirt. The curl of his lip told her he was speculating about her breasts. As she watched him, he stood up slowly and pulled his chair next to hers. His eyes raked up and down her body.

Diana's thoughts began racing. In an attempt to appear indifferent toward him she reached for her glass but, before she was able to grasp it, the man had snatched her wrist, not hurtfully, but firmly. He smiled into her eyes, and his thumb played with the flesh on the back of her hand.

Diana tried to pull away, but he held her with surprising strength, using just enough force to keep her from escaping. He was amused. "You like Honduras men?"

"Not you!" she snapped. "Let go of me!"

He laughed more loudly and glanced at his friend, who remained at the door, grinning.

Suddenly Diana imagined herself being dragged outside and into an alley. She jerked her arm as forcefully as she could, but to no avail. Then, clenching her free fist, she swung at the man's head but he deflected the blow, grabbing her other arm. His face was inches from hers, and the stale tobacco smell of his breath filled her nostrils. Diana was terrified.

"Help!" she screamed.

The racket in the back room ceased. A fat man with a large drooping mustache appeared at the kitchen door. He called several words to her captor, then returned to the kitchen.

"Please, help!" Diana called after him, struggling and pulling with all her might.

All at once the front door to the restaurant flew open, banging hard against the stucco wall. A Honduran in fatigues carrying an M-16 filled the doorway, then another entered pointing his weapon at Diana and her attacker. Before she could assimilate what was happening, an officer, a short thin man, walked in. His weapon, a forty-five, was on his hip.

Both Diana and her captor were momentarily stunned. The man released her and backed away until a grunt and several sharp words from the officer froze him in his tracks.

Gradually Diana realized that these men were police of some sort and that she had been rescued. A broad smile crept across her face as the officer walked toward her. He casually examined her, letting his eyes roam from the epaulets of her cotton shirt to her dusty Frye boots.

The gleam of a gold tooth preceded his words. "Señorita Hillyer?" he pronounced in a firm voice.

"Yes?"

"In the name of the Honduras nation, you are under arrest."

Diana's mouth dropped. "But why?"

"Please come with me, *señorita*. We talk later." He pointed at her shoulder bag hanging on the back of her chair, which Diana took.

Before they had gone two steps the waiter was before them, his face imploring as he addressed the officer in a low respectful tone. The other turned to Diana. "The man says the bill is not paid. It is four lempiras."

She opened her bag and fished out some coins, which she placed in the waiter's hand.

He bowed politely. *"Muchas gracias, señora."*

As they proceeded out of the restaurant and into the bright sunlight, one of the soldiers took Diana firmly by the arm. Two jeeps and several more soldiers waited in the dusty street. A small crowd of mostly children and teenagers had gathered, moving back as the entourage exited the building. There was a low murmur at the unexpected sight of the beautiful, tall *norteamericana* in the custody of the police.

"Please," the officer said, as he gestured for Diana to get into the back of the nearest jeep.

"Where are you taking me?" she demanded, jerking her arm free from the soldier's grasp.

There was a touch of impatience on the officer's face, but he smiled just enough for the tooth to gleam again. "Now is not the time to talk. Please," he added more emphatically, and pointed to the back seat.

"I demand—"

"Silence!"

Curt orders were given, and two soldiers stepped forward and grasped Diana by each arm. One took her purse from her and handed it to the officer. Then she was dragged into the jeep and wedged between the soldiers in the back seat. Diana felt tendrils of hair, which had been pulled back in a bun, falling against the sides of her face and neck.

She sensed by the reaction of the crowd the gravity of her plight. A feeling of desperation struck her. Nowhere in the sea of spectators was a friendly face.

Diana watched the pompous officer walk around to the passenger side of the vehicle and climb in. Before they pulled away, she was struck by the pungent smell of the men who held her. She looked down at the dirty fingernails on the hands clutching her arms and realized that this nightmare was real.

The small convoy of military vehicles with Diana's jeep in the lead made its way through the streets of Comayagua, stopping finally in front of a substantial building hidden behind high walls. A Honduran flag hung limply on a pole in the courtyard.

Diana was led into the building. The central room was dank, cool and poorly lit. There were a few desks, chairs and benches scattered around, and wooden bookshelves lined the walls. Two naked light bulbs hung on cords from the high ceiling at opposite ends of the room.

Diana was standing between her two guards when a wide door on one side of the room opened, revealing what appeared to be a cell block. She shuddered at the sight. Then she noticed a man in the gloom holding a white, blood-stained cloth to the side of his face. It was Raul! He had been captured!

The door to the cell block closed, cutting off her view of the young man she had ridden into town with on the bus that morning. That explained why the police had come for her at the restaurant, knowing her name.

"Come with me, Señorita Hillyer," the officer said, and led her to an adjoining room. It was small, with a tiny barred window on one wall eight or ten feet above the floor. In the center of the room was a wooden table with a single chair under it. Two other chairs were against the wall.

Diana turned to confront the officer, who was behind her in the doorway. "I saw Raul," she said defiantly. "What have you done with the girl?"

The man smirked. "The *señorita* is safe with her employer."

"Employer!" Diana shrieked. "Her jailer you mean!"

He scoffed.

"That girl is a slave and you know it!"

The man's glare was hard now.

"What kind of a policeman are you?" Her voice had become shrill, and she was on the verge of tears.

"Sit down!" he commanded, his finger pointing threateningly at Diana, then at the table and chair. On the officer's order a guard stepped into the room and sat in one of the chairs against the wall. His superior stalked out, slamming the door.

The utter starkness of her surroundings told Diana that she was in an interrogation room. Thinking again of Raul's battered face, she wondered if they would become violent with her, as well. Surely an American citizen would be accorded some measure of propriety.

Sitting in silence, Diana decided her only recourse was to forcefully assert her rights. If she could just speak with an American consular official.... Get word to the capital.... Whatever happened, she knew she would not betray Marta, for not even Raul knew that she had come to Honduras at her friend's request. Marta's work was too important. Not even Elena's freedom was worth that. No, she would never betray her friend.

In the midst of Diana's reverie the door to the room opened. The guard rose to his feet as the officer entered.

Diana saw that he held a passport in his hand—her passport.

He stood before her. "Señorita Hillyer, this passport says that your name is Diana Emerson Hillyer."

"Yes, that's correct."

"Is this name 'Emerson' a family name?"

Diana was surprised at the question. "Yes, it was my mother's maiden name."

"*Señorita*, do you have relatives in the American military?"

The question was unexpected, but by the concern she detected on the officer's face, the possibility that she did have such relatives was of moment. But was the prospect of a connection in her interest or against it? She decided it was more likely to be in her interest.

"Yes. My mother's family has a long tradition in the military," she said with assurance, though she knew it wasn't true.

A dark look came over him. He turned and marched from the room, calling the guard to come with him. When they had gone, Diana went to the door. Carefully she turned the knob. It was locked. She thought about her lie and wondered what she had done.

THE SOUND OF MARIACHI MUSIC drifted across the compound to where Lieutenant Colonel Cleve Emerson sat at his gray metal desk. He looked out the open window toward his villa where the brassy tunes originated and pictured his plump housekeeper working to the sound of the music. Recently he had begun regretting the dispensation he had granted her to play the radio while she cleaned.

During the three weeks since his return to Honduras, the music had bothered him more than usual. In truth, he

knew that everything about the place was beginning to
annoy him. Was it that late-autumn snow in Washington
or just the glimpse of "civilization" that had soured him
on his life in this remote corner of the world?

Whatever it was, Cleve knew that if he didn't get back
to form he would lose his reputation. *El Paciente*, The
Patient One, was what the Hondurans called him, because he had learned to deal with them at their own pace.
In fact, Cleve had become a rather popular figure in the
country. Between his *indulgencia* of local ways, his
fluency in Spanish and a social status based on his re-
puted charm with the ladies, Cleve was everybody's favorite American—not only at Palmerola Air Base, but in
nearby Comayagua, the provincial capital, as well.

During the past few weeks he had spent hours thinking about his life. His illness and the brief sojourn in
Washington had left him in a malaise that even the frenetic preparations for the joint Honduran-American
maneuvers coming up in January would not cure. Something had happened to him.

That snowy night at Jack Dawson's party had reminded him of three things: there was life outside the
army, making love in English was a different experience
from in Spanish, and it was possible for him to become
obsessed with a woman.

Jack's offer had been tempting. And the blond cocktail waitress had been more—much more—than he had
hoped, but she meant nothing to him, melting from his
mind like the autumn snow. No, it was that face, that
woman, who had haunted him these past few weeks, even
in his sleep. The wide, sensuous mouth smiling through
that crystalline beauty. *Diana*. It was she who tormented
him.

Cleve Emerson's reverie was broken by the sound of aircraft in the skies. He listened for a moment and decided that it was another C-130 with supplies and materiel for Chaparral, the code name for January's operation. The American compound took up only a small area of the Honduran air base, but Cleve knew the Hondurans had no aircraft that large; it had to be American. He was trying to remember what had been scheduled in that day when there was a knock at his door.

The clerk, Spec Four O'Malley, stuck his head in. "Sir, there's a call for you on the civilian line. It's Captain Lopez of the police in Comayagua."

"At this time of day?"

"Yes sir."

"He couldn't have picked up any of our people; it's not a Friday or Saturday night."

O'Malley shrugged, and Cleve stood up and strode around his desk to the outer office.

"Hello, Captain Lopez? *¿Cómo está?*"

"Thank you, I am fine," Lopez said in Spanish. "I am sorry to disturb you, Colonel, but I have in custody here in Comayagua one of your countrymen, and I thought I should tell you about it."

"Army or air force personnel, Captain?"

"Neither, Colonel. A civilian, a beautiful young woman—beautiful like on the television."

An image came to Cleve's mind, and his interest quickened. "I see.... What did she do?"

"A small problem at one of the cantinas..."

"She's a prostitute?" Cleve asked in surprise.

"Oh no. It is not that. She was...how shall I say...interfering."

"Why are you calling me, Captain?"

"It is a courtesy to you, sir. You see, the girl is of the family name Emerson, on her mother's side. She says it is a military family. If there is a relationship, I thought you should know. Her surname is Hillyer. Could there be a connection?"

Cleve thought. He had no relatives fitting the description, but the notion of a beautiful young American intrigued him. The matter clearly was not in his jurisdiction, but the distraction might be interesting. Besides, he didn't want to appear insensitive to the influential police official.

"I very much appreciate the call, Captain Lopez. Perhaps I should come to your headquarters. With your indulgence, I'll be there as soon as possible."

Cleve hung up and turned to his clerk. "O'Malley," he said, feeling the malaise lifting, "get me a jeep."

DIANA HILLYER WONDERED what was transpiring outside the locked door, what they would do with her. From where she sat at the table, she could hear voices occasionally, but mostly there was silence. A feeling of helplessness seized her and she shivered. For the first time in her life, she felt totally out of control.

After a few minutes Diana heard the doorknob rattle, and she looked up as the short officer entered the room. But behind him another man appeared in the doorway. This one tall, fair, wearing jungle fatigues rather than solid green like the others. On his head was a red beret, tilted rakishly.

She engaged his eyes and, as she did, saw his mouth drop slightly open under his sandy mustache. The man seemed frozen, immobile in the doorway, his strong, tanned forearms hanging bare at his sides, his boots planted on the cement floor.

Gradually, out of the numbness of her brain, she realized that the handsome man with soft brown eyes staring at her in disbelief was not Honduran. He, like she, was different. With tears of relief welling in her eyes, she rose to her feet, staring at the welcome face that suddenly looked familiar to her.

"Diana!" the man half whispered, half spoke in a voice pregnant with disbelief. "What are you doing here?"

English! He's an American! She searched the man's face. Then it came to her—the officer at that party, the attractive man in uniform who had looked at her so hauntingly, provocatively.

Suddenly the terror she had felt for the past hour receded, and she was flooded with joy. The hand he extended told her he was a friend. Almost as though some external force was responsible, Diana felt her legs propelling her toward the man, the last steps almost at a run. She threw herself into his arms. Tears of relief ran down her cheeks, soaking the front of the man's uniform, and she felt safe.

Cleve Emerson let his arms protectively encircle the weeping woman. It was an instinctive thing for a man to do. He held her frail, lithe body against him. Lowering his face, he let his cheek graze her hair. The scent of her was soft, delicious. Closing his eyes, he remembered the haunting face reflected in the dark glass that snowy night, and he couldn't believe that now that very woman was in his arms.

From the corner of his eye he saw Captain Lopez shifting uncomfortably, apparently assuming their spontaneous embrace was the affection of relatives. Cleve knew that an explanation would be required and that it was imperative he get Diana out of there. He needed a strategy. Lopez spoke English too well for them to talk openly in front of him. They had to have a moment alone.

Cleve looked up at Captain Lopez, smiling. "Captain, it is most fortunate you called me," he said in Spanish. "Señorita Hillyer-Emerson is indeed my cousin. She is the daughter of an aunt I have not seen in a number of years. The last time I saw her, she was just a young girl."

The Honduran police official nodded respectfully.

"Could I ask your indulgence, Captain, and have a word alone with my cousin?"

The man clicked his heels smartly, coming to attention. "Certainly, Colonel. I am at your disposal. Please come to my office when you are ready."

Diana had pulled back slightly as the man spoke. She wiped the tears from her eyes with the back of her hand and tried to regain her composure.

Lopez slipped past the couple and Diana studied Cleve's face inquisitively, as though she might understand from his eyes what had happened. He smiled gently and led her away from the door so that they would not be overheard.

"Did you understand that?" he asked. "Do you speak Spanish?"

"Very little. What's happening?"

"Well, I'm going to try and get you out of here, but I'll need your cooperation. Lopez thinks we're cousins...."

"But why? Who are you?"

One side of Cleve's mouth twitched back in a grin. "Apparently your middle name is Emerson, my last name is Emerson, and it would be very convenient for *you* if we were related." He studied her for a moment, his face still tinged with disbelief. "Listen, what the hell are you doing here, anyway? Why aren't you back in Washington?''

"Me? How about you?" She looked squarely into his eyes. "What are *you* doing here?"

"I live here."

"But you were the one I saw at that party in Washington a few weeks ago, aren't you?"

Cleve grinned. "I was wondering how long it would take you to find me."

"Find you? I came down here to help out a friend."

His look was ironic. "Yeah, Lopez told me he caught you trying to rescue a prostitute. Surely your friends don't—"

Diana's mouth was forming words of protest when he cut her off.

"Never mind, we don't have time for polemics. We've got to get in there and sweet-talk Lopez."

Diana resented feeling chastened, but this man was her rescuer. "Okay, Mr. Emerson, what do you want me to do?"

"For starters, don't call me *Mr.* Emerson."

"What shall I call you? Sergeant Emerson?"

He smiled indulgently. "Listen, princess, Lopez told me you're from a military family. Most army brats know the difference between an officer and an enlisted man. You see this insignia—" he pointed to his collar, then sighed "—oh, never mind. I'll explain it later. I'm Colonel Emerson, Lieutenant Colonel Emerson."

"I'm sorry," she said contritely. "Did I offend you?"

He dismissed the question with a wave of his hand. "Of course not."

"It's Colonel Emerson, then?"

"No, to you it's 'Cleve.' That's what my family calls me."

Her wide mouth broke into a tentative smile, and Cleve remembered that image of her at Jack Dawson's party.

"I guess that includes me?"

"It does for the time being, at least until I get you out of here. We'd better go see Lopez, he'll be wondering."

"What are you going to tell him?"

"I'll handle that. All you have to remember is that your mother is my aunt, and we haven't seen each other since you were a young girl." Cleve let his eyes drift casually down, then up the woman. "In fact, the less you say the better. If you have to do anything you can cry a little . . . it certainly got to me."

Diana shot Cleve a sarcastic look, lifted her hand to her forehead and awkwardly saluted the handsome soldier.

"We'll have to work on that, too, Diana," he said playfully. Then he took her by the hand and led her to the office of Capitán Humberto Lopez-Molina.

The Honduran police officer was sitting at his desk when Diana and Cleve were shown in. He rose, then went around to greet them as though they were visiting dignitaries from the capital. He invited Diana to sit in a comfortable armchair to one side and motioned for Cleve to take the chair across the desk from his own.

"I consider it most fortunate," the captain said in English, "that your family connection was discovered at this early stage."

Cleve responded immediately in Spanish, effectively freezing Diana out. She would have been resentful except that he undoubtedly intended it so, in order to control the discussion. He had done well so far; she decided to trust him.

Diana listened to what sounded like rather convivial banter with only an occasional word being intelligible.

After a while there was a knock at the door, and a soldier entered carrying a small tray with a bottle and three glasses.

"Ah, some refreshment," Captain Lopez said in English. "Señorita Hillyer-Emerson, may I offer you a little Spanish sherry?"

"Thank you, Captain. Please."

The officer stood, poured healthy portions into two of the glasses and a comfortable splash into the third. Picking up the modest serving, he carried it to Diana and handed it to her in a cavalier manner. Returning to the desk, he offered Cleve a glass and took the other himself. With a respectful nod toward each of them in turn, he spoke. "I propose a toast to the happy reunion of the cousins present and to the respected and honorable Emerson family."

Just before her glass touched her lip Diana saw Cleve wink at her discreetly. The gesture was daring, just as the man himself, and she decided that she liked him.

While the men resumed their conversation in Spanish, Diana was left alone to enjoy her sherry and the sight of her rescuer. Her view of him was in profile, enabling her to examine him candidly. Though the Army Ranger uniform was completely different from what he had worn in Washington, the demeanor, the self-assured manner was the same one that had intrigued her. He had watched her so boldly, so unapologetically....

Only with the relaxing effect of the sherry did the high drama, which had so agitated Diana, start to dissipate. She began appreciating how truly good-looking this dashing soldier was. Military men had never particularly appealed to her...and yet, this man was different.

The stream of words between the men had become a blur. Occasionally, one or the other would gesture in her direction, almost as though this protracted negotiation was over the price she would bring as a prized concubine.

The contempt on her face must have been evident, because she saw Cleve's brow furrow with concern when their eyes briefly met. Remembering his admonition, she quickly smiled—her way of lending encouragement to her champion. *Pay what you must, Colonel Emerson, but for God's sake make the purchase,* she implored.

Just when Diana thought the bargaining would surely end, the men sallied forth into a new round of give and take, pausing once to refill their glasses, she being rewarded for her modesty with another splash of sherry and a respectful smile.

The whole business was absurd, really. Her only crime was a little foolishness. The corrupt little vulture behind the desk who had lately clothed himself in genteel propriety would probably have done his worst with her already if it wasn't for Cleve Emerson.

Looking at the captain and trying to hide her contempt, Diana remembered her battered comrade in his cell. *Poor Raul,* she thought. He believed all he had to do was get Elena into Diana's custody and she would be safe—they all had.

Her disturbing thoughts were interrupted by the laughter of Captain Lopez and she looked at him, trying to affect a gracious expression. They exchanged nods, and she again caught the audacious wink of her compatriot. She sensed the bargain had been struck.

Before long the two officers rose, Captain Lopez strode around his desk and they grasped hands firmly, each grinning broadly. The Honduran even flashed his gold-toothed smile at Diana. He seemed pleased to be getting rid of her. She couldn't help feeling a bit like a piece of merchandise.

"Señorita Hillyer-Emerson," he said with a formal air. "I have the pleasure to inform you of my decision to release you. I have no doubt Colonel Emerson will see to your protection and welfare."

Diana glanced at Cleve, who was looking rather pleased with himself. "I'm very grateful, Captain," she replied in a firm but respectful tone. She wanted to say more, but there was a sign of warning on the American officer's face, so she bit her lip.

"Because of the fine reputation of the Emerson family," Lopez said, "and because of my personal regard for your cousin, Colonel Emerson, I have decided *he* is best suited to reform you. Better, *señorita*, that you profit from his guidance, rather than pass time in prison."

Diana lowered her eyes, not in contrition—though it appeared that way—but rather to avoid the rage that seeing his face would provoke. "Thank you," she said through gritted teeth.

"Well, Colonel," Lopez enthused, seemingly pleased with Diana's response, "we have taken a great deal of your time, and I am as grateful as Señorita Hillyer-Emerson, I am certain."

"Thank you, Captain Lopez, for your understanding and generosity." Cleve stepped to Diana's side and put his arm around her shoulders. "Diana and I will have a long talk. You made the right decision."

She hadn't raised her eyes from the floor, barely able to contain herself with all the pompous, arrogant, self-righteous dribble these men were bandying at her expense.

Captain Lopez went back to his desk, removed Diana's purse and passport from a drawer, then delivered them to her. With a respectful bow he offered Diana his hand, which she took, reluctantly.

A moment later she was following Lieutenant Colonel Cleve Emerson out of the police captain's office.

CHAPTER TWO

As they descended the steps of the police station Diana looked up at Cleve. "Oh, what I wouldn't give to get my hands on that pompous bastard," she said through her teeth. "What did I cost you? Two pigs and a chicken?"

Cleve threw back his head and laughed. "More like a case of that Spanish sherry."

They stopped at Cleve's jeep, and she turned to him. "Is that *all*?"

He reached up and pinched her cheek. "If you weren't so damned pretty, I probably could have gotten off with three or four bottles."

Diana's eyes flashed. "You can cut the *macho* chauvinism, Colonel Emerson. We're alone now."

"What kind of gratitude is that?" he asked as he helped Diana into the vehicle. "I pay a premium price for you, and all I get is criticism."

She watched as he walked around the jeep and climbed in beside her. "You didn't *really* give him sherry for my freedom?"

Cleve smiled and rather brazenly savored her beauty. What he seemed to be saying with his eyes was more inflammatory than all his bravado with the Honduran. His mustache twitched with amusement. "Not formally, no. I'm aware of his tastes, and now I'm indebted to the man. The sherry I give him in the future will only be a token of my gratitude. I just hope that someday he won't ask a favor that will be difficult to grant.''

''Well, I don't know about the favor he'll ask,'' she said, opening her purse, ''but I can certainly pay you for a case of sherry. Will you take my check?''

Cleve reached over and grabbed her hands before she could pull out her checkbook. Diana looked at him in surprise.

''I would consider that an insult.'' His eyes froze her as surely as his strong grip.

Diana found herself complying in the face of his commanding tone, though she resented his patronizing manner. ''Very well, *Colonel*.''

''Until you put on a uniform, Diana, 'Cleve' will do.''

Suddenly she became acutely aware of his touch. She looked down at the large hand that had captured both of hers. ''Okay, Cleve.''

He smiled and released her. ''Let's get out of here.''

Cleve went to turn the ignition key when Diana touched his arm. ''Wait, what about Raul?''

''Raul?''

''Yes, Raul. I was helping him to free the girl—Elena. They're cousins. Raul was arrested, too. I saw him in a cell.''

Cleve frowned. ''Well, I'm afraid your friend Raul will have to fend for himself. I don't have any Honduran cousins.''

''But we can't leave him here.''

''Look, Diana, consider yourself lucky you're not in a cell yourself.''

''But Cleve, we've got to try. Couldn't you ask Captain Lopez? He respects you. Tell him I'm upset...tell him you'll give him another case of sherry. I'll pay for it.''

Cleve turned his head away and sighed. Finally he looked at her with a stern face. "You know, I get the distinct feeling you think I run this country."

"He's just a poor peasant boy. What do they care about him? I'd think one word from a big-shot colonel like you, and they'd let him out."

Cleve's eyes flashed. "Was that meant as sarcasm?"

Diana immediately saw she'd gone too far. "I'm sorry. I didn't mean it that way."

"Look, if this Raul is going to do something stupid like mess with the authorities, he'll just have to take the consequences. There's nothing I can do about it."

"*I* was doing the same thing. *I* was in on the deal as much as Raul!"

"Yes, I was going to mention that later. What are you doing mixed up in a dumb stunt like this, anyway?"

Diana's eyes first widened, then narrowed in anger. "Is that what you meant when you told Captain Lopez you would have a long talk with me?"

Cleve glared at her, but did not respond.

"Well?"

"As a matter of fact, yes."

"Well, of all the nerve!" Diana started to climb out of the jeep when Cleve grabbed her arm.

"Where do you think you're going?"

"To bail Raul out . . . or bribe him out . . . or whatever the custom is in this godforsaken town!"

"You walk in that door, and you won't come out in one piece, Diana."

She paused, not wanting to stay, but suddenly afraid to go. "Then take me to the bus station. I'll go back to La Esperanza. I've been staying with my friend in a village not far from there. She'll help me get Raul out."

"There aren't any buses this late. You'll have to stay."

Diana knew there was no way to reach her friend, since Marta didn't have a phone, and she wouldn't be going into La Esperanza to collect her messages at the post office until the next day. And because Marta didn't have a car to come and get her, the bus was the only way for Diana to get back. "All right, I'll go to a hotel then."

"You won't be safe in town." He hesitated. "The only hotel of consequence, the El Presidente, doubles as a house of ill repute. It's not a safe place for a woman alone. I think you'd better come back to the air base with me."

"With you!" Her tone of voice made the prospect seem heinous.

Cleve started the engine. "I think it would be best. Captain Lopez told me he rescued you from a rather nasty situation. He suggested you wouldn't be safe in town, and I think he's right. This isn't Palm Beach, you know. Comayagua is no place to abandon a lady." He grinned. "Certainly not a cousin of mine."

Diana studied Cleve's face. "You're trying to tell me I'd be better off as *your* prisoner instead of his?"

Cleve put the jeep in gear. "I prefer to regard you as my guest," he said dryly. The vehicle began moving toward the gate of the compound.

"I think I prefer jail."

Cleve slammed the brakes so hard that Diana nearly went into the windshield. "I can drink the sherry myself," he said coldly. "The jail's behind us if you prefer that to *my* hospitality."

Diana gave him a scathing look, and decided she wouldn't be intimidated. "All right, Colonel Emerson...I mean Cousin Cleve. Drink your damn sherry. See if I care." With that she stepped out of the jeep and started walking briskly toward the police headquarters building, twenty yards away. She waited for his voice, but it didn't come. Stealing a glance over her shoulder, she saw him sitting there, immobile, his back to her.

In the rearview mirror Cleve watched the willowy beauty move away, but the closer she got to the door of the building, the slower she seemed to walk. By the time she reached the steps she had almost come to a stop. He saw her raise her foot to the first riser, then freeze. She stood stock-still, as if uncertain what to do. Then she turned and marched back toward him, her face grim, her boots crunching in the gravel. When she arrived at the jeep, she climbed into the seat beside him. Cleve did not turn to look at her.

"Damn you," she muttered under her breath.

Lieutenant Colonel Cleve Emerson of the Army Rangers put the jeep in gear and drove out onto the road. There was the faintest of smiles on his face, but Diana Hillyer wouldn't give him the satisfaction of noticing it.

They drove through the mostly unpaved streets of Comayagua in silence. Diana was still angry, but the wind in her face from riding in the open jeep felt good. It represented freedom, and despite his pompous arrogance, the company of Colonel Emerson was infinitely preferable to that of Captain Lopez. She hadn't yet considered what the consequences of going to the air base with him would be, but if he had any designs on her, she'd straighten him out real fast.

Cleve Emerson glanced at Diana several times, but her face remained the same: jaw set, eyes fixed on the road ahead, her proud head erect. She was as stubborn as a mule, but it didn't diminish her allure in the least. She posed a formidable challenge, and that pleased him.

They soon came to the edge of town and turned onto a narrow paved road running through the dusty, open country. Autumn was the beginning of the dry season in Honduras, and the green grasses of the intermontane valleys and savannas had begun to blanch as the ground-waters had dissipated and the rainy days of summer had faded away. They were headed north across the high valley containing both Comayagua and Palmerola Air Base, and Diana could see verdant mountains in all directions, partially obscured under a veil of blue-gray haze.

"Are you thirsty?" he finally asked, breaking the long silence.

"No," she replied, without looking at him.

"Good, we'll stop for a drink then." Cleve slowed the jeep and pulled off the road.

Diana glared at him, but he paid her little attention.

They stopped in front of a small adobe building that sat under a few large shade trees. The spot was almost like an oasis in the expanse of barren, vacant land. Under the trees in the dirt were some tables, but no people, no sign of life except for several chickens scratching at the dusty soil.

Diana folded her arms and looked at Cleve.

He had turned off the jeep's engine, and the last of the dust cloud that had been pursuing them drifted by. "This is a favorite haunt of the Americans on the base," he said. "We call it Uncle Ernie's. The proprietor is Ernesto, and he speaks English. That in itself is enough to get him the business. No one else for miles speaks more than a few words."

"I see," she said icily.

"Ernie's a good old boy, anyway," Cleve continued, ignoring her frosty disinterest. "Everybody likes him. Come on, you'll want to meet him."

He climbed out of the jeep, but Diana hesitated, contemplating what she ought to do. Finally she decided the hostility she felt was a product of wounded pride and that to pout would only lower her to his level. The best tack was to rise above the situation, so she got out of the jeep and followed Cleve to one of the tables.

They sat in silence for a time. He stretched his legs, tilted his beret forward over the bridge of his nose and leaned back with his hands behind his head. It seemed as though he was preparing to doze off. Diana watched him with surprise, then began to feel irritation at his apparent indifference.

Unwilling to let his cavalier attitude upset her, she looked around. The most notable thing was the silence. There was no traffic on the road. Leaving Comayagua there had been a few vehicles, some donkeys and lots of people on foot, but in this isolated spot there was no one. Even the leaves in the boughs of the trees above them seemed to have been silenced by the hush that lay over the land. Occasionally there would be a low cluck from one of the chickens and, when their scraping hit harder soil, there would be a little scratching sound, but even they seemed obedient to the pervading quiet.

Diana glanced at her companion who—incredibly—seemed to have fallen asleep. On top of everything, the man had no social graces. She tried to contain her pique, telling herself not to take it personally. He was a boor, that's all. It had nothing to do with her.

Diana looked around again, thinking how bizarre the circumstances were. How strange to be sitting at a table with this soldier, under a tree, in a godforsaken spot in the middle of nowhere. Where was this "Uncle Ernie"? What about the drink Cleve wanted? Why was he making her sit here watching him snooze? What gall!

She decided if he could play this game, she could, too. She tried to relax and enjoy the air. Fortunately it was mild. The temperature had been most pleasant since her arrival in the country five days earlier. Although it was now December, Honduras was in the tropics and Diana had expected steamy jungles. Marta had told her that it was that way on the coasts, but in the mountains, which made up most of the country, the climate was much more temperate. It seemed everything about this trip was turning out to be a surprise.

Diana looked at Cleve again and contemplated him, sensing that he was aware of her observation. He was quite good-looking. His mouth had an appealing, self-satisfied curl to it. The jaw was as strong as he. Cleve Emerson was rugged, tanned—a physical man—aesthetically pleasing, but not her type. That she was quite sure of. But in spite of the strong resentment she felt toward him, she realized that deep down there was an intense attraction, as well.

Physical attraction was nice, but it had never been very important to her. Of course she enjoyed a handsome face and a good physique as much as the next woman, but that sort of thing was for magazines and beaches. It was a man's mind and personality that had always captured Diana's fancy. Good-looking or not, she told herself, this man was not much more than an uncouth soldier—at the moment feigning sleep in a chicken yard. It was really very funny. She laughed to herself, enjoying the feeling, especially because it was at his expense.

As she watched him, a fly came meandering along and lit on the tip of his beret. Diana followed its progress as it walked slowly toward Cleve's nose, which protruded from under the edge of the hat. When it finally stepped onto his nose, Cleve twitched and the fly buzzed away.

Diana couldn't help letting out a little laugh and he opened one eye, giving her a sideward glance.

"Service is kind of slow around here, for being a big hangout, isn't it?" she said with a hint of sarcasm.

"Ernesto will be along in a while," Cleve replied, closing his eyes again.

By now, Diana was truly annoyed at his aloofness. "What's the matter, Colonel Emerson, don't you have anything to say?"

Cleve lifted his beret off his nose and turned to look at her. "I was under the impression you had no interest in talking with me."

"I don't."

He shrugged and started to pull his beret down over his nose.

"But I think we ought to get several things straight...."

Cleve slowly sat up again and turned to her.

"First of all," Diana began, "I have rights, and I refuse to be pushed around by Captain Lopez *or* by you."

"I hardly think what I've done for you could be called 'pushing you around,' but okay, what do you want to do?"

"I want to get to a phone so I can try and reach my friend. *Somebody* has got to help Raul."

"All right. You can phone from the air base. But," he added emphatically, "I'll have to ask you to be discreet about my involvement in this business. If you don't mind, it might be better not to mention you'll be staying at Palmerola."

"Why?"

"Because Lopez released you as a personal favor to me. It has nothing to do with my official position. I'm in the military, Diana. Civilian matters are completely outside my realm of authority."

"What's the harm in my friend knowing where I am?"

"There's no harm, so long as it doesn't get back to my superiors or to the embassy in Tegucigalpa."

"You'd think I was a leper."

"No, but according to Lopez you were involved in a conspiracy to defraud a merchant."

"Defraud a merchant! I was trying to help a girl who's being held as a sex slave get back to her family!"

"All right, all right, don't yell at me. I'm not the prosecutor, I'm the guy who got you out of the snake pit, remember?"

Diana saw the anger and indignation on Cleve's face and realized she'd been unfair. She had been accusing him, when she really should have been thanking him. "Listen, Cleve," she said, leaning across the table toward him, "I'm sorry. I've been upset and I keep seeing you as part of the problem, when I know I'd be in a terrible mess if it wasn't for you. I'm sorry I got angry."

Cleve started to respond, but was interrupted by a jovial voice behind them.

"Colonel Emerson! It is you, yourself. I am honored."

Diana looked back and saw a heavy man with a bald head waddling toward them. A large white cloth was tied around his waist as an apron.

"Ernesto! ¿Cómo está?"

"Oh, Colonel!" he said, his eyes widening as he looked at Diana. "What is this beautiful creature? You have taken a wife?"

Cleve chuckled. "No, I'm afraid not, Ernesto. This is my friend, Diana Hillyer."

"Welcome, señorita," the man said, beaming. He clasped his hands together. "The colonel is so lucky to have such a friend." He bowed slightly and Diana smiled.

"Please, *señorita*. I hope you will permit this..." He turned and shouted back toward the house.

After a moment a woman stuck her head out the door and exchanged a few words with Ernesto, before retreating back inside. Then, in an instant, she came hurrying out again with a child in tow. The woman and the child— a girl of about five—came up to the table.

"This is my wife, Maria," he said proudly of the plump little woman. "And this girl is my...how do you say it, Colonel Emerson...*nieta*?"

"Granddaughter."

"Yes, granddaughter."

Diana nodded politely to the woman. "*Señora*." Then she smiled at the girl, who cowered at her grandmother's side, her large dark eyes round at the sight of this stranger.

"My granddaughter has never seen an American woman before," Ernesto explained.

Diana smiled understandingly. "*¿Cómo se llama?*"

"Rosa," the child managed in a tiny voice.

"*Buenos días, Rosa.*"

They all laughed. Maria turned back to the house, muttering her farewells, and the girl stood beside her grandfather, gazing at Diana as the man chatted with Cleve.

Ernesto finished what he had to say and went back to the house himself, leaving Rosa in the company of the American couple. The girl had grown a little braver and came and stood next to Diana.

"I think you've made a friend," Cleve said.

"Isn't she pretty," Diana replied. "Those big black eyes of hers."

Rosa stood there watching her, and they exchanged admiring smiles.

Soon Ernesto was back with two bottles of beer and two glasses on a tray. He placed the drinks in front of the couple, bustling about in an almost comical fashion, then he left.

"If you aren't used to the water yet," Cleve said, "you might want to drink out of the bottle."

Each took a beer and, holding his bottle in the air, Cleve leaned toward her. For the first time she saw a warmth and softness in his eyes. "To the most beautiful woman in Honduras," he said, then glancing at the child he added, "by popular acclamation."

They touched bottles and sipped the beer.

"I was afraid for a moment you were going to belie all the other times you've made that toast."

Cleve looked hurt. "What makes you think I've said that before?"

She let her eyes trail down the man before meeting his gaze again. "Woman's intuition."

His grin mocked her and he took a long drink from his bottle, tilting back his head to permit the cool liquid to flow down his throat. Diana saw the ripple in the cords of his neck as he swallowed, noted his square, angular jaw, the muscular arms. Curiously, she felt overwhelmed with a sense of his masculinity.

She took a modest sip of her beer and watched Cleve with growing fascination. She would have thought him crude compared to the educated and sophisticated men she associated with at home, but somehow he was becoming less and less offensive. Perhaps she was getting habituated to this rugged environment, which he seemed to complement so well.

As she observed the man, Diana was struck with the realization that she would be spending the night with him—there was really no alternative to accepting his hospitality. What was this air base he was taking her to like, and what sort of arrangements did he have in mind? The combination of the primitive circumstances and the uncertainty about what to expect sent a tremor through her.

Diana shivered noticeably, then realized that the little girl, Rosa, had run her fingers lightly along her arm. The child looked up at her with a happy, shy expression on her face. Diana took the girl's hand in one of her own, then ran her fingers along the child's chubby arm. Rosa giggled and Diana turned to Cleve, smiling.

It was the smiling face at Jack's party he saw now. The sophisticated woman with pearls in her ears and elegant clothes—a creature from that other world. Those face-less twits she had associated with were replaced by a Honduran child, yet the woman remained immutable. The jeans, the boots, the cotton shirt, the loose tendrils of hair couldn't disguise her elegance. Unbelievably, in this isolated corner of the universe, Diana had come to him.

So lost had Cleve become in the vision that it took a moment before he realized her eyes were questioning him.

"What is it?" she asked.

"I was thinking how beautiful you are...about that first night I saw you in Washington."

His comment was totally unexpected and caught Diana off guard. Her eyes dropped and she turned distractedly to the child, pinching the girl's round cheeks. She felt Cleve's eyes, but couldn't bring herself to look at them. Apparently her idle reveries earlier weren't unilateral. Uncertainty gripped her, and Diana felt more vulnerable now than at any time since Lopez had released her into Cleve's custody.

"Forgive me for asking a stupid question, Diana," he said as though his last comment hadn't been uttered, "but what exactly are you doing in Honduras?"

She looked up at him, not having thought until now whether she could take him into her confidence.

He saw her hesitation. "Are you part of some sort of international ring dedicated to rescuing prostitutes?"

"No."

He chafed under her circumspection. "Would you mind telling me just who you are and what you're doing here?"

"I don't know whether I should trust you."

"I haven't exactly thrown you to the wolves so far."

Diana studied Cleve, lightly drumming the beer bottle with her nails, thinking. "A friend is involved," she began hesitantly, "an American here in Honduras. Can I trust you not to betray a confidence?"

"As long as it doesn't affect my duties and responsibilities, sure."

"Oh, it has nothing to do with the military or anything like that."

"Okay, what's your story?"

"A very dear friend of mine, someone I've been friends with since childhood, actually, is here in Honduras in the Peace Corps. Her name's Marta. She wrote to me in Washington a number of months ago about a girl from the village where she works who was kidnapped and made a sex slave in a bordello in Comayagua. Marta had no luck in getting help here in Honduras and hoped I could get someone in the government at home interested in the case."

"Why you?"

"I'm a lobbyist and do consulting work in the social, education and health fields. Marta was aware that I knew people on Capitol Hill and around Washington, and thought I might be able to spread around Elena's story—get someone fired up about it.''

Cleve grinned. ''So the president sent you down here to straighten out Honduras?''

Diana gave him a scathing look. ''Very funny, Colonel.''

''Sorry. I was just wondering why they would send someone like you here.''

''I'm not sure what you mean by that, but the fact of the matter is nobody sent me. I couldn't get anyone in the government interested in the case. Basically I got the same response Marta got when she talked to her superiors in the Peace Corps—'Don't interfere in Honduran affairs, stay out of politics!'''

''So you came on your own?''

''Not exactly. I went to all the international humanitarian organizations I could think of. Finally I got the ear of an official at Freedom International. They were very sympathetic, but they said it would be six months to a year before they could conduct an investigation.

''By then I really felt the need to do something personally. I had gotten emotionally involved in what was happening to these girls and I felt an obligation to Marta, who I knew was terribly upset by it. I just couldn't let her down. She was counting on me.

''I don't have international credentials, but my experience is otherwise relevant, so I asked the people at Freedom International if there wasn't something I could do. They told me that they would welcome a fact-finding mission and report. I took a leave of absence from my job and . . . well, here I am.''

Cleve had been listening closely. His hand was on his chin. "You must feel pretty strongly about this to take a leave of absence and come all the way down here."

"I do, Cleve. And now that I've seen for myself and heard other stories, I feel more strongly than ever. The worst part is that nobody seems willing to do anything about it. Nobody cares."

"So how did your fact-finding mission turn into a conspiracy to kidnap—pardon me, liberate—the girl from the cantina?"

Diana's cheeks reddened, but she saw he intended no malice. If there was mild sarcasm in his tone, she probably deserved it. What she had done was rather foolish. Embarrassment seized her, and she bowed her head. "Well, I hadn't intended it. I guess I got so involved emotionally that before I knew it we had decided to get Elena out of there and not wait for help."

"You mean you and this friend of yours, Raul."

"He's not really a friend. I only met him five days ago when I arrived in Honduras."

He sighed and looked at her sadly.

"Cleve, if you only knew. She's just a girl—seventeen. She was kidnapped almost a year ago and forced into prostitution. And now they won't let her go."

"You mean the proprietors of the cantina won't let her go?"

"Yes, they have this phony story that she owes them money, and unless the debt is paid she can't leave. They keep these girls there under armed guard. It's a common practice. It's slavery."

Cleve nodded. "Yes, I know."

"What I don't understand is why somebody doesn't do something about it. How can the police, men like Captain Lopez, just stand by and let this sort of thing happen to an innocent girl?''

''I'm afraid it's a little more complicated than that, Diana. You're not just talking about an isolated abuse. The cantina system is part of a very complex social environment.''

''What do you mean?''

''These people have a very different society from ours—''

''Well, it's barbaric!'' she snapped.

''Perhaps to you, but to—''

''It's not to you? Do you mean to tell me you condone what they do to these girls?''

''Not all of the girls in the cantinas are held against their will. Some of them—''

''Wait a minute, you didn't answer my question. Do *you* condone what's happening?''

''No, of course I don't condone it.''

''Then how can you just sit there smugly shrugging your shoulders?''

Cleve's temper flared. ''What do you expect me to do? Organize a raiding party to clean out the town of Comayagua?''

''No.... I want you to help me free Elena.''

He looked at her, his face registering both annoyance and exasperation. ''No, Diana.''

''Why not?''

''This might come as a surprise to you, but I'm not the U.S. Cavalry, and these people aren't Indians.''

''Well, from what I've heard, you aren't exactly missionaries, either. Marta tells me the American troops are major customers in the cantinas.''

"Good Lord, Diana, soldiering and prostitution have been with us since antiquity! Are you going to hold me responsible for that, too?"

"Judging by the way everybody kowtows to you around here, you seem to have authority."

"I can't change human nature!"

"Far be it from me to expect any help from you."

"Look, Diana, I know you're well-meaning, but forgive me, you're a little naive. My job is not to 'civilize' the world. No, I don't personally approve of the cantina system, but I don't think it's my place to tell other societies how to function, either."

"How can you just ignore other people's suffering?"

"This is hardly the place for polemics, Diana, but let me tell you a little about Honduras. True, this is not the most advanced society on earth, but the people have dignity and they have their virtues, too, notwithstanding the problems you see. In every society some people suffer at the hands of others. This girl, Elena, was probably without a protector, a *patrón*, which in effect made her a fair target.

"Women in Central America have a very different status from what you're used to. The whole society is organized around paternalism. It can be bad, but it can also be good. You had a taste of it today, as a matter of fact."

"You mean *your* paternalism?" Diana asked dryly.

"In a way, yes. Before you were recognized as a member of my family, you were fair game for anyone. Once our relationship became known, you were accorded all the respect and deference 'our' family entitled you to."

"Captain Lopez is a hypocritical bastard."

"Hard as it might be for you to believe, his deference was totally sincere—once your status and credentials were known."

Diana scoffed. "What about *me*, Cleve? What about my dignity as a human being? What about Elena? Are we women only validated by our connection with some *man*?"

"I'm afraid it's not the most enlightened philosophy, but it does have its advantages. There are women here who are very happy and wouldn't change their lives for all the independence and 'dignity' an American woman could show them."

"Well, I don't care what you say. What has happened to Elena is barbaric, and I intend to see her freed and back in her village, even without your help."

"You shouldn't interfere, Diana."

"Politics won't stop me from doing what's right."

"It's dangerous, and it's wrong. You have no right to tell these people how to live."

Her eyes flashed. "And you have no right to tell *me* what to do!"

Cleve lifted his hands in sign of surrender just as Ernesto approached. "Colonel Emerson, would you and your lady like another beer? For the lovely lady thees one is—how you say it?—on the house."

Diana rolled her eyes at the irony of the café proprietor's words, but she couldn't help smiling at the sight of Cleve Emerson as he dissolved into laughter.

CHAPTER THREE

WHEN THE JEEP ROLLED to a stop in front of an old stucco building on the American side of the air base, Cleve turned to Diana. "This is my office. You can call your friend from here. Then I'll take you over to my villa and Lupe, my housekeeper, can help you settle in."

"Without any luggage, there'll hardly be any settling in to do. Besides, I won't be imposing for more than a night."

"You're free to do as you please, but you're welcome to stay on the base as long as you'd like. You'd be safer here than anywhere else in Honduras."

"Thanks, but I expect I'll be returning to Marta's."

"Well, talk it over with her, but remember my doors are always open to an Emerson."

Diana laughed, then watched him climb out of the vehicle, wondering just what the accommodations at Cleve's villa would be like. But she couldn't worry about that now. The first order of business was to get word to Marta about what had happened to Elena and Raul.

Cleve came around the jeep and helped her out, his hand warm and strong to the touch.

"Just to keep my boys' tongues from wagging," he said as they mounted the few steps to the door, "the party line is that you're down from Washington on an investigation for an international organization."

"Okay, Colonel." Diana glanced at him as he held the door, sensing affection in his smile.

"O'Malley!" Cleve called as he looked around the Spartan offices. "My clerk must have stepped out," he said, then pointed to an ancient telephone on a wooden desk. "You can use the civilian line."

Diana went to the desk, then turned to catch his eyes as they raked over her. "How do I get through to La Esperanza? Is there an area code or something?"

"No, you'll have to talk to the operator." He hesitated, then walked casually over to her. "Maybe I should place the call for you."

Cleve was standing very close to her and, as he reached past her to take the receiver, she was touched by the faint fragrance of his cologne. Though he had held her briefly in his arms at the police station, she hadn't been as aware of him then as she was now. He depressed the hook several times, then waited for the operator. "What's her number in La Esperanza?"

"Marta doesn't have a phone. I'm to leave a number at the post office, and she'll call back when she comes into town."

Cleve smiled wryly. "Is there a secret code, or aren't you at liberty to disclose it?"

Diana feigned a dirty look, but he turned his attention to the operator. She listened to his Spanish, not understanding a word, but was acutely aware of him, his nearness. The starched front of his fatigue shirt was wrinkled where her tears had spoiled it and she felt a momentary flash of embarrassment, remembering the emotional scene at the police station.

"What's your friend's name? Marta, is it?" Cleve asked while he waited to be connected.

"Yes. Marta Ronan."

"Unusual name."

"Her mother is Mexican-American, her father Irish."

Cleve nodded and after a moment began speaking again into the receiver. Then he stopped and extended the instrument toward Diana. "Would you care to give the clerk the message?"

She took the phone hesitantly. "Do they understand English?"

Cleve took back the receiver. *"¿Habla inglés, señora?"* he asked, still looking at Diana. He waited, then shook his head. "Want me to leave a message?"

Diana sighed. "Just ask her to have Marta Ronan call me as soon as possible. At this number . . . if it's okay."

He started to speak into the phone, then stopped. "I'm on the table," he said. "The Honduran version of being put on hold."

She laughed and Cleve sat on the edge of the desk, gazing into her eyes as he waited. After a while Diana began to feel uncomfortable under his scrutiny.

"You know, it's still hard for me to believe that the beautiful woman at Jack Dawson's party is right here in my office."

Diana felt her cheeks color and she looked down. Then Cleve took her left hand and rubbed her bare ring finger with his thumb.

"I take it that the fellow you were with was just a friend?"

She blinked, conscious of his touch even more than the directness of his question. "Tom? Yes, he's a friend. A close friend," she added, pulling her hand free.

Cleve started to say something, but the clerk came back on the line and he turned his attention to passing on Diana's message. When he finished he replaced the receiver on the cradle and announced, "Mission accomplished."

As he stood up she felt a curious awareness of him and edged back. She looked up into his eyes.

"Do I frighten you, Diana?"

"No, certainly not. Why do you ask?"

Cleve shrugged. "I don't know. You seem shier to me than you did that night in Washington."

"Oh? How did I seem then?"

"Icy and aloof... but beautiful."

Diana turned and walked across the office, then stopped and looked back at him, feeling braver for the distance. "I'm flattered by your compliments, Cleve, but... I don't want you to get the wrong idea...."

He grinned, amused.

"What's so funny?"

"I was just noticing that standing over there you seem more like you did that night at Jack's."

"Icy and aloof?"

He smiled. "Actually, I was thinking more the beautiful part, but... maybe that, too."

"I'm sorry to disappoint you."

"No disappointment at all. True, you aren't wearing the pearl earrings, that low-cut blouse or the fur, but the elegance is still there, notwithstanding the pants and boots."

"I'm glad you approve."

He didn't reply; he just watched her.

Diana tried to meet his gaze, but couldn't for long. She turned and went to the window, staring out at the flat, barren expanse of the air base. She was conscious of him behind her and wondered why the man disconcerted her so.

"Would you like to see your quarters?" he asked. "If you like, we can walk. It's just across the compound."

Diana's heart raced at the prospect of getting outside in the air. "Yes, I'd like that," she said, turning.

She watched Cleve walking slowly toward her, and she felt more vulnerable and feminine just then than at any time she could ever remember. Recalling the attractive officer in the mirrored glass that snowy night, she understood the emotion Cleve must have felt when he, too, remembered that evening.

DIANA STOOD at the window following his progress back across the compound, his bearing erect, his strides long and purposeful. Several other soldiers also in red berets passed him, saluting smartly. He was alien to what she had known and he irritated her, but Diana found Cleve Emerson fascinating. Despite the yawning chasm separating them, despite the disparity of their experiences and beliefs, she was intrigued by him. . . .

Diana did not turn away from the window until he had disappeared into his offices. Then a fleeting sense of anxiety passed through her, though she wasn't quite sure why.

Behind her Cleve's housekeeper, Lupe, was watching from the table where she sat sewing. The smile on her round face was a knowing one. "He es a wonderful man, no?"

Being discovered so easily embarrassed Diana. "Colonel Emerson is a nice man, yes."

"No, *señorita*. 'Nice' es not a word good enough for our Colonel Emerson. He es much more than thees. He es *caudillo*. I cannot say it in English."

Diana did not recognize the word. She shook her head.

"You know, *macho*, *señorita*? It es the quality of a good man. A *macho* man es not afraid. He holds his head high up. He takes action."

"Yes, Lupe, I know *macho*."

"Well, *señorita*, the *caudillo* es the *macho* man, but he es more. He es leader because he es strong. But not the strong muscle, the strong character."

Diana could not help but be amused at the expressive face of the woman. She was passionate and Diana loved her fiery enthusiasm, but Lupe also brought Cleve's comments about Honduran women to mind. Diana's instincts told her that Lupe was not just a dupe, and that this adulation of the male character was sincere. Still, she couldn't help but believe that if Lupe had seen the other side she'd feel differently.

"You see, *señorita*, the *caudillo* has the—how you say it?—the magnet that draws to him all the other men, all the other peoples." Lupe laughed. "Especially the beautiful *señoritas*, like you."

Diana smiled. "Perhaps you are right, Lupe, but I believe what's in a man's mind and his heart is also important. Women shouldn't only admire a man because he is strong and others follow him."

"Yes, *señorita*. But what woman cannot see into a man's heart if her eyes are open? Thees is the gift of the woman to know the things the men cannot see. The *caudillo* must be good in the heart. The strong and wise woman knows."

Diana understood Lupe's words, but she also knew the two of them were from different worlds. What's more, the man they each knew as Colonel Cleve Emerson was, for all intents and purposes, two different men.

The housekeeper returned to her sewing and Diana sat in a leather armchair, thinking. Cleve's villa was Spartan, but totally comfortable by the standards of the country. It had a cement floor, which made it somewhat exclusive considering the majority of the dwellings in Honduras still had dirt floors. There was a rag carpet in the sitting room, the large wooden table the housekeeper was using and an assortment of furniture of both Honduran and U.S. military origin.

The tour that Lupe had proudly taken Diana on revealed, in addition to the sitting room, two bedrooms, a bath and a kitchen. There was a small room off the kitchen for Lupe's use when she spent the night, which was only occasionally.

Cleve's room had a double bed, a night table, a dresser and chair. Against one wall was a wooden bookcase filled with dozens of hardbound books and a number of paperbacks. In the corner was a small closet covered by a bright red flowered curtain. This Lupe took pains to show Diana because of all the neatly pressed uniforms and shirts hanging there in orderly fashion, ready for the officer's use.

The guest room, which Diana was to use, contained a twin bed, sagging slightly in the middle, with lumps evident beneath the neat bedding. There was also a small dresser and a straight wooden chair. The "closet" consisted of a three-foot wooden pole supported between two metal brackets on the wall. The curtains throughout the house were a deep red, except for those in the guest room, which were aqua blue.

The house had seemed to Diana to be scrubbed within an inch of its life, and Lupe confirmed the impression during the tour by lifting cushions, opening cupboards, sliding dressers and even handing Diana items on shelves so that she could inspect for dirt and dust.

"Lupe," Diana had concluded, "even my own mother was not as good as you." With that the cherub-faced woman, who didn't come to Diana's shoulder, had hugged her gratefully.

Diana glanced at Lupe, who was still sewing busily. She was glad for her presence, glad there was someone besides Cleve to talk to. Even though she had only known the housekeeper for half an hour, she was already fond of her.

As Diana looked around the room, she was grateful for this small house on a remote Honduran air base, which would be her place of refuge—at least for the night. She knew that she was fortunate to be there, fortunate that Cleve Emerson had come along when he had.

THE SUN WAS BEGINNING to fall behind the mountains to the west, casting long shadows over the parched ground of the air base. From time to time Diana would look out across the compound toward the building where Cleve worked, but mostly she talked to Lupe or worried about the mess her friends were in. Despite everything, she felt safe in Cleve Emerson's house.

She had been telling Lupe about her life in Washington, about working as a lobbyist, urging members of Congress to pass certain laws and not others, and was having trouble convincing her that a woman—a single woman in particular—could do these things. Although impressed with Diana's professional life, the housekeeper simply could not understand that it wasn't shameful to reach the age of twenty-eight without marrying. And Lupe couldn't believe that a woman would leave her father's house to live alone, without taking a husband.

Diana realized that there was no point in trying to explain her way of life—it was so different from Lupe's experiences that it didn't translate well. She was recalling what Cleve had said earlier about Honduran society when there was a knock at the door. Lupe went to see who it was.

"I have a message for Miss Hillyer from Colonel Emerson," Diana heard a man say. The housekeeper turned to her, and she rose and went to the door.

A young, ruddy-faced soldier was standing outside. His mouth dropped open at the sight of Diana. She smiled to herself, realizing it must have been some time since he had been home. She hadn't had this much attention since her days as a cheerleader in high school when she used to ride the bus with the football team to games.

"Beg pardon, ma'am, but Colonel Emerson asked me to tell you he wouldn't be home for dinner like he said. He had to get on a plane, and he won't be back till late tonight."

"A plane. Where'd he go?"

"He didn't say, ma'am, but I imagine it was one of the bases in Olancho province. That's where they usually go."

"Olancho? Where's that?"

"Clear at the other end of the country, ma'am."

"I'm afraid I don't know Honduras very well yet."

"Yeah. Colonel Emerson said you were here on business from Washington. We see all kinds going through here, so I'm not surprised."

"You work with Colonel Emerson, do you?"

"Yes, ma'am. I'm Spec Four O'Malley, the colonel's clerk."

"I see." Diana was curious about Cleve and wondered what she might learn from the young soldier. "Have you been working with Colonel Emerson long?"

"About a year, ma'am."

"It must be interesting working with a man like him."

O'Malley broke into a broad grin. "More than interesting, ma'am. Ole P&P's a hell of a guy."

"P&P?"

"Whoops!" he exclaimed, turning red.

"Don't worry, I won't tell him." She laughed. "What does it mean?"

"Well..."

"It's okay."

"Ole P&P is short for Old Pain and Pleasure. That's what we call him, er, I don't myself much, but—"

"Pain and Pleasure? Why that?"

"He's had that name since Vietnam, ma'am. 'Pain' because he knows how to dish it out. They say when he was in Nam he was shot down in a chopper in Cambodia in the middle of a VC regiment and fought his way ten miles back to the border. Course I don't know, that was before my time."

"And the 'pleasure'?"

"Well, er, you're a lady ma'am, and you must have noticed yourself, ma'am."

"You mean he's popular with women?"

The soldier looked down, embarrassed. "That's a nice way to put it. Yes, ma'am."

Diana couldn't help laughing. "Well, thank you, Spec Four O'Malley. I appreciate you bringing the message from Colonel Emerson."

"You're welcome, ma'am. Oh!" he said, reaching into his pocket. "The colonel asked me to give you this, too." He handed Diana an envelope.

"Thank you. It was nice to have met you."

The young man saluted her casually and turned and walked back across the compound. Lupe had gone into the kitchen, so Diana returned to her chair with the envelope. She tore it open and began reading.

Diana, talked to Lopez again this afternoon. He agreed to let your friend Raul out on "bail" until his trial sometime next month. I had Ernesto drive him back to his village.

If you can hold out two more days, Saturday I'll take you to your friend's place, if that's where you decide to go.

I have to leave first thing tomorrow for the field and will be gone all day, so I won't see you till dinner tomorrow evening. Tell Lupe to fix something special.

Cleve

Diana sat in the fading light and reread Cleve's note several times, trying to discern his state of mind, his attitude, his feelings toward her. The news about Raul pleased her. Obviously that was Cleve's intent in getting him released. She wondered whether it had been difficult, or if he had just been stubborn when he refused to help Raul initially.

She decided the overall flavor of the note was conciliatory, yet there was a straightforwardness, almost familiarity implicit in the tone. The fact that he had taken it for granted that she would still be there the next night had not gone unnoticed. It was as though a relationship was assumed between them.

Diana stared vacantly at Cleve's clean, bold hand and thought of Lupe's admiration of the man—*caudillo*, she had called him. His young clerk had been full of praise, as well. Captain Lopez respected him. Ernesto seemed fond of him. Perhaps there was something to this *caudillo* business, something about a primitive environment that made a basic man like Cleve Emerson stand out.

She mused at how very different her own world was. Experiencing Honduras and this Colonel Emerson was, for a woman like Diana, something of a time warp. Yet he was fascinating and, to her surprise, seemed to touch something basic in her, too.

When Diana went into the kitchen to talk to Lupe, the housekeeper had anticipated her request and had a bowl of soup and tortillas waiting on the small table. She had put away the food she had intended to prepare for their meal and was cleaning the kitchen. Diana related Cleve's request for a special dinner the next evening and Lupe's eyes lit at the prospect.

"But what will you wear, *señorita*?" the woman asked as she looked at Diana in dismay.

"This, if I'm still here."

"You cannot be thinking of leaving us, *señorita*?"

"Well, I'll probably be joining my friend in La Esperanza. I won't know for sure until I talk with her."

"Then tomorrow I bring you something from a shop in the village—just in case."

"That's not necessary. Thank you, but please don't."

But the housekeeper was shaking her head. "*Señorita*," she admonished, "thees es for a special dinner with Colonel Emerson—*caudillo*, remember? You must be beautiful. Not in boots like a man."

Diana could see it was futile to argue with Lupe, and not wanting the woman to waste her own money, she went to fetch her purse. Returning, she handed the woman a large bill.

Lupe's eyes rounded in surprise. "*Jesús, María, señorita*. I said I would buy a dress, not the store."

"Well, buy two dresses then and something for yourself. You must be beautiful, too."

Lupe put her arms around Diana. "*Señorita*, you are a great lady... even in the boots."

Diana laughed.

"I will tell you something my heart tells me," the round-faced little woman added in a conspiratorial tone.

"Yes?"

"May the priests forgive me, but you would be a wonderful wife for Colonel Emerson."

"Wife?"

"My heart tells me," she said with assurance.

Diana smiled, secretly amused at the woman's naïveté. A rugged soldier, however attractive, however charming even, was not the sort of man she had envisioned for her husband. The polished and sophisticated men she dealt with in her work were far more likely candidates.

After a friendly glance at Lupe, Diana turned to the bowl of soup on the table and began eating enthusiastically. She was hungry and hadn't eaten since breakfast. Lupe, apparently satisfied that she had made her point, left Diana to her meal.

Diana thought about Lupe's passionate words as she ate. How simple the housekeeper saw life to be. Maybe that wasn't all bad, as Cleve had said. But as for Lupe's matchmaking scheme, Diana had to laugh.

After dinner the women listened to Latin music on the radio for a while, sitting in the living room under the single light bulb hanging from the ceiling. Lupe tried to sew, but her eyes tired in the poor light. The woman seemed fatigued.

"When do you go home, Lupe?" Diana asked with concern.

"I will stay with you until our colonel comes."

"Not for my sake, I hope. What about your family?"

"I have a grown daughter who es sixteen. She takes care of the others. It es not important, *señorita*."

"No, I insist you go. Besides, I'm tired. I'm going to take a bath and go to bed."

Lupe consented, but insisted on helping Diana find what she needed. They went into the bath and found some shampoo, but no hair dryer. It didn't matter though, there was no place to plug one in, anyway. Lupe gave Diana a towel, and they discussed what she might wear for nightclothes.

The women went into Cleve's room and Lupe looked through the drawers, hoping to find something suitable. They decided on one of Cleve's T-shirts. They were all olive drab, army issue, but one was old and the fabric had stretched enough that it would hang discreetly to the middle of Diana's thighs.

Having done all she could to make Diana comfortable, Lupe bid her goodbye and left. It was nine by the time Diana had finished bathing, towel-dried her hair and washed out her lingerie. She went into her room, turned off the light and climbed into the bed, which she found hard and uncomfortable. With nightfall the air had cooled considerably, and Diana was grateful for the army blanket over the coarse linen sheets.

For a long time she lay listening to the quiet. There was an occasional bark of a dog off in the distance, and several times she heard a vehicle traversing some distant corner of the base, but little else. Diana felt a deep, abiding sense of loneliness in this alien place.

Her mind trailed over the events and traumas of the day. She pictured Elena, a girl she'd never seen, in some dank bordello, her face reflecting misery, her spirit broken. The vision made Diana hate this cruel society and she trembled. But the reel of mental images turned on, and she saw the angelic face of the little girl, Rosa. What would be *her* fate?

Diana tried to erase it all from her mind and find a conducive path to sleep. She fought the melancholy of her circumstances, but could think of nothing or no one to look to for relief. Frustration began building and the prospect of sleep receded, causing her to toss and turn in her bed.

Finally she decided to get up and find some distraction. She remembered the bookcase in Cleve's room. Perhaps he wouldn't mind if she borrowed something for bedtime reading.

Diana stole into his bedroom, turned on the light and went to the bookshelves. She was shocked at the variety of titles and subjects she found. Poetry in French, Spanish and English vied with *The Education of Henry Adams* and the selected works of Mao Tse-tung. Political science textbooks were intermixed with the revolutionary writings of Che Guevara and Regis Debray. There was even some Iris Murdoch and D.H. Lawrence.

She had just pulled out an old battered copy of George Kennan's *American Diplomacy*, wondering whether she had been hasty in her judgment of Cleve, when she heard the front door open. Her eyes widened in horror, and she anguished at the thought of being caught in the skimpy T-shirt.

Diana wanted to scamper to her room, but before she could, Cleve appeared at the bedroom door. The surprise on his handsome face slowly, incrementally, turned to delight.

"Well, a literatus I see. But aren't you out of uniform?" Cleve asked with a crooked smile. His eyes moved from the dark cloud of hair hanging past her shoulders, down her scantily clad body, to her bare legs and feet.

Diana tugged at the tail of the T-shirt, trying to cover more of her thighs. "Oh, Cleve, I'm sorry. I couldn't sleep. I was looking for a book."

"No need to apologize. Borrow my books anytime." Cleve unfastened the utility belt around his waist, and Diana noticed for the first time the forty-five as he swung it off his hip. Wrapping the belt around the holstered weapon, he stuck it in a drawer and tossed his beret on top of the chest.

Without hesitating, he sauntered over to Diana. "What book did you pick?" He took it from her hand and glanced at the cover. "An aspiring diplomat?" he asked, before tossing it on top of the bookcase.

Her lips opened in an attempt to respond, but she couldn't say anything. His presence was overpowering. He smelled of vegetation and earth, and there was also a hint of aviation fuel mixed with his own natural musk.

She knew he would try to kiss her. Diana also knew it would be difficult to resist him. Still, somehow, she had to. She saw his lip curl under the sandy fringe of his mustache as his head started inclining toward her. Diana realized that if she was to act, it must be now. Before his mouth touched hers, she turned abruptly away.

He reached out and took her arm just as his words vaulted the narrow space between them. "Have you changed your mind?"

For an instant she couldn't look at him. His presumption sparked her anger. When Diana's turquoise eyes finally met his, they were defiant.

The expression on his face told her he wasn't accustomed to this sort of reception. His fingers clamped tighter and he pulled her a bit closer, his eyes narrowing slightly, but more with determination, it seemed, than anger.

Diana glared at him. "This might be Honduras, Colonel Emerson, but I'm not one of the local *señoritas*."

The ironic smile on his face showed he was unmoved. "That's apparent enough, Diana."

She saw he was unchastened. "This *macho* business might be big stuff here, but it means nothing to me," she snapped. "*I'm* not impressed."

There must have been more challenge in her voice than rebuke because Cleve immediately responded by taking her face in his hand and doing what he intended from the beginning. He bent down and covered her mouth with his own.

When she finally gathered herself after the surprise of his attack, Diana recoiled from his kiss, pushing at his chest with her hands. If Cleve noticed her resistance, he paid little attention to it, wrapping his arms around her slender body and gathering her closer.

For an instant she resisted, but then Cleve began easing back, his kiss becoming softer, the embrace more gentle. Diana's fear, sparked by the unexpected intimacy, persisted, but she also sensed a germ of ambivalence growing deep inside.

Cleve seemed to sense this first evidence of her crumbling defenses. His tongue gently probed her mouth, and his hands, moving lightly over her shoulders and back, seemed more to explore than to dominate.

The flimsy T-shirt had ridden up Diana's thighs, and she suddenly realized how vulnerable and near naked she was. Cleve, too, must have discovered that she wore nothing but the shirt, because his hands ran up under the tail of it, capturing the roundness of her bottom.

Diana felt alternating waves of desire and fear. She moaned softly in spite of herself, realizing too late it would only encourage him, but not knowing for sure what it was she really wanted. Her palms were still against his chest, but she no longer pushed at him, no longer tried to evade him.

Cleve lightly kissed her neck, his hands still caressing her buttocks.

"Please don't," she managed in a husky half whisper.

But he ignored her, plying and caressing her skin with his lips. In response she writhed slightly, and before she knew it, another damning moan emitted from her throat.

Cleve took the fullness of her bottom in his hands and lifted her so that her pelvis slid up the front of him. For a moment he held her against him, only the tips of her toes touching the floor. Then he let her ride down him again, his hardness igniting her soft femininity.

While his lips and tongue played at her neck, he lifted her again, then again and again, in a slow, rhythmic motion that gradually caused the front of her shirt to ride up over her hips. The soft down of her femininity now pressed directly against his uniform, the resulting sensation so strong that Diana was powerless to resist.

Acutely aware of the growing swell under his clothing, she realized that the same friction that had inflamed her had aroused him, as well. Her desire was unequivocal now, but she knew that it represented danger, more even than the man himself.

"I want you, Diana," he whispered into her hair.

For a moment she couldn't utter her words of refusal, her mind and body were so fully engrossed in the exquisite, intimate friction. Diana shook her head. "No," she finally muttered, but without conviction.

She pulled her head back to look into his face, to tell him no with her eyes, but again he ignored her. "Please," she implored, sensing the futility of her request, knowing he was reacting to what she wanted, not what she said.

Cleve looked at her for a long time, but he seemed locked in some inner dialogue. Then his mouth curled, and he bent down and lifted her into his arms. He traversed the few short steps to his bed and laid her across it so that her lower legs dangled over the side.

Diana looked up at Cleve, uncertain what he would do next. Behind him was the light bulb, hanging from a cord, exposing her near-naked body, but hiding his expression from her. Any clue to his intent was hidden in his shadowed face.

She tugged at the T-shirt, which was bunched at her waist, and tried to press her knees together, but Cleve's legs were between hers. He looked down at her, savoring what he saw. Then, without warning, he dropped to his knees, pressing his face into the soft flesh of her stomach.

As he began kissing her with surprising tenderness, Diana felt her body quiver. She was torn between knowing she should shove him away and wanting to crush him into her. Caught in the void of indecision she lay passively, staring at the ceiling, waiting.

Cleve began stroking the velvety skin of her stomach with his tongue, scoring it with icy fire. He nibbled at her, kissing her lightly from her navel to the fringe of her downy mound. Then he made his way across her pelvis and down her legs, letting the strong hands that held her waist slide to her hips. As he kissed the soft flesh of her inner thighs, she began throbbing in expectation.

Those earlier traitorous forces within her were now fully in league with the man. She hated that she craved his touch, but she did. Utterly at his mercy, Diana forced herself to remain still, forbade herself to encourage him or beg for the touch that could bring her satisfaction. Yet she could hardly ignore the growing ecstasy wrought by his touch. Never, *never* had she experienced such yearning. Just when she was sure that his tortures would drive her mad, Cleve wedged open her thighs.

During the eternity that she waited, tiny, prescient tremors radiated from her pelvis to every corner of her being. Her nails dug into the coarse wool blanket beneath her and she knew what was imminent, for the warmth of his breath was on her. Never having experienced this, Diana had no idea what to expect, but knew with all her soul that she wanted it.

The first touch was a kiss, soft as a butterfly's wing on the wind, so sweetly gentle that Diana found herself surrendering to it completely—her fear evaporating under his tenderness. Then, there was a serpentine stroke of his tongue, electrifying her, charging and discharging energies throughout her in an eruption of sensation.

He was doing his will with her. Each lap of his tongue subjugated and incited her. Spasms rippled through her at *his* command, not hers.

Though she struggled to remain passive, she could wait no longer. Her pelvis arched toward him. "Oh God," she moaned, and he fell upon her.

Moments later she was at the point of climax, the pulsations racking her so deeply and thoroughly that her body began rocking spontaneously. Cries of ecstasy emitted from her throat just as the eruption came. For an instant she felt as though she had been served up to death itself.

In the minutes that followed, life slowly reclaimed her, and Diana found herself somewhere between heaven and earth. Cleve had pulled away, permitting cool air to wash over her. She was in control again.

Amid the silence that ensued, Diana suddenly became aware that he was standing beside the bed, undressing. It was then that she realized that this quiet moment had been the intermezzo before the finale.

CHAPTER FOUR

FOR A LONG TIME Cleve lay with his face in the crook of Diana's neck, his arm draped across her stomach. She listened to his breathing and the quiet of the Honduran night, piecing sensation and experience into the patchwork of reality. What had happened to her during the past hour was unmatched by any single event or happening, whether real or forged in her imagination.

He had been a fantastic lover: giving her pleasure unselfishly, titillating her, possessing her, skillfully mixing tenderness and passion. Her body still glowed from their lovemaking. But along with the pleasure there was an emptiness, and as the minutes passed Diana became progressively more aware of what was missing.

Who was this man sleeping beside her, anyway? She really didn't know him. He was like a phantom, an apparition that had visited her, a man in a dream.

How could she have let this happen? Diana had always been able to resist men when she wished, even attractive men. This was hardly the time or place to slip. A soldier—particularly one who had her alone in an isolated corner of the world—was not the sort of man she should have let seduce her.

There was no doubt in her mind that he had wanted her, but what he wanted was the sexual intimacy she afforded—not the person she was. She had never been closer to a man physically, yet so removed from him spiritually.

It was a sad thing in a way, but she had no one to blame but herself. She had been foolish. The question was, what should she do now? It was obvious that she couldn't let it happen again. He had assumed that she was his for the taking, and she had made the mistake of letting him believe it. Changing that assumption would be the first step.

The first step. The thought amused her. Why should there be any future steps? Was he so irresistible that she wanted more of him...even on her own terms? This *caudillo* business was no more a part of Diana than the alien culture she found herself in.

Lying in Cleve Emerson's embrace, Diana thought about the cavalier manner in which he had taken what he wanted. She knew she had been used, beautifully used, but used nonetheless. The more she thought about it, the more resentful she felt. With her hostility toward Cleve mounting, she couldn't stay in his arms. She had to be by herself, get to her own bed.

Slipping carefully away from the sleeping man, Diana stole silently back to her room and climbed into her bed. She felt relief immediately. Separation, distance, control were what she craved.

But after a few minutes, she began to feel uncomfortable in the foreign surroundings. The room was not really hers; it was borrowed. The house, the air base, the country—all alien. And the day had been among the more harrowing she had ever experienced: the man in the café who had assaulted her, the police, a battered and bleeding Raul in jail, and this sexual liaison with Cleve Emerson, a stranger. It was a lot for a person to go through in a single day—extremes of terror and passion, fear and pleasure. It was a lot for anyone.

In spite of her resolve, Diana felt her emotions welling. She needed to cry, to purge herself. Overwhelmed, Diana let the tears fall, and she began weeping softly. Her body was still aglow, but filled with resentment, anger... and fear.

CLEVE WAS GRADUALLY COAXED from sleep by the chill of the night air. He shifted his body, seeking warmth, felt the scratchy wool blanket under him and wondered why he wasn't between his sheets.

Then he remembered Diana. He felt the bed beside him. She was gone!

Cleve sat up, searching the darkness until he realized she must have returned to her room. He turned his ear to the silence, then heard her crying softly. But why? Had he hurt her?

Cleve got to his feet and, taking a cotton robe from the closet, went quietly to her room. He could not see her in the darkness, but he heard her.

"Diana," he said softly. "What is it? Are you all right?"

She stopped abruptly, and he heard her bed creak as she turned. She did not respond.

Cleve walked over and looked down at her, unable to see more than her silhouette. He sat on the edge of the bed. Diana lay motionless, like a small animal caught in an open field.

"Did I hurt you?"

"No," she said, only a trace of emotion evident in her voice.

"I heard you crying. I was afraid something was wrong."

"I just needed to be alone."

"But why were you crying?"

"Women do that sometimes, Cleve. I've had a rather trying day." Her voice softened. "I felt like crying."

"Nothing I did?"

"No."

He studied her shadowed image on the bed, seeing the fan of her dark hair on the pillowcase. He touched her cheek with the back of his fingers, feeling the dampness of the tears on her skin. "I'm sorry I fell asleep like that. It wasn't very considerate."

Diana shook her head as if to tell him it was not that, but she did not speak. The tiny sounds she made told him how upset she was. He leaned down and softly kissed her mouth. It was a brief, tender kiss, intended to heal, but it only served to make her turn away.

"Come back to my bed, Diana, so I can hold you."

She shook her head again. "No, I want to stay here."

Cleve gently pushed her hair back from her face, then stroked her head like a father might a child. "What have I done?"

"Nothing."

He knew there was something wrong and chafed at Diana's circumspection. "You didn't enjoy it?"

She hesitated. "Yes," she replied finally, her voice brittle.

Cleve was getting nowhere, and his frustration was mounting. "Whatever I did wrong, I'm sorry."

Diana didn't reply. She lay motionless.

He started to stroke her head again, but she gently pushed his hand away. "Please don't, Cleve."

"I wish you'd just tell me what's bothering you."

She didn't respond.

"Diana?"

"Isn't it obvious? I wish I hadn't made love with you."

"Why?"

"Because I don't do that sort of thing . . . normally."

"I don't think badly of you, if that's what you're worried about."

The little laugh she gave was vaguely derisive.

"What's wrong with that?"

"Nothing's wrong, Cleve. I just want to be alone." She turned to him. "Look, I made a mistake tonight. I'm not interested in casual sex, and I'm sorry I let it happen. I don't blame you. It was my fault. There's no need to take it personally."

"But I do take it personally. I'm not interested in casual sex, either. Not with you, anyway."

Again she gave a little laugh.

"I wish you wouldn't do that."

"I'm sorry. It's just the irony, the circumstances. I think it would be best if we forget the whole thing."

"Maybe I don't want to forget it."

"In a few days I'll be leaving, Cleve, returning to Washington."

He felt annoyance at the remark. "You don't have to be so pleased about it."

"I'm being realistic."

Now Cleve fell silent. There was no disputing her statement. But . . . what was he thinking? That it could be otherwise?

Cleve wondered what it was that he truly wanted. Casual sex? No, he wanted what he couldn't have—a relationship, a woman he cared about. It was ironic, actually. He had seen Diana at that party, knowing that in twenty-four hours he'd be thousands of miles away. She had been little more than an image in the mirrored glass, and now here she was, fresh from his bed and just as elusive, just as untouchable.

He caressed her cheek with his fingers, his heart wrenching at the thought of having her and not having her. Diana turned away, stifling a little sob. Cleve bent down and kissed her, his lips moistened by her tears. "Can we be friends?" he asked in a husky whisper.

She nodded, biting back another sob.

"Friends should help each other," he said softly. "If you're going to cry, you must do it right." Cleve swung his legs up on the bed beside her and slipped his arm under her head, gathering her to him. Then he kissed her forehead and began stroking her temple with his hand. "Crying is an art," he whispered. "Now you can do it right."

After a brief hesitation Diana began weeping as though every burden and sorrow in her life could be purged in one tumultuous cataclysm. Cleve held her close, kissing her tenderly and feeling as though in their unhappiness they had touched each other—more really than when they had made love.

He held Diana close, but he could not erase from his mind the fact that he would have her only for days, hours. He was a soldier and she a traveler passing through his life. His career would allow no more than the briefest relationship, at least not without suffering. Sadly he realized that Diana Hillyer was—could be—no more than a lovely vision destined to become a memory.

THE MORNING SUN shining through the curtains cast a yellowy-green tint over Diana's room. She awoke, blinking at her surroundings in the strange light, puzzling over the confusing wash of thoughts that buffeted her. Then she remembered Cleve, the powerful effect of his love-making, the masterful way he had aroused her...the shameful submission that followed.

But Diana also remembered her sadness afterward, and his tenderness, which she now regarded more as a form of apology than a true reflection of his feelings. He had had his way with her, gotten what he wanted. The sensitivity was probably an investment in the future, in other nights. The man was not a fool.

Though Cleve had taken advantage of her, Diana recognized that ultimately she was the one accountable. There was nothing to do but chalk it up as another lesson. Last night was over, but today and tomorrow were still within her control.

Diana turned her attention to her major concerns: Elena, Raul and Marta. Her friend, her closest friend in the world, would be calling sometime that morning. She would be upset and worried, and Diana would have nothing to show for the ordeal they had all been through except failure. They would have to regroup—that was obvious enough—but deciding what would happen next would have to wait.

Diana threw back the sheets and climbed from the bed, aware for the first time of Latin music playing softly in the kitchen. It was probably Lupe. And she was probably wondering what Diana was doing in bed so late.

Walking across the cold cement floor, Diana glanced down at Cleve Emerson's olive-drab T-shirt on her otherwise naked body. She shivered at the awareness of her vulnerability. However the day developed, she knew she'd have to be strong.

"*¡Señorita!* Good morning!" Lupe exclaimed when Diana came out of the bedroom after bathing and dressing. She was clearly delighted to see her. "Did you sleep well in the house of our Colonel Emerson?"

There seemed to be a knowing smile on the housekeeper's face, and Diana hoped Cleve hadn't said anything. He couldn't have, surely.

"Come, *señorita*," Lupe said, taking her hand and
leading her toward the kitchen. "You must have your
coffee, and I will bring to you the little surprise."

"What surprise, Lupe?"

"The clothes from the village. Don't you remember it?
We are to make you look like a woman today, no?"

Diana sat at the table, and Lupe put a steaming cup of
coffee before her. Then she disappeared into the other
room. A few moments later she was back with a neat
package of brown paper tied with simple cord. "I hope
that you like thees as much as I."

Diana smiled at the beaming woman and began removing the wrapping. Inside was a peasant blouse, pale
lemon in color, a turquoise muslin skirt, full and soft,
and a pair of sandals with low heels.

"They're lovely, Lupe. Thank you so much." She
squeezed the woman's hand.

"Now you will be ready for tonight. And the skirt es
even the color of your lovely blue eyes. The colonel will
see that you can be a woman, too, *señorita*."

Diana thought of Cleve Emerson's hands under her T-
shirt and blushed, knowing that he was already more
aware of her feminine attributes than she would have
liked. She looked down at the clothes Lupe had brought,
thinking how foreign they seemed—much like Honduras and the man in whose house she had taken refuge.

After she had her coffee, some bread and jam, Diana
put her new outfit in her room, deciding she would wear
it that evening to please Lupe, assuming that she ended
up staying. The change of clothes would be welcome,
though she'd have preferred some of her own things.

The housekeeper was folding laundry on the table in the living room when she returned. Diana had been there less than a day, and she was already beginning to chafe with a feeling of confinement. She wandered over to the window and looked across the compound toward Cleve's office. The man drifted into her mind again.

What a surprise it must have been for him to find her in his room, virtually naked—a ripe fruit waiting to be picked. And how easy it had been for him. Diana shivered with humiliation.

She turned to see a knowing smile on Lupe's face.

"Our Colonel Emerson es not in his office today, *señorita*. He won't return to us until tonight."

"Yes, I know, Lupe." Diana was annoyed at the housekeeper's assumption that she had been thinking about Cleve. She was even more annoyed that it was correct. "He said in the note he sent that he would be in the field all day," she said casually.

"Yes, he left very early I think. Already he was gone when I came to the house thees morning."

Diana was pleased with his absence. It would be nice, in fact, if he had to be away until she left the air base. She preferred the benefit of the refuge Cleve Emerson afforded without having to contend with him.

"I'm expecting an important phone call," Diana said, suddenly remembering Marta. "I hope someone knows to come for me if my friend calls."

"*Sí*, I think so. I am sure that by now *all* the soldiers know there es a beautiful *señorita* in the house of the colonel."

"I'm just a guest here, Lupe. I hope they realize that," Diana replied, hearing the defensiveness in her own voice. She saw, though, that the housekeeper didn't understand her point.

"Do not worry about the soldiers. There will be no problem, it es certain. But I will protect you. If you must go out while the colonel es not here, I will go with you. You will be safe with me, *señorita*."

"Yes, Lupe, I understand that. It's not what I..." She saw there was no use in explaining. "Thank you, but you needn't worry about me."

"It es my job. The colonel would expect thees of me, I know it."

Diana smiled and turned to the window again. Beyond the compound were the mountains, blue-gray in the distance, remote from this military island she found herself on, this isolated patch of concrete in the center of the broad valley.

Most of the populace, she had come to know, lived in the mountains, eking out a living on postage-stamp farms, gathering in clusters of earthen buildings that were their villages. Most of them were happy in their sequestered lives, though sometimes, as in the case of Elena, vulnerable to the outside world.

Elena. She had to think about what could be done to free the girl. Marta had been skeptical about finding anyone willing to put their neck on the line for Elena, but surely there was someone. It was clear from Diana's experience with the police the previous day that the government would not be likely to help. Perhaps the church. She and Marta hadn't discussed that prospect. Maybe it was worth pursuing. When her friend called, she would ask her about it.

Just before noon, Spec Four O'Malley came to the door with word that there was a telephone call for Diana. Despite Diana's objection, Lupe insisted on walking with her to Cleve's office, apparently taking seriously her perceived duty to protect her charge. The three hurried across the dusty compound. Sensing Diana might want privacy, O'Malley and Lupe left her alone in the office.

"Marta!" Diana exclaimed upon hearing her friend. "It's so good to hear your voice."

"Diana, are you all right? What are you doing at Palmerola?"

"I'm staying with the American commander, an army colonel. He rescued me from the police in Comayagua yesterday."

"The police? Were you arrested, too?"

"Yes, at the café where I was supposed to meet Raul and Elena. A police captain named Lopez stormed the place and arrested me. You'd have thought I was leading a revolution or something."

"Good Lord. You poor thing."

"It was pretty harrowing. For a while I thought I was going to be tortured or raped, but I wasn't hurt, not a scratch."

"Thank God. Raul wasn't sure what had happened to you."

"How is Raul?"

"I'm afraid he wasn't as lucky."

"Was he hurt badly? I guess he got back all right."

"Yes, he got back last night. They beat him up, but nothing terribly serious, fortunately—a broken nose and some bruises."

"I had a glimpse of him in the police station when they brought me in, but I didn't get to talk to him. I saw that he was bleeding."

"He was more devastated by the failure to get Elena than by the beating, I think."

"What happened with Elena, anyway?"

"Raul said they caught them going out the back door. The guards grabbed them both, then called the police.

They took Elena back upstairs. Raul didn't see her again, so apparently she's still at the cantina, probably being watched more closely than ever."

Diana felt her stomach twist in a knot. "Marta, how can they do that? How can they get away with it?"

"It's hard to believe, but they do. It's the system. I thought maybe because of your involvement they might let her go, but I guess we were wrong.... So, what's with this colonel? How'd he get involved?"

"Cleve's a friend of Lopez, the head of the police. The whole thing is a curious coincidence I'll tell you about later, but he had influence and came along just in the nick of time, thank God."

"He *must* have influence, Diana. Apparently he was responsible for getting Raul out, too. Sounds like quite a guy."

Marta's words struck Diana as ironic under the circumstances. The recollection of him standing in the doorway at the police station in Comayagua came to mind, followed closely by the image of him at the door of his room when he had caught her there, scantily clad, looking for a book. "Yes," she mumbled, "he is."

"What's his name? Cleve?"

"Yes, Cleve Emerson. Lieutenant Colonel Cleve Emerson of the Army Rangers."

"Sounds pretty important. Could he help with Elena?"

"I already asked, but he refused."

"Why?"

"Same old thing. He doesn't want to interfere—the same bull the Peace Corps gave you about respecting the way other people want to live."

"I'm not surprised."

"Well, I'm indignant about it. I can't forgive him for not trying."

"Probably doesn't want to put his neck on the line. I suppose you can't expect otherwise. After all, he doesn't know Elena."

"That's true, Marta, but he didn't know me, either."

"You're an American. He probably didn't consider that interference."

"Why are you defending him? I think it's a shame, an embarrassment. Undoubtedly, he could get Elena out if he really wanted to."

There was silence.

"So what do you plan to do, Diana?"

"I'm going to get Elena out of that place one way or another."

"You've already done a lot—taken a big risk. If the police are on to you, you'd better not take any more chances."

"Well, I can't quit. Not now. I know something can be done, and I'm going to do it."

"You can go back to Washington and write a report for Freedom International. That would be a help—a help to other girls, if not Elena."

"I've got to get *her* out, Marta. I'm hooked."

"Well, don't do anything foolish. I never should have let you and Raul go into Comayagua like that. It was dumb."

"Maybe in retrospect, but it might have worked."

"What are you going to do, come back here?"

"I don't know. What do you think, Marta? Where can I do the most good?"

"To be honest, I think back in Washington, working with Freedom International."

"I'm not leaving! Not until I've given it my best shot."
She sighed with frustration. "How about the church?
Would they help?"

"Unfortunately, the church in Honduras is not strong.
There's a shortage of priests. The people are very reli-
gious, but their religion is virtually without the benefit of
clergy. Some villages are lucky if they see a priest once or
twice a year."

"I thought Latin America was full of churches."

"Oh, there are churches, but no clergy. Most of the
priests live like carpetbaggers, running around the countryside performing weddings months after the fact, saying prayers over people long since buried."

"In Comayagua, too?"

"I don't know for sure, but it's more likely there'll be
clergy in a town of that size. There's supposed to be a
bishop there, I believe."

"Maybe I should talk to him."

"Try if you wish, but be careful not to offend anyone.
The church is sort of in the same shoes as the Peace
Corps and the American military—in Honduras at the
pleasure of the government."

"You mean they won't want to rock the boat, either?"

"That'd be my guess."

"I can't believe the whole country—the whole world—
doesn't care about that girl, Marta."

"You're beginning to understand *my* frustration."

"Any suggestions?" Diana waited, knowing Marta
was as disappointed as she.

"That American officer at Palmerola might be your
best bet. Even if he won't help directly, he may be able to
put you in touch with somebody who can and will."

"Like who?"

"It would probably be somebody in the capital, Tegucigalpa, someone with authority. Power is highly centralized in Honduras."

"Sounds like you're saying I should stay here, Marta."

"There's not much you can do from here, that's for sure."

Diana thought. "I'll come to get my things, though, as soon as I can arrange it. Probably sometime Saturday, unless I can find a way to get there sooner."

"Okay." There was a pause. "Listen, Diana, take care of yourself."

She heard emotion in her friend's voice. "Don't worry about me."

"And thanks for all you've done...."

"Don't thank me yet, Marta. Wait till I get Elena out of that cantina."

DIANA ATE the lunch Lupe put before her, but without enthusiasm. She only half listened to the patter of the housekeeper, her mind still immersed in her conversation with Marta and the problem facing her. Cleve Emerson, it seemed, held the key, but he had taken a contrary position, giving every sign of being intractable on the issue.

It was frustrating, but not hopeless. Diana earned a living persuading stubborn congressmen to change their position on an issue, to take risks, to do the honorable thing even when it wasn't clearly in their self-interest. If she could handle them, she ought to be able to handle Cleve Emerson.

Unfortunately, this situation was a little different—not so much because Cleve was in the military instead of Congress, and not so much because this was Honduras and not the States. The problem, quite simply, was that she had slept with him.

Never in her professional life had Diana considered having a relationship with someone she was lobbying, though occasionally men would drop hints. But here she was, an important issue on the line and already at a disadvantage because of one foolish mistake. Getting Cleve Emerson to cooperate was going to be a formidable challenge, but she would do it—do it without becoming his concubine.

"You know, *señorita*," Lupe said, interrupting Diana's thoughts, "you are going to be so beautiful tonight in your new clothes. I cannot wait to see the eyes of Colonel Emerson!"

CHAPTER FIVE

SEVERAL HUNDRED YARDS AHEAD, coming toward them on the dusty road, was a man and a donkey. Diana watched them with curiosity, thinking how unlikely it all seemed. Walking beside her Lupe was silent, though she had been chattering away most of the time since they had left the villa.

Diana breathed deeply. The air was warm and still. The only sound was their footsteps. She looked down at her boots as she walked, aware suddenly of how masculine they looked compared to Lupe's sandals. In fact, everything about her and Lupe seemed different. But, despite their vast dissimilarities, Diana felt a strong bond with the housekeeper.

After lunch they had talked for a long time, and both had been pleased to learn that Ernesto and his wife, Maria, were mutual friends. When the housekeeper had suggested paying the couple a social call, it sounded like an interesting diversion to Diana, a way to get out of the house. Now, though, she felt rather conspicuous in her boots and pants, and wished she had worn the peasant outfit Lupe had brought that morning.

As the man and the donkey approached, Diana had a real sense of the primitive society in which she found herself. Walking along the road like a peasant was a great equalizer. She felt stripped of all her trappings of independence and self-sufficiency. She was just a young woman with her *acompañadora* going to pay a social call on some friends.

The traveler coming toward them, Diana could see now, was rather elderly, and when he was very near he looked at the two women with curiosity: Diana because she was tall, fair-skinned, wearing pants and boots, obviously a foreigner, Lupe because she was with Diana. The housekeeper greeted the man, who mumbled a response, his mouth a little agape. When he had passed, Lupe turned to Diana.

"I think when we go into the world, *señorita*, you should wear the clothes of a woman," she said matter-of-factly. "You are too much—how you say it?—seen."

"'Obvious' is the word you want, Lupe."

"Yes, perhaps."

"Do I embarrass you?"

"Oh no. I am very proud for you." She touched Diana's arm. "But, I think it es a problem for you to look like you want to be a man."

"Lupe, I don't want to be a man. I find these clothes convenient. I dress differently at different times."

"*Sí, señorita,* I believe thees, but I worry for you. It es not safe."

"What do you mean?"

"A woman who es not as a woman should be es not safe because the men do not like it. Do you understand thees?"

"I'm not sure, unless you're saying women who are not conventional threaten men."

The housekeeper looked perplexed. "I don't know what thees words say, *señorita*, but the woman who is not as the woman should be makes problems."

"Problems for men, perhaps. But I'm not sure that is necessarily bad. If the world is to improve, people—all people, including women—must take action to change it. Evils and problems can't be overcome without change.''

"Change, *señorita*? What do you want to change? You want to change your life to find a husband? Thees I understand. But the woman does not find the husband by having the revolution. It es the opposite of thees. The man looks for the beauty, the love, the softness he needs for his life in the woman. The revolution he has with the other men. That es for his spirit, not for his heart." She glanced at Diana. "Believe me, thees es true. If you knew thees yourself, you would already have the husband and the children."

Diana sighed but said nothing, knowing there was no point in trying to explain her conviction that sometimes, for some women, a husband and children were not the primary objectives in life, not necessary to their happiness.

Lupe, apparently reading Diana's thoughts, said, "I know that all of you *norteamericana* do not believe thees and that you think you will be happier if you can wear the man's boots, but I believe in my heart it es not true."

"I understand why you feel that way, Lupe, but I think that a woman, like a man, must do what her heart tells her to do, no matter what others say."

Lupe looked at her uncertainly.

"Do you know why I am in Honduras, Lupe?"

"No, *señorita*, it es not my business to know."

"Well, perhaps if you knew you would understand me better." Diana then related the gist of her mission in Honduras—the details of Elena's circumstance and her need to rectify the wrong. Afterward Lupe fell silent. Then she spoke.

"You have a very large heart for the other peoples. I know of thees girls of which you speak. It es very sad, very sad. For a woman to be without the protection of a man es a terrible—how you say it?—tragedy?''

"Do you think I am wrong to try to help Elena, Lupe?''

"You are not wrong, no *señorita*. It is the way you try to help that I cannot understand.''

"You mean I should send a husband to help?''

A smile spread across Lupe's round face. "*Pero no, señorita*. For you that es the problem. You don't have one to send. You have only the boots!''

They had arrived at Uncle Ernie's, and Lupe was still chuckling as they left the road and headed across the dusty ground toward the café nestled under the large shade trees. Maria called a greeting from the window, and Ernesto, who was serving a customer at one of the tables under the trees, turned and waved.

"Welcome, Señorita Hillyer,'' he said, beaming as the women approached. "Come. Sit here and I will bring you something cool to drink.''

Lupe signaled for Diana to sit. "I go to the kitchen to talk with Maria. It es cooler for you here under the trees.''

Diana was glad to rest after the long walk in the sun. She watched Ernesto and Lupe go into the café, then saw Rosa appear at the doorway. With a little squeal, she ran out to Diana.

"*Buenos días, señorita,*'' the child said, stopping a few feet from where Diana sat.

"*Hola*, Rosa!'' she replied. They beamed at each other.

"Well, well, *señorita*,'' Ernesto said a few minutes later as he placed a beer before Diana, "to what do I owe this very great honor of your visit?''

"Lupe wanted to call on Maria, so I thought I would come along."

"You are most welcome." The man smiled graciously. "Would you be offended if I sit with you?" he asked, gesturing toward the chair opposite.

"Not at all. Please."

As he seated himself Rosa moved to his side, still beaming at Diana.

"I hope you will permit this, Señorita Hillyer, but in the few minutes I was inside, I already learned of the purpose of your visit to our country."

Diana smiled. "Word certainly travels fast."

Ernesto shrugged. "I don't know if it is the same in your country, but here the women talk. Lupe was telling it to Maria while I was getting the beer for you. Then my wife says to me I should come and talk to you about this."

"You don't approve of my purpose in coming to Honduras, I take it."

"It is not my place to judge this, *señorita*."

Diana studied Ernesto's face. "Then why did you want to talk to me about it?"

"Maria thought perhaps I should explain—and Lupe, too."

"Well, I understand the cantina system well enough, Ernesto. What I don't understand is why something isn't done about it."

The man sighed, his expression sad. "It is very complicated, Señorita Hillyer. But I want to tell you I do not approve of what is done. My country is not a perfect place, I know. When I took this boy, Raul, back to his village for Colonel Emerson, he told me about his cousin Elena and all that has happened, though he said not a word about you."

"Didn't what has happened to Elena upset you, Ernesto?"

"Yes, certainly, *señorita*. As I said to you, I do not approve of what they do in these cantinas."

"What about other people? Do others oppose the practice of kidnapping these girls and making them prostitutes?"

"It is not a popular thing, certainly. Of course those most affected by this, the poor people, are most against it, but others, also, like me."

"Won't the government listen to the wishes of the people?"

"Like I said before, it is complicated. I think, also, you have the problem in your own country that we do not understand. The gangsters, for example—what you call them?—Mafias, I think."

"Yes, the Mafia."

"We hear all these stories about the Mafias that make so much money doing the crimes against the American people. They bring the drugs into the country to kill the young people. They are criminals, I know, but we ask ourselves why this big, powerful country like the U.S.A., with all the police and computers and lawyers, cannot catch a few Mafias and put them in the prison. Once I asked the Colonel Emerson this, and he told to me it is because of the rights of the constitution that the police cannot do more. Perhaps sometimes also the money goes to the police or to the judges. I don't believe the people in your country likes these things, but they happen."

"You're right, Ernesto. There are problems and injustices everywhere. But if there are ways to fight them, they must be used. What I'm wondering is if there is a way to help Elena. How can I get her out of that place?"

"The problem is that many important people have an interest in the money of the cantina system, *señorita*. To help this girl, someone important must wish it."

"Who can I ask? The bishop in Comayagua? Would he help?"

"I don't believe the church can be of much help in this matter. The bishop seat has been empty for many months now, and the priests have too much to do to fight with the owners of the cantinas. There are other serious troubles."

"Then who?"

"I think it would be a man of importance in Tegucigalpa."

"Which man?"

"*Señorita*, I am just the proprietor of a small café. I am not of the big families. It is to them that you must go if you wish the influence."

Diana could sense Ernesto's sincerity, but she felt frustration nonetheless. There appeared to be no solution, unless it lay in the capital.

"I am sorry, Señorita Hillyer, because I can see that you care for this very much. Please know that I will do what I can to help you in this matter, but I am afraid my influence is very small."

"Thank you, Ernesto. I appreciate your offer."

The customer at the other table called for another drink, and Ernesto excused himself to serve the man. While he was gone, Diana tickled the arm of Rosa as she had the day before, and they laughed, but her mind was on the increasingly frustrating problem of Elena. It seemed more apparent than ever that Cleve Emerson was the key. If it meant making the air base her headquarters, she would, and it occurred to her that the sooner she got her things from Marta's place, the better.

When Ernesto returned, Diana asked him if he would be willing to drive her to the Peace Corps station near La Esperanza in exchange for a tank of gas. He said he would, and they agreed that she should come to the café first thing the next morning so that they could get an early start.

"I admire you greatly, *señorita*," Ernesto said when it was time for Diana and Lupe to return to the villa, "but I must warn you to be very careful. There are powerful men in Comayagua who will not be happy when you step on their toes with your boots."

DIANA CLOSED the door to her room and went to the bed, where the clothes Lupe had brought were laying. Picking up the blouse, she saw immediately that because of the off-the-shoulder design, she wouldn't be able to wear her bra. She thought of Cleve, the expectations he undoubtedly had for the evening and the inference he might draw from the provocative clothing. She nearly decided to scrap the idea of the peasant outfit, but thought of Lupe's expectation and realized she had to wear it. *Besides,* she reasoned, *he couldn't expect a woman to turn down a change of clothes. I'll just have to make my disinterest in him clear.*

Diana eagerly removed her boots, pants, shirt and bra, then slipped on the blouse and skirt. The garments felt light and feminine, but she had no mirror to evaluate the visual effect. She decided to go into the bath to glean what she could from the small mirror over the basin.

Standing on her toes, Diana was able to see the top of the blouse, the bare skin of her chest to where the neckline came, but nothing more. She looked down in frustration at the skirt. The length seemed okay, and the flared style had always been a flattering one on her, but she would have liked to have seen what Cleve would see.

Catching her reflection in the mirror, Diana wondered about her hair. She had been wearing it up, but down would be more casual and in keeping with the spirit of the outfit. Perhaps she should wear it down. She would ask Lupe.

Remembering that she hadn't yet tried on the sandals, Diana stole back to her room and slipped them on. They were a little tight for comfort, but she wouldn't have to walk in them, so they would do. When she went into the kitchen where Lupe was busily at work, Diana felt the curious vanity of a girl in her first prom dress.

"¡Qué bonita, señorita!" Lupe exclaimed when she saw Diana. "You are wonderful in the skirt. So beautiful!"

Diana smiled. "But what about my hair? Shall I wear it down?"

The housekeeper studied her charge for a moment. *"Sí, señorita.* I think it es better for thees clothes. Get for me your brush. I will do it."

Diana sat in the living room as Lupe brushed out her hair, feeling pampered and cared for. It was silly, and a rather strange experience, but she liked it.

"There," the woman said, stepping back after a few minutes to examine her work. Then she gave a toothy smile. "Yes, thees es better. Wait, I will take the mirror from the wall so you, too, can see."

Lupe left the room, then returned a moment later with the small bathroom mirror. Standing in front of Diana, the housekeeper held the glass for her. The reflection Diana saw was familiar, but Lupe's brushing and teasing had given her hair unaccustomed fullness. The image did not really look like her, but the soft effect was in concert with the outfit, so she decided it was acceptable.

"Have you seen the clothes yet, *señorita*?" Lupe asked, tilting the mirror. "Stand up, and I will show you how beautiful you are. You must know what our colonel will see."

The joy in Lupe's laugh sent a little surge of excitement through Diana, and she peered into the mirror with the expectation of a schoolgirl.

SOMEWHERE IN THE DISTANCE Diana heard the drone of aircraft approaching and wondered if it might be Cleve returning from the field. She went to the window of her room and pulled back the curtain. Dusk had fallen, and though the sky beyond the mountain ridges still glowed muted tones of yellow and orange, stars were beginning to appear.

She listened to the sound of the airplane drawing near and her heart quickened. There was still no sign of it, but she was certain it must be Cleve. Her hand went to the bare flesh of her chest and, feeling suddenly vulnerable, she wasn't sure whether she wanted to see him.

Lupe had sent Diana to her room to wait for his arrival, but now the idea struck her as rather silly. Humoring the housekeeper was one thing, but she oughtn't to permit the matchmaking scheme. Even if it hurt Lupe's feelings, she should make it clear that she had no interest in the revered colonel.

As she looked out the window a streak of light swept across the airfield beyond the trees, and Diana knew that a plane had landed. She returned to her bed and sat on the edge.

Fifteen minutes later she heard a vehicle outside, Cleve greeting the housekeeper as he entered the villa, then, after a moment, Lupe knocking softly on the bedroom door.

"*Señorita*, the colonel is home. Will you come out now?"

"Yes, Lupe."

Diana opened the door, was greeted by the beaming housekeeper and followed her into the living room. Cleve was at the table, pouring bourbon into a glass. He looked up and, seeing her, froze momentarily. After his eyes had taken her in, a friendly smile eased over his face.

"Well..." he said, his tone warm, "don't you look lovely."

The sincerity of his admiration made Diana blush, but she kept her poise. "I was desperate for a change of clothes, and Lupe was good enough to pick some things up for me in the village."

They both glanced at the housekeeper who, still smiling, nodded politely and withdrew to the kitchen. Cleve chuckled softly. "I was told to notice your outfit, Diana, but the advice wasn't necessary. You're as beautiful a *señorita* as you are a *norteamericana*."

"Thank you. But I'm a *señorita* only temporarily, and only by accident."

"A lovely interlude, then. May I offer you a drink?"

"Thank you." Diana moved toward the table, feeling drawn to him, feeling feminine under his eyes.

When she was next to him, Cleve leaned down suddenly and kissed her softly on the cheek. "Good evening, Diana." He smiled. "How was your day?"

The gesture caught her off guard, but she managed with an effort to act indifferent. "Quiet. How was yours?"

"Busy. We've got a joint operation coming up with the Honduran military after the first of the year." He was fiddling with the bottles and glasses Lupe had on the table. "Bourbon, vodka and rum seem to be the choices."

"Vodka would be nice."

"Tonic?"

"Please."

Cleve mixed her drink quickly, using several of the precious ice cubes Lupe had requisitioned from the mess hall, then led Diana to the couch.

"I'm told I'll have time for my bath before dinner, but I thought we could have a drink first."

"Oh, don't go to any trouble on my account. Just stick to your normal routine."

"In case you haven't noticed," Cleve said, "things around here haven't been normal since your arrival. Delightfully abnormal, as a matter of fact."

They sipped their drinks, Diana studying him, trying to gauge the bent of his thinking, his intentions. Their eyes met. He savored her, and as he did she remembered their lovemaking. Her cheeks colored. Diana sipped her drink and couldn't look at him for a moment.

"I want to apologize for last night," he said softly.

She looked up at him boldly. "There's no need to apologize. I'm a mature woman. I take responsibility for what I do—for my mistakes."

"There was no mistake, other than my insensitivity."

"I'm afraid there was. I gave you the wrong impression, and I hope to rectify it." Diana felt her resolve harden. "I don't intend to sleep with you again."

She watched him look at her, his expression calm.

"Naturally, I wouldn't want you to do anything you don't wish to, but—"

"I don't want that kind of a relationship with you, Cleve."

He slowly took a drink, a touch of consternation on his face.

Diana went on, "As a matter of fact, I think it would be best if I moved out."

Cleve blinked. "Because you don't trust me?"

"No...that's not it." Diana wondered if it might not be because she didn't trust herself. Not liking the implications of the thought, she quickly pushed it from her mind. "It doesn't look right...and I don't want you or anyone else to get the wrong idea."

"Wrong idea?"

"About my purpose in being here. I'm serious about freeing Elena, Cleve. With or without your help."

A look passed over his face, and he quickly took another drink. Just then Lupe stuck her head in the door.

"Colonel Emerson, the dinner will be ready in about twenty minutes."

Cleve nodded. "Okay. Thank you, Lupe." He smiled at Diana, then, touching her hand affectionately, rose to his feet. "Excuse me. I'll just get cleaned up before dinner."

She watched the tall, sandy-haired man as he strode across the room, thinking how the jungle fatigues he wore belied a depth to him she sensed, but hadn't yet fully comprehended. He had the bearing of a military man, yet there was something about him that didn't compute—or was it that her reaction to him didn't compute? And why did she feel the need to thwart him so? Was he *that* threatening?

Diana was confused, but there was one glaring fact she couldn't ignore: Cleve Emerson was the first stranger who had ever seduced her. She tried to decide whether she hated him because of it or whether it made him intriguing. One thing was certain, this enigmatic soldier had taught her a lesson. He would be the last to succeed at that particular game.

Twenty minutes later, Diana was draining the last of her cocktail from her glass when Cleve reappeared. For a moment he stood immobile in the doorway. He was wearing a dress shirt, open at the neck, and a pair of dark slacks. Seeing her reaction to him, the lip under the fringe of his sandy mustache bent into a smile.

"I wasn't born in a uniform, you know," he said with a laugh. "Although sometimes it seems like I was." He walked over and sat down beside her, closer than before.

Diana was struck immediately by his musky cologne. The scent was familiar from the previous night, but freshly applied after his bath it was much more noticeable and arousing.

"You look nice," she said, striving for an impression of casual indifference.

He patted her hand.

"Oh, Colonel Emerson," Lupe said, entering the room with a casserole dish in her hands, "you are just in time." She placed the dish on the table, which she had set during Cleve's absence. Wiping her hands on her apron, the housekeeper turned to the couple and beamed. "Please come."

They rose to their feet and Cleve offered Diana his arm, which she took, feeling a little shy.

"Oh!" Lupe exclaimed. "You are both so beautiful!"

Cleve laughed as he helped Diana with her chair. "Señorita Hillyer is beautiful, Lupe."

"As you say it, Colonel." Turning to the table, Lupe let out a little gasp. "Goodness! I forgot to light up the candle." Quickly she struck a match and lit the single taper in the middle of the table. Then she took her shawl and bag from a nearby chair and went to the door. "Enjoy your dinner. And please don't worry for the dishes. I will do them in the morning." Still beaming, she turned off the light and stepped out into the darkness.

When she had gone Cleve and Diana looked at each other. Amusement, uncertainty, suspicion and anticipation were alternately on their faces. Diana held out her hand, requesting Cleve's plate. "I think one of us should talk to Lupe, Cleve. She definitely has the wrong idea."

"Wrong idea about what?"

"About us." She served him some casserole and vegetables. "On the other hand, with me moving out, maybe she'll get the picture."

"Yes," he said, taking the plate. "I wanted to talk to you about that."

Diana glanced up. Cleve looked particularly handsome in the candlelight. His expression was gentle, soft, but there was a lingering danger in his obvious masculinity. "What do you mean?"

Cleve poured some wine into Diana's glass. "Your safety is the most important thing. I think you should stay here with me."

"No."

"Why?"

"Because."

He smiled. "Devastating argument."

"Because of last night."

Cleve had poured himself some wine and picked up the glass, sipping the ruby liquid carefully. "You didn't enjoy it?"

"No."

His eyebrows rose.

"Well, at the time it was . . . uh . . ." Diana sighed with exasperation. "Cleve, you know what I mean. I have no intention of—"

"I understand," he cut in. "You needn't explain."

"Then why did you ask me if I enjoyed it? That was hardly a gentlemanly thing to do."

"I was curious."

"Well, couldn't you tell?" Diana turned bright red. "I mean, what a person does under unusual circumstances has no bearing on their feelings." She glared at him, hating the handsome face as much as the ambivalence his nearness provoked.

"Yes, I could tell. That's why I was surprised by your denial."

Diana took a large drink of wine. "Obviously, tactfulness is not part of an officer's training."

"I apologize."

She looked at his face that, for the moment, did seem benign, apologetic. "Have you noticed how apology seems to have become a pattern for you?"

"I'm sorry."

They both laughed.

"I suppose the point is," Cleve began, "that you either don't trust me or you're afraid of me."

"I'm not afraid of you."

"Then it's a matter of trust."

"It's a matter of decorum and common sense."

"Forgive me, Diana, but if you had any common sense, you'd be back in Washington where you belong. And as for decorum, well, this isn't exactly wartime, but the circumstances are hardly conventional."

"What are you trying to say?"

"I'm trying to say I think you should stay and that I'll give you whatever guarantees or promises you require."

Diana smiled. "You mean your word as a gentle-man?"

"Despite the implicit sarcasm, Miss Do-Good-er...yes."

She watched him as he ate, knowing he had already assumed victory. "If it wasn't for Elena, Cleve, I wouldn't consider staying. To be honest, though, I real-ize my best chance to help her is here...with you."

Cleve looked at her as though he knew that another appeal for help was in the offing. "I'll do what I can to facilitate your work. But, as I've said, I can't get in-volved personally."

"Can't or won't?"

"Can't *and* won't."

"If you'll at least point me in the right direction, I will agree to stay."

There was resignation on Cleve's face. "You're a stubborn little thing, aren't you?"

"Determined."

"Okay, Diana, I'll do what I can to keep you out of trouble."

CHAPTER SIX

THE VAST PLAIN, stretching far beyond the perimeter of Palmerola Air Base, was bathed in moonlight. After dinner, Cleve and Diana strolled leisurely in the dappled shadow of the trees.

They stopped for a minute and listened to the night. "Mind if I risk your ire by asking a provocative question?" he asked after a while.

"No," she said, laughing, "if you're prepared to take the consequences."

He grinned at her in the darkness. "I said provocative, not indecent."

"Okay, what's your provocative question?"

"What are you *really* doing here in Honduras?"

"I told you; I'm here to help Elena."

"Because your friend Marta asked you to?" he said with a touch of incredulity.

"Marta's much more than just a friend. She's virtually family to me. We grew up together. There's nothing I wouldn't do for her."

"That's quite a friendship."

"Marta was there for me once when I really needed her—her whole family, actually. When I was fifteen my father died, and it devastated both my mother and me. I adored him. Mother and I were overly dependent upon him and, for a few months after his death, Mother lost it. She just cracked up.

"I went to the only other person I had—my best friend, Marta. I ended up moving in with her family for the rest of that school year. Her father, Dan, became a second father to me, the Ronans treated me like another daughter. In a way, that saved my life."

"Where was that?"

"In Washington—the Maryland suburbs. My father was a lawyer with the Justice Department, Marta's father was with the Department of the Interior—nothing very celebrated, but he's a wonderful man."

"Your mother still live in Washington?"

"No, she remarried while I was in college, at George Washington. She and my stepfather live in Southern California now."

"So, from George Washington you became a lobbyist?"

"With a few detours along the way. After college Marta and I spent six months in Europe bumming around. Then I became a VISTA volunteer in the Appalachias for two years."

"A pattern of public service, I see."

They fell into silence, listening again to the sounds of night.

"How did you come to be a soldier?" Diana finally asked, breaking the quiet.

"I was born into it."

"Your father was in the army?"

"Father, grandfather, uncle—we're a military family."

Diana looked up at him, seeing his teeth and the white of his shirt distinctly in the muted light. "You do seem like a soldier, but in another way you don't."

"Despite the fact that it's the only job I've ever had, I do know a little about life on the outside."

"You say that, Cleve, as though you were an inmate and this were jail."

"Is it that obvious?" He grinned. "I suppose the military can be like jail. There are limitations, restrictions on your freedom.... But, disadvantages notwithstanding, I love it—most things about it, anyway."

"But you really have nothing to compare it with."

"Oh, I've been around some, too. I spent several years in England after I graduated from West Point."

"You were stationed there?"

"Not exactly. I was studying at Oxford."

"Oxford? While you were in the army?"

"The military's not completely anti-intellectual, Diana. There's almost always someone from the academies in contention for a Rhodes scholarship."

"You were a Rhodes scholar?" She couldn't help the surprise in her voice.

"Incredible as that may seem."

"I'm sorry, I didn't mean to—"

"Don't worry, I sometimes think back on it myself and wonder how it ever happened. Slogging through the back country of Honduras is a far cry from rowing on the Thames in the Cambridge race."

Diana fell silent, surprised at the revelation. The man beside her began taking on a new dimension in her mind. This crude soldier who seemed so at home in the wilds of Honduras, this American *caudillo* was, underneath the facade, a man of intellect, a true gentleman. She remembered the impressive library in his bedroom. "I guess those books in your room weren't just left over from the previous tenant then."

"No, I always manage to drag a few around with me, wherever I go."

They had stopped at the end of the row of trees not far from the runway. Off in the distance a small plane was approaching the field, its running lights bright in the moonlit sky. Cleve leaned against a tree and watched the plane. Diana studied his strongly chiseled profile in the half light, wondering about the man, realizing there was much more to him than she had surmised.

"You have your books, Cleve, but no wife or family. Is that because of you or because of the army?"

"I did have a wife once. That was because of me. We were divorced—I like to think that was because of the army."

"Was it?"

"In fairness to the service, no. It was just that . . . Carolyn was not enamored with my career, to put it mildly."

"She didn't fit in?"

"Military life can be very tough for a woman—for dependents. If a man's life goal is becoming a general and he devotes himself to it body and soul, I suppose it's not surprising a woman might feel shunted."

"Did she?"

Cleve stared at her in the darkness for a moment. "That was the accusation, but I'm not sure that was really the problem. I'm really not."

Diana wondered about his marriage, what Carolyn must have been like. An unhappy, broken marriage in his past explained a lot. The touch of melancholy beneath his tough veneer made sense to her now. "People choose their lives, Cleve. They aren't mandated by fate."

"Yes, I chose, she chose, we all do. You're right about that."

She could feel his eyes on her, though she couldn't see what they were saying. His presence was intense, close, powerful. It was like the night before, when he returned to find her in his room. Only now he had promised to respect her wishes, he had given his word, and she had had a glimpse inside him. As a result, he was less threatening, but the intimacy of their conversation was frightening in a different way.

"Do you regret your choice at all?" she asked, feeling herself inching away from him.

"Sometimes I do."

"Like when?" For some strange reason she felt compelled to understand him.

"Do you really want to know?" His voice hinted at something ominous.

She hesitated, not certain how to respond.

"That night in Washington, in the lobby of that building, when you were standing not ten feet from me and I thought I'd never see you again—I regretted it then." His voice grew husky and low to the point of a whisper. "I regret it now."

Diana turned at the sound of the aircraft touching the runway a hundred yards away. She trembled, not knowing why she had let the conversation take the turn it had.

"Some guys, like Jack Dawson, solve the problem by getting out," Cleve went on. "Now he's got a three-piece suit, a house in the suburbs and the third kid on the way."

"But that's not what you want?"

"What I'd like is something I can't have."

"What?"

He grasped her bare arm, then stood motionless, his touch restrained, yet firm. Diana looked questioningly into the shadows of his face.

"I wish you were going to be here longer than just a few days."

She felt the warmth of his hand as it tightened slightly, as if to emphasize the point he had made. Involuntarily she stiffened.

"I had only one reason for coming to Honduras, Cleve. When I've done what I came to do, I'm leaving."

He released her, then turned to watch the small plane taxi along the runway. Diana waited, sensing his frustration.

"Why is it you're so driven by this thing?" he asked finally. "Running off half-cocked to free some girl you don't even know? This whole damn world is full of problems, Diana. You don't have to go looking for them."

"I'm mainly here because of Marta, because of something dreadful that's happened to someone she cares about. Marta's like a sister to me, Cleve. If she needs my help, I'll do whatever's necessary to help her."

He sighed. "That doesn't make it any less foolish."

"Foolish? I think you make the mistake of confusing compassion with foolishness. It's unfortunate that you aren't equally touched by Elena's tragedy. With your help, I might get her freed."

"Dammit, Diana. Why do you insist on pressuring me about this scheme of yours?"

"Pressuring you?" She felt her blood rising. "It hardly speaks well of you that you have to be pressured to do the decent thing."

"I've already made my position clear."

"Yes, your position is quite clear. Your head is nicely buried in the sand."

"That's unfair," he seethed, his voice low and hard.

"But accurate."

"Look, don't you learn from your mistakes?"

"You're right, Colonel Emerson. I should have realized by now that you're incorrigible. I can't—any more than the next guy—squeeze compassion out of an insensitive bureaucrat in uniform!"

"Dammit, Diana, that's nonsense. I resent it." He took her arm again, but she jerked it away.

"I'll thank you not to manhandle me!" She turned and began walking briskly toward the villa.

Cleve watched her go, feeling irritation but also regret. He thought of their conversation, the apparent understanding between them, and wondered how the evening had gone wrong. *Duty,* he thought. *Duty will always be between me and what I want.*

CLEVE LINGERED at the breakfast table longer than he should have, but he hoped to see Diana before he left. He had to go over to Olancho in the eastern zone again and wouldn't be getting back until late. The notion of leaving her all day with last night's spat unresolved didn't sit well with him. He wanted to clear the air before going, if only with another apology.

Lupe had been chattering away nonstop since her arrival that morning, but Cleve could tell that she, too, was anxious to see Diana. He hoped that the tension of the previous night wouldn't be obvious to the housekeeper, because it was apparent that she expected to see bliss on Diana's face. He didn't want to fail either of them, but most particularly, he didn't want to fail himself.

"I'm so glad you liked the dinner, Colonel," Lupe said in Spanish. "It was the same dinner my mother prepared for the family of my brother-in-law before he asked to marry my sister. It brings good fortune."

"You are very thoughtful, Lupe, but I don't think Miss Hillyer is even remotely thinking in terms of marriage—to me or anyone else."

The housekeeper looked at him with surprise. "Did she tell you this?"

"Not in so many words, but she didn't have to. She is my countryman, I understand her."

Lupe looked concerned. "But how can she do this, Colonel? She is not thinking clearly. Not thinking of her future."

"Lupe, you're assuming too much."

"With all respect, Colonel, I assume nothing. I speak of the things that I feel and see."

"I appreciate your good intentions, but I think it best if this talk of marriage not continue. Miss Hillyer knows her mind as well as I know mine. There is nothing to be gained from this talk."

Lupe dropped her head in contrition, but Cleve could see that inwardly she resisted.

"As you wish it, Colonel."

Cleve accepted another cup of coffee from the housekeeper, though he didn't really want it, hoping still that Diana might come out. He glanced at his watch, then toward the bedrooms, and saw that Lupe had seen him. He wondered whether she could really tell just how deep his feelings were for Diana.

These games of the heart were unfamiliar to Cleve. He couldn't remember playing them before—certainly not growing up. And there had been no cat and mouse with Carolyn. Their relationship seemed pretty straightforward from the beginning: a brief period of very positive feelings, followed by a long period of negative ones, culminating in rupture.

He sipped his coffee, though his stomach was already rebelling, and wondered why he had even let himself get involved, sucked into this conundrum with Diana Hillyer. Obviously he was just indulging himself. There was no point in it. There was no plausible outcome other than disappointment.

Was it the sex? Cleve thought of her in his bed—their wonderfully spontaneous lovemaking, the unexpected excitement that seemed to have carried them both away. Together they had been like two strains of an exquisitely euphonious melody, intertwined and consonant. It had been so lovely, so fulfilling, that the discord that had followed seemed painfully wrong, criminal. Yet, what else could he expect?

"*Señorita*, good morning!"

At the sound of Lupe's voice Cleve looked up and saw Diana standing in the doorway, her hand resting on the doorframe, her eyes uncertain, shy. She had on the clothes she had worn the first day when he had rescued her from Lopez.

"Good morning, Cleve." There was no tension in her voice, though there was hesitation, wariness.

"Well, good morning. How did you sleep?" He managed to sound upbeat and cheerful.

"I slept well." Diana came to the table, and he watched her sit down.

They waited in silence until Lupe poured Diana's coffee and put some bread and jam before her. The housekeeper must have sensed the repressed feelings, because after a moment she left the kitchen to give them greater privacy.

"I won't bore you with another apology, Diana, though I am sorry about last night. I want you to understand I'm not being insensitive or callous about not helping Elena. If I could help without stepping on toes, I would. But I know these people, and I know what it would cost in terms of soured relations.''

"I understand you have a job to do.''

Her acquiescence took him by surprise. Cleve studied her, skeptical. "Do you really understand?''

"Yes, I understand. It doesn't mean I share your priorities, but I understand.''

He felt the gap between them and hated it even more than when they had argued over his refusal to help. Somehow, the distance was more painful than the anger. He felt an overwhelming need to touch her, but it wouldn't be well received, he could tell.

Cleve thought of what he had said to her the night before, about how she had made him regret his military career. He wanted to say it again, to express how much he hated the clash of duty and feelings, but there was no point in it. He picked up his coffee cup, then put it down, knowing his stomach didn't want any more.

"I'm running late, Diana. I'd better go.''

She nodded. There was no hostility in her manner, only aloofness.

"I'll be back late tonight. I've told Lupe I won't be home for dinner, so I'm afraid you'll have to eat alone.''

"That's all right. I don't mind.''

Their eyes met.

"Please don't worry about me, Cleve. You've got enough to think about.''

The distance was excruciating. "I'm not worried, I just regret not being able to get back for dinner. I'd much rather spend the evening with you.''

Her smile was polite—not in the least unkind—but it didn't say what he wanted it to.

"I'm sorry you've had to rough it for a couple days, but tomorrow I'll see that your things are picked up from the Peace Corps station."

"I'll survive, but I appreciate your concern."

Cleve was feeling more and more anxious, knowing he had to leave and regretting that things were not as he wanted them. He stood, then took his beret from the back of his chair. Diana smiled at him, looking wonderfully beautiful. Cleve touched her cheek, unable to resist. "See you tonight."

Diana watched him exit the kitchen, the heat of his touch still glowing on her cheek. She tried to cool the spot with her fingertips but the feeling persisted, lingering about her as the man did himself. His restraint, the pent-up passion in him, suffocated her when they were together. Letting him take her as she had that first night was easier than this. Diana knew she had to get away.

Lupe returned to the kitchen. "I hope you enjoyed the dinner last night, *señorita*."

"Yes, Lupe, it was lovely. We both enjoyed it very much."

The housekeeper was searching her face, but didn't comment further. She just gave Diana her cherubic smile and began clearing the dishes. It was obvious she knew things hadn't gone well.

"What are your plans for the day, *señorita*?"

"I'm going to visit my friend who lives near La Esperanza. I've asked Ernesto to take me."

"Does the colonel know thees?"

"I didn't tell him because I didn't want to upset him. He's very busy, and I don't want him to feel badly about being unable to look after me."

"I am sure he likes it, *señorita*."

"He's very kind. Everyone I've met has been very kind—with the exception of several gentlemen in Comayagua—but I don't want to impose any more than necessary. Will you tell the colonel that I arranged a ride, and that I'll come back tomorrow with whoever he was going to send for my things?"

"*Sí, señorita*. Whatever you wish."

Diana took a last sip of coffee. "I'd better get going. Ernesto is expecting me."

THE ANCIENT PICKUP TRUCK bumped its way up the mountain road, leaving a cloud of dust in its wake and Diana's bones crying for relief. The seat springs were long since battered flat, and only the cushion that Ernesto had given her had saved Diana from certain bruises. After a particularly harsh jolt, the café proprietor looked at her and smiled.

"It is not much farther, Señorita Hillyer. You will make it, I assure you."

"The spirit is willing, but I'm afraid the flesh is weaker than I thought, Ernesto."

"*¿Señorita?*"

Diana laughed. "I'll make it. I've just been spoiled by four-lane interstate highways, that's all."

"I bet you've never seen a road so bad as this one."

She smiled, despite another jolt. "The scenery's wonderful, Ernesto."

"Yes, what Honduras lacks in pleasure for the body it makes up for in pleasure for the eyes." He grinned. "And to be fat like me has its advantages on the road like this one."

A short time later they arrived in the village where Marta Ronan had worked for nearly two years as a Peace Corps volunteer. The petite redhead appeared at the front window to her house when Ernesto's truck creaked to a stop.

Before Diana had managed to get out, Marta ran to the truck and pulled open the passenger door. "Diana! I didn't expect you until tomorrow. Are you all right?"

Diana stepped down onto the dusty road and embraced her friend, feeling truly safe for the first time in days. "Oh, it's so good to see you!" She pulled back and looked into Marta's happy green eyes.

The two women, their arms around each other, stepped from the road to the small porch of Marta's house as Ernesto came around the truck. He was smiling.

"Buenos días."

Diana introduced Ernesto.

Marta extended her hand. "Oh, you're the man who brought Raul back from Comayagua."

"Sí, señorita. How is my young friend, Raul?" Ernesto asked as he shook Marta's hand. "Is his nose straight, or still curved like the mountain road?"

"He's better, but I think his nose will be a souvenir of his adventure in Comayagua."

"Oh, Marta," Diana said, "that's dreadful. Will he be terribly disfigured?"

"No, fortunately it's not that bad, but the doctor said his nose won't be as symmetrical as before." She pushed aside the strips of plastic hanging in the doorway, which were designed to admit the air but discourage flies and the hot rays of the sun. "Come on in, you'll both want something to drink after your trip."

DIANA AND MARTA WAVED farewell to Ernesto from the porch as he climbed into the truck, Diana again calling out her thanks for his help. They waited as the vehicle coughed back to life and the man turned it around in the middle of the narrow village road, momentarily holding up half a dozen pedestrians and several donkeys. Having pointed his truck in the right direction, Ernesto waved and headed off.

The two women went into the house, an adobe structure with a neatly packed earth floor. They sat down at the table, and Diana felt herself sag with relief at being back with her friend.

"Was it dreadful, Diana?"

She nodded. "Yes, especially the disappointment at having failed. But it's good to be here. Almost as good as being home."

"Didn't you like Palmerola?"

"Yes and no."

Marta looked at her, apparently hearing something in her voice. "Which part is yes and which part is no?"

"It was pleasant enough, but I haven't made any progress in trying to help Elena. The past few days have been frustrating."

"That all?"

"Yes and no."

There was a knowing smile on Marta's face. "Is it that colonel?"

"Yes and..." She grimaced. "Yes, to be honest."

"What happened?"

"His men call him 'Old Pain and Pleasure'. The nickname's an apt one."

"Is he good-looking?"

"Unfortunately."

"Why 'unfortunately'?"

"It would be better if he wasn't, that's all."

Diana could see by Marta's expression that she knew. "Come on. Give. What happened?"

"I went to bed with him."

"You didn't!"

"I did. The first night I was there."

"Lord, that's not like you, Diana. He must be great."

"Oh, he's perfectly wonderful. He's even a Rhodes scholar, though I didn't know that when I let him seduce me. He's charming, witty, attractive as hell and obviously irresistible."

"Well?"

"He's a bastard, too—at least he is about Elena."

"Maybe he'll come around."

"I doubt it. We argued about it again last night. We're completely at cross-purposes about it."

"But you obviously like him."

"I let things get out of control, Marta. I made a stupid mistake getting involved with him, and now I regret it."

"You don't like him?"

"How could I? He's not my type. We have nothing in common. And there's absolutely no possibility anything could come of it."

"You *do* like him!"

"Oh, Marta! Of course I like him...in a way. But in another way I don't. I'm attracted to him, but I don't know him, so how can I care for him?"

"It would be just fine with you if you never saw him again?" Marta asked skeptically.

"Yes, of course. You know how I love my job and Washington. It's everything to me. And there's Tom— we've been dating for more than a year now."

"But you don't love Tom. I mean, it's not serious."

"No, but it might become serious someday."

Marta stared silently.

Diana knew what the look meant. "What?"

"I think the lady doth protest too much."

Diana laughed. "That's absurd."

"Maybe, but there's something in your manner that doesn't match your words."

"The man's attractive, I've admitted that. He really turned me on. I mean . . . he's incredible. But so what?"

"So what?" Marta's tone was full of incredulity.

"So...there's no future in it. I might as well fall in love with the chairman of the Soviet Communist Party."

"Now we're all the way to the point of falling in love?"

"Marta, what is this? The Grand Inquisition? I think you've been in Honduras too long."

"Sorry. I'm just giving you feedback, playing back what you're saying minus the static."

Diana reached over and touched her friend's hand. "I'm sorry, too. You know I love you. It's just that I've had a few rough days. A couple hours on stable ground and I'll be my old self."

Marta smiled sympathetically. "No need to apologize. I've been rocked in my boots by a guy before myself."

Diana opened her mouth to protest, but stopped. She remembered Marta's words, *"The lady doth protest too much."* She decided that if she was going to quell the emotional tempest stirred up by Cleve Emerson, she'd better stop protesting now. Perhaps that had been her mistake in dealing with him the past few days. Her outbursts were only adding fuel to the fire. The best way to stifle a flame, she decided, was to let it die a natural death.

"So what do you think we ought to do about Elena?" Marta asked. "Is there anything more you can do in Honduras, or is it a matter of going back to Washington and lighting a fire under Freedom International?"

"The options are narrowing, that's for sure. I checked into the possibility of getting help from the church, but the bishopric in Comayagua is vacant, and you were right about the limits of their ability to influence a matter like this. I've pretty well concluded we'll find the solution in Tegucigalpa, or not at all."

"Any ideas?"

"Nothing specific, but Cleve agreed to at least point me in the right direction. I'm not sure where that'll lead me, or even how sincere he was, but I'm going to give it a shot."

Marta grinned. "You're going to endure him for the sake of the cause?"

"Don't get smart, Señorita Ronan. My fall from grace was all because of you."

The other laughed. "Yeah. That's like my father used to blame his big stomach on my mother's good cooking. Some foods—and some men—are just irresistible."

There was a man's voice outside the house. *"Hola. ¿Señorita Ronan?"*

Marta got up and went to the door. Diana heard her friend exchanging words with someone in Spanish before stepping back and admitting a young, slender Honduran into the room.

"Raul!" Diana exclaimed.

He grinned under a large white bandage on his nose. *"¿Señorita Hillyer, cómo está?"*

She rose, extending her hands, which the young man took. "More importantly, how are you?"

"I okay," he replied with a bashful grin. "I worry for you in the jail."

"I saw you there, you know. They arrested me, too."

The young man nodded.

"It must have been terrible for Elena."

He didn't understand and Marta translated.

"She cried when thees mens take her."

A mental picture of a weeping girl being dragged away struck Diana, and her face twisted at the image. "God, I wish we had succeeded." She turned to Marta. "Did they nearly make it or wasn't there a chance?"

"Raul told me that he got to her room all right, just as we planned. They were able to talk, and he explained what she was to do. Then they made it downstairs okay and to the kitchen, but they were caught going out the back door."

Diana squeezed Raul's hand. "I'm so sorry, Raul. I haven't given up. I'm going to keep trying."

"*Muchas gracias, señorita.* I am happy for your help."

"Has it been terrible for Elena? I'm sure she's miserable. Were you able to talk at all?"

Marta translated, and Raul responded at length in Spanish. "He says that she was very frightened when they first took her to the cantina, a year ago," Marta explained, "but now it is the loneliness and dreariness of her life that's hardest to bear. She wants desperately to return to the village or go somewhere to start a new life."

"Poor thing." Diana felt tears welling in her eyes. "Do they badly mistreat her?"

"Raul has told me that the food is adequate and the clothes, as well. The girls are supplied with cosmetics and beauty aids, which they are charged for—it all augments the debt that supposedly justifies keeping them in the cantina."

"Maybe we should have waited until she was outside and kidnapped her back."

Marta shook her head. "Apparently there's no way to predict when she might be out of the cantina, and Raul said they're always escorted."

The young man spoke again, and Diana waited for Marta's translation.

"He says that Elena has been given a few privileges because she has become a favorite of some of the American servicemen, who pay better than the other customers."

"Americans? From the air base?"

"Apparently so."

Diana's anger flared, her neck turning red.

"You knew they frequented the cantinas, Diana. I told you that when you first arrived."

"Yes, but if Elena is a favorite, the proprietors of the cantina may be keeping her just for that purpose. She may be of extra value to them."

"Who knows?"

"Marta, Cleve's men are keeping her in that cantina!"

"You don't know that, Diana."

"They're a factor. That much is sure."

"Don't get yourself worked up about it. Let's just get Elena out of there. This fellow, Cleve, may be our best bet. Let's use him to our advantage, not make an enemy of him."

Diana exhaled, but the tension she felt wouldn't abate. At that particular moment she would have liked to give Old Pain and Pleasure a little pain, but Marta was suggesting the opposite. She could see it was coming down to the old vinegar and honey dichotomy. The question was, how nice she could make herself—or let herself—be?

CHAPTER SEVEN

DIANA WAS PINNING her hair up, barely able to see herself in the tiny mirror on the bedroom wall, when a clamor of children's voices came from the road outside the house. Marta had been in the kitchen doing the breakfast dishes, and Diana heard her go outside.

She listened as she quickly finished with her hair, but couldn't make out what all the excitement was about. The noise seemed to move farther down the road by the time she had gotten to the living room. Diana went to the door and pushed through the plastic strips to look out.

Squinting into the bright morning sun, she saw a crowd of children gathered around a car at the lower end of the village. Marta was in the center of the group with a tall man in a dark brown leather jacket. He was fair, with sandy-colored hair and, as he turned, she saw his mustache. It was Cleve.

He and Marta were talking, both smiling and gesturing. Surprised and fascinated, Diana shrank back into the doorway, where she could watch without being seen.

As the children dispersed, she could see Cleve was wearing buff-colored trousers tucked into high-topped leather boots. The image was rather dashing, and it surprised Diana to see him in civilian clothes. Though he hadn't exactly said what he had intended to do about getting her clothes back to the air base, she had assumed he would be sending someone else.

After another moment of conversation, Cleve and Marta began walking up the road toward the house. Some of the smaller children tagged along, but the others lost interest and began drifting away. From her place just inside the door and behind the plastic, Diana had a good view of Cleve strolling next to her friend. They were an incongruous couple, and yet seeing them together was, in a funny way, reassuring. Was it the civilian clothes or Marta's presence that made him seem more beneficent?

When they were near, Diana retreated into the bedroom, deciding it would be uncomely to be caught spying. Besides, she wanted her surprise at seeing him to appear spontaneous.

"Diana!" Marta called from the living room a few moments later. "You've got a guest."

After a final glance in the mirror, then at her pearl-gray slacks and cranberry cotton sweater, Diana pushed aside the heavy curtain over the doorway and stepped into the other room.

Cleve felt his chest tighten as the curtain slid open, revealing the woman he had come for. Her eyes rounded and her lips dropped slightly open at the sight of him. Her dark tresses were softly pinned, with errant tendrils touching her neck and face. The same gentle smile from breakfast the previous day touched her lips.

"Cleve, I hadn't expected you—personally, I mean."

"You didn't think I would leave such a delicate mission to someone else, did you?"

She smiled. "What's so delicate? The controversy?"

"I was thinking of the cargo. You." He saw her glance at Marta, who was listening with a bemused little smile on her face. Then she looked back at him.

"I guess you met Marta?"

"Yes, with the help of half the children of the village. I figured once I had tracked her down you couldn't be far away."

"You make me sound like a fugitive."

"Yes, I do, don't I?"

The air was alive with tension, restraint on both sides. There was both ice and challenge in her manner.

"Why don't the two of you sit down," Marta said, pulling a chair out from the table and gesturing to Cleve. "I'll make some coffee."

Diana moved to the side of the table opposite him like a she-cat, equally capable of attack or flight. His loins warmed at her nearness. Were it not for that girl—Elena—they might be in each other's arms. But her resolve in the matter was apparent.

To Diana, Cleve seemed studied, even careful, though he maintained an easy manner. He was very friendly and charming, thoroughly likable as he asked Marta about her work and experiences in Honduras. She seemed to react positively to him, and Diana found herself silently warning her friend to be cautious, not to be taken in by him, wanting her to see everything, not just the beguiling facade.

After they had finished their coffee, Marta asked to be excused for half an hour or so to deal with a problem at the station. She invited them to stay for lunch before heading back to Palmerola. They agreed, and Cleve suggested to Diana that they take a walk in the morning air while Marta was busy.

Outside, Cleve and Diana were soon joined by several of the children in the village, and he bantered with them as they walked up the road, much to the youngsters' delight.

"Do you really like children, Cleve, or is this just part of a military public-relations program?" Diana's question was more caustic than she had intended, and she was glad when he let it pass without taking offense.

"I like children, though I've never been around them much," he replied simply.

She saw the hurt on his face. "I didn't mean that how it sounded."

"Oh, don't worry. When you're in the middle, people have a tendency to shoot in your direction."

"Is that how you feel—that I'm taking shots at you?"

"Let's just say I'm acutely aware of an outstanding point of disagreement between us."

She smiled at Cleve's phraseology. "I'm beginning to understand the reason for your books on diplomacy."

They came to the edge of the village, and the last of the children left them. They wandered up the road alone. Neither of them said anything for a while, each seemingly engrossed in the verdant mountain scenery, but their mutual awareness was acute.

Diana took a deep breath, savoring the fresh pine-scented air. "The smell of the forest is wonderful, isn't it?"

She glanced at Cleve who nodded, more aware of her, it seemed, than what she had said. But he responded anyway.

"Shall we leave the road and walk through the woods for a while? There seem to be a number of trails."

She agreed, and they wandered off into the woods, which were still cool from the night air. For a time they walked side by side, but despite their proximity, the distance between them was evident. Diana would have liked to take Cleve's arm, if only as a friendly gesture of companionability, but "the outstanding point of disagreement" stood in the way. The serenity of the forest made the tension in the air seem particularly unfitting.

Then Cleve spoke, arcing the gap between them. "You know, I was really disappointed to get home last night and find you had gone."

"Oh? I would have thought you'd have been relieved."

"Why?"

Diana couldn't help a little laugh. "I've been nothing but trouble for you."

"Not in the least."

"Oh come on, Cleve. You don't have to be diplomatic with me. I know I've been a pain in the neck. I'm embarrassed to think about it—especially considering how much you've done for me. I feel badly until..."

"Until what?"

"Until I think what it is we disagree about."

Cleve smiled thinly. "Yeah. It would be a lot more convenient if you were here to investigate Honduran crop rotation."

"If it wasn't for Elena, I'd probably be on Capitol Hill right now twisting an unwilling arm."

Cleve reached over and tweaked her cheek. "Well, at least you won't have lost your arm-twisting skills on this trip."

Diana was glad for his touch, for his having breached the gap, even if the remark was at her expense. "You see, in a moment of candor you admit I *have* been a pain."

He grinned. "Perhaps I'm a masochist."

"You certainly picked a funny way to get your torture."

"Now that's certainly hyperbole. Your company is hardly torture."

She let the silence hold.

"Then again . . ." he volunteered after a moment.

Diana laughed. "I suppose it's a good sign that we can laugh about our differences."

Cleve took her arm as the path they had been following became a little rocky. Again, she liked the feel of his hand on her.

"Nothing's simple, is it?" he asked wistfully.

"Should it be?"

"It is in one's fantasies. People have a compulsion to idealize, don't you think?"

"I suppose."

"Take for example our encounter in Washington. Who would have thought we'd have ended up at opposite ends of a gun barrel?"

Diana glanced at him. "Is that where we are?"

He grinned. "Perhaps we'd better avoid the subject. I'm sorry I brought it up."

She reflected on his mood, not sure what he was thinking. "Did you really have an impression of what I was like that night? I mean, we didn't even speak. I remember seeing you at the party, but I don't recall any particular thoughts about you, other than curiositv."

"Only curiosity?"

"Yes, I'd say that's what it was."

"In what sense?"

Diana smiled. "I wondered why you were staring at me so."

"You captivated me, Diana." He took her arm again as she stepped over a small log. "You were the most beautiful creature I had ever seen."

"Until reality set in," she replied with a shy glance.

"No, you still are." Cleve stopped suddenly, pulling Diana to a stop a second later.

She turned toward him and looked into his eyes, feeling the emotion that had welled up in him.

He still held her arm, tightly, with urgency. "I hate this business that's between us," he said, searching her eyes as though he might find concurrence.

"Cleve..."

Before she could say more, his mouth descended on hers, taking it certainly, but tenderly. Diana stood motionless, frozen with surprise as his arms wrapped around her.

The mesmerizing caress of his lips and his familiar masculine aroma instantly breached her defenses. Diana accepted his kiss without thinking, but when he whispered his desire for her, she came to her senses.

She pushed him away. "No, Cleve, I can't."

"Diana..."

"Don't you understand?" she implored, feeling tears brim in her eyes. "You promised."

"Promised what?"

Her jaw hardened. "It was understood that...that our relationship is strictly business."

He searched her face. "I know how you feel about that girl, but..." He grasped her shoulder, but she pushed his hand away.

"Don't make it any harder than it is, please." Her expression was beseeching. The hurt on Cleve's face told her how completely at odds their desires were. Without another word, Diana turned and ran back down the path as fast as she could go.

CLEVE APPROACHED the village, wondering what he would find when he arrived. Kissing Diana had obviously been a dumb thing to do, but it was a product of frustration, not miscalculation. He had done as he wished, and there had been nothing in her behavior that told him the gesture would be unwelcome. To the contrary, it seemed that she had craved the affection as much as he.

Arriving at Marta's door, he knocked on the frame. To his surprise, Diana appeared almost immediately.

"I've only one bag," she said, pushing a suitcase through the dangling plastic strips. "Would you mind carrying it to the car for me?"

She hadn't looked him in the eye, and her matter-of-fact manner caught him totally by surprise.

"Sure, I—"

"Marta!" Diana called, retreating into the house. "We're going now."

"I'll be right out," he heard the other woman call from a back room.

A moment later Diana stepped out into the sunlight with her purse and a small overnight bag in hand. "It's warming up," she said, shooting him a perfunctory look.

"Warmer than I would have expected."

"Look," she said in a low voice, "I overreacted back there in the woods. Can we just forget it? I've got some serious issues to discuss with you."

"Sounds ominous," he said under his breath. They heard Marta coming.

"Strictly business," she assured him.

Marta stepped outside. "Well, can't I convince you to stay for lunch?"

"Thank you, but I hadn't realized Cleve was under a tight schedule. We'll barely make it back in time as it is. Right, Cleve?"

"Oh…yeah. I've got some serious matters to tend to— heavy discussions." He glanced at Diana, who was watching him warily.

"Well, I'm glad you came up anyway, Cleve," Marta said sweetly. "It was awfully nice to have met you." She extended her hand, which he took. "We seem to be dealing with opposite extremes of Honduran society, but it's nice to know another American in the neighborhood."

"By all means, Marta. If I can ever be of help, let me know. They keep us on a pretty short leash, but sometimes there are unofficial means."

"I'm terribly grateful for the help you're giving Diana with Elena. And I don't know what we would have done if you hadn't gotten her out of jail. My opportunities to do much are extremely limited because of my role here. Everything I've done has been strictly outside channels."

"That's what I understand. Fortunately we've got Diana, who can do things without governmental constraints—if she can manage to stay out of jail, that is."

Diana shot him a withering glance.

Marta seemed aware of the tension now, as well. She touched Diana's arm. "Take care, kiddo."

Diana smiled, and they embraced. "I'll let you know what happens, Marta. If I can, I'll come back to see you before I return to the States."

They said goodbye again, and Cleve and Diana walked down the village road to the car. He helped her in and went around to the driver's side.

"That was rather cynical, Cleve," Diana said as he climbed in.

"What?"

"Your comment to Marta about your being fortunate to have *my* help."

"We *are* fortunate."

"*We?* You make it sound like you're on our side when you aren't."

"Well, I'm not on any other side." He started the engine.

"There's no such thing as neutrality in a matter like this."

They slowly drove out of the village under the curious eyes of the populace. "Is that what you wanted to say to me?" Cleve asked, knowing his annoyance was beginning to show.

"No, there's something else."

He looked at her.

"I'm sorry, Cleve, but I spoke with Raul yesterday and learned something that has really upset me. That's why I reacted so strangely earlier."

"What is it?"

"According to Raul, Elena has become a favorite of the American servicemen."

"Oh, God." He rolled his eyes and sighed with exasperation.

"I'm sorry. I'm no more pleased about it than you are."

"So now, I take it, my obligation is undeniable. Is that what you're trying to say?"

"I'd hoped it would open your mind, if not your heart."

"They *are* open. Believe me." He felt the frustration mounting.

"Then why don't you do something?"

Cleve looked at her, knowing that to respond would only add fuel to the fire. Ahead the road curved along the side of the mountain. He stared at it, his fists tightening on the wheel.

They drove down the mountain in virtual silence. Cleve turned the situation over in his mind repeatedly, looking for a way to accommodate Diana without neglecting his duty. What did she expect him to do? Confine his troops to quarters for their entire tour of duty?

"Could I ask a question?" she asked, breaking the silence. Her voice was calm, unaccusing.

"Certainly."

"Is there anyone in authority in this country who would be sufficiently moved by Elena's plight to do something about it?"

"I would imagine so. The problem is that prostitution is endemic to this society. People accept it, without personally liking it or approving of it."

"But Elena's not a prostitute. She's a sex slave."

"The distinctions tend to blur."

"But the distinction is significant, Cleve."

"Not when you're from the wrong side of the tracks. Everything that happens to the lower classes is regrettable. Frankly, people in authority haven't experienced these things personally. I don't think they know what it's like in a cantina."

"Do you?"

"No."

"Well, maybe that's the problem. If you saw the suffering yourself, you might have a little more compassion."

"Please, let's not start bickering again."

"Am I wrong?"

"I don't know that you're right. You haven't been in a cantina, either."

"Maybe we *both* should go and find out."

"Go to a cantina? That's absurd."

"Why not? We've been arguing over something neither of us knows about firsthand. Let's go to the cantina district when we get back to Comayagua."

"No."

"What's the matter? Afraid of what you'll see? I'm not."

"Okay, Diana. We'll go to the cantina district. You're right. There's no point in dealing with shadows."

It was midafternoon by the time they reached Comayagua. Cleve drove past the main square and the church to the edge of town, where they came to several dirt streets lined with shabby adobe buildings with red tile roofs. Sewage was running along the open ditches on either side of the road, and pigs rooted in the dusty earth around some of the cantinas.

"Lord, it's worse than I thought," Diana said as they inched along. "I wonder which one Elena's in?"

"Do you know the name?"

"Raul said it's the biggest one. A two-story building. The name had the word *noche* in it, I believe."

Cleve read the names as they passed each cantina. "Ah, this must be it," he said, pausing in the road. "It's called My Glorious Night."

"I want to go inside, Cleve."

"No, Diana, you can't."

Before he knew what had happened, Diana jumped from the car and ran to the front door of the cantina. Cleve quickly pulled to the side of the road and got out, his heart pumping as he ran after her. Diana had been stopped just inside the door by a guard. The man was shouting at her, ordering her out.

"Wait a minute, friend," Cleve said to the man in Spanish. "We are looking for someone."

"No one you or this lady knows would be here. You are mistaken."

"Please, just give us a moment to look."

The man stared at them suspiciously, then moved half a step back. He turned and glanced with them around the murky room.

Several men were drinking beer at a rough-hewn bar. They looked over their shoulders at the commotion. At a nearby table was a middle-aged man wearing a dirty shirt. There were dark circles under his eyes, and he hadn't shaved for a day or two. A cigarette hung from his lip. Catching Cleve's eye, he turned away.

Farther into the darkness, against the back wall, were half a dozen wooden chairs and a bench. Two girls sat apart, one in a tattered red slip, her hands resting on her knees, the other in a low-cut cotton dress, her elbow on the back of the chair next to her, the side of her head in her hand. Cleve saw Diana staring at the girls.

"Elena?" she called out hesitantly.

Neither girl moved. Both stared vacantly.

"You have seen," the guard said. "Now go." He stepped toward them.

"Elena?" Diana called more insistently.

"Come on," Cleve said gently. "I doubt if either of them is Elena. She's probably not here now. Let's go, this won't do any good."

She looked up at him, her eyes brimming with anger and emotion. "But, Cleve..."

"Come on," he said, taking her arm.

Another guard with a carbine suddenly appeared at the rear of the room.

"Let's go before there's trouble." He pulled her to the doorway, but Diana went reluctantly, her head turned back toward the two young women, neither of whom had moved.

As soon as they were outside Diana sank against him and he put his arm around her shoulders, walking her to the car. When they were inside, Cleve started the engine and glanced over at Diana. Tears were running down her cheeks.

"I never should have agreed to bring you here," he mumbled, feeling irresponsible and foolish.

Diana said nothing; she just stared blankly down the road, and Cleve knew he could no longer let matters drift.

THERE WAS LITTLE ACTIVITY on the air base that afternoon. It seemed unusually quiet as Diana sat in the living room, thinking. But feeling tired from the trip and emotionally drained by the incident at the cantina, she decided to go to her room and lie down until Cleve returned from town, where he had gone to drop off the car he had rented for the trip to Marta's.

What a strange twist the day had taken. Cleve had come for her in civilian clothes, a rented car—all to be inconspicuous—and in the end he had thrown caution to the wind and gone to the cantina. The whole business was ironic and bitterly sad.

For the first time in years, Diana felt helpless. She wanted desperately to get Elena out of that hellhole, but she didn't know how to go about it. Her frustration was unbearable. Cleve may have been right; it was probably a mistake to go to the cantina. It only served to upset her and confirm her worst fears.

Cleve seemed to be affected by the experience, too, though he hardly said anything on the drive back to Palmerola. However, if his eyes had been opened by the visit, it may have been worthwhile after all.

At the moment Diana was alone in the house. Lupe only worked in the morning on Saturdays and had already gone home. Waiting, Diana felt a little melancholy, but tried to cheer herself by thinking about Washington and her job.

The thought of being back at her desk and caught up in the frenetic pace of her lobbying activities was a pleasing one. It represented a return to normalcy—an end to this bizarre, emotionally charged experience in Honduras.

It would also mean an end to her time with Cleve Emerson and the tension his presence produced. Whenever he was around, her control and self-assurance were continually under siege. It was a sure sign of a faulty relationship, incompatibility.

On the other hand, Diana knew it was more complex than that. There was a tremendous attraction between them that befuddled her. In fact, she was rather ashamed of the way she had acted—she had lost her cool with him half a dozen times, and that wasn't like her. But Diana couldn't believe there was any great significance in the fact. Physical attraction—that was all it was.

She closed her eyes and pictured him in the village walking up the road with Marta. Those high-topped boots with the trousers tucked in, the leather jacket and that cocky, challenging look that never seemed to leave his face—it was an alluring image. The man was damned attractive, there was no denying it. Too damned attractive.

And then he had kissed her in the woods, knowing it was the wrong thing to do. But he did it anyway, forcing her to react, challenging her to resist him. And yet, in spite of everything, the kiss had not been pernicious— just presumptuous, inconsiderate.

But could she honestly say he was insensitive? What had happened at the cantina seemed to have upset him as much as it had her. What *really* was inside the man?

Gradually Diana's fatigue overcame her, and she began to drift into sleep. Cleve Emerson was at the periphery of her consciousness, holding her, protecting her, permitting her to take refuge in his arms. It was a sweet sleep.

BLINKING AWAKE in the semidarkness, Diana felt the warmth of his hand on her head. He was stroking it gently, with great affection. She smiled up at him, liking the feeling of his proximity and warmth. Then she realized it was really he.

"Cleve..."

"Sorry to awaken you, but I've fixed some dinner. I thought you ought to eat something since you missed lunch."

"What happened?"

He smiled down at her. "You've been sleeping. Deeply it seems." He leaned down and kissed her on the forehead.

She touched her cheeks with her fingers, feeling numb. She blinked at him, still not fully understanding. "How long have I been asleep?"

"I don't know, but I've been home for an hour and a half." He stroked her hair. "I've got good news."

"What?"

"I stopped by the office earlier and put in a call to a friend of mine in Tegucigalpa, a man named Alberto Esparza-Padilla. He's not in the government at the moment, but he's very wealthy and influential."

"You talked to him about Elena?"

"Yes, the bottom line is he's agreed to check with people and see if something can be done."

"Cleve, that's wonderful!"

"Well, don't get your hopes up too much. It's just a start. It's not certain that Alberto can help."

"But you said he's influential."

"We had a long talk on the phone. A very candid conversation. He confirmed my suspicions about the virulence of the cantina system. Off the record, he told me that the take makes its way to some of those in the highest circles in Honduras. Elements in the army control the cantinas. He estimated that Comayagua alone is worth fifty thousand dollars a month to them."

"What does that mean?"

"It means we're not just up against a cantina owner and some corrupt police officials. Prostitution is legal, and Alberto told me that these businesses are cloaked in all the trappings of propriety. They've got the required licenses, the girls are all certified, and so forth."

"You mean Elena's presence in that place has been sanctioned by the government?"

"I don't know about her in particular. I would guess that they've got the necessary papers, though if she's a minor like you say, the documents were probably falsified. Minors can't be licensed."

"Lord. Do you think this friend of yours will be able to help?"

"I don't know, but he and his wife, Isabel, are willing to try. She is interested in women's causes herself. I told Alberto about your coming to Honduras because of Elena—though I didn't say anything about Marta—and he was impressed. In fact, he was thinking that you might be helpful in getting something done for Elena."

"Me? How?"

"He and Isabel will have to work that out, but they think the foreign influence might make it easier for them. The point is, they want you to go to Tegucigalpa."

"When?"

"Well, I told them that you were my guest, so they've invited us to spend Christmas with them at their estate outside the capital. It's a big time for social gatherings, and various VIP's will be visiting over the holidays."

"But, Cleve, I've got to be back in Washington."

"It would be an excellent opportunity to help Elena. Isn't there some way you could extend your trip a few days?"

"Frankly, I was hoping to be at work this coming week. And, since my mother and stepfather are going to be on a cruise, I have tentative plans to spend Christmas with a friend and his family in Philadelphia."

"Would your boss give you another week or so?"

"I suppose I could take some more time without pay. Fortunately Congress is in recess, so it's a slow time."

"How important is this friend?"

Diana could detect a hint of hesitation in his voice. "All my friends are important, Cleve."

He smiled, apparently taking her response to mean that Tom was not special. "Shall I tell the Esparzas we'll make it, then?"

Diana wondered if she shouldn't have taken the opportunity to establish her interest in another man, in order to cool Cleve's ardor. It may have been the smart thing to do, but it wouldn't have been entirely honest.

This invitation to go to Tegucigalpa came as a surprise. Why was Cleve so anxious for her to go to the capital? Then it struck her. He would be extending their time together. His interest in the exercise was probably a selfish one. She looked at the attractive face above her. *But then,* she thought, *what of it? As long as he's willing to help with Elena, there's really no harm—so long as I'm careful.*

Diana nodded. "Okay, I'll go to Tegucigalpa."

The smile that spread across his face told her he was happy. Very happy indeed.

CHAPTER EIGHT

SUNDAY, DIANA WOULD have to spend alone. It was Lupe's day off, and Cleve was scheduled to fly out early in the morning to Panama. He was to spend all day Monday there, planning logistics for Operation Chaparral and wouldn't be back until late that night.

Before Cleve's departure they had breakfast together, a quiet interlude that Diana found more comfortable than any other time they'd shared since they had met. The previous night at dinner there had been only a lingering air of tension, but they were both much more relaxed and had spent a quiet evening reading and talking.

After breakfast Cleve gathered his things and Diana walked out onto the porch with him to say goodbye. She looked up at him. His red beret was tilted rakishly to one side, his broad shoulders near and strong. His lips curled into a smile under the soft fringe of his mustache. Then he bent down and kissed her softly on the lips, as naturally as could be.

It didn't come as a surprise to Diana. There had been an intimacy that morning that made the kiss seem so natural, so honest.

After their lips parted, Cleve held her close for a moment, his face indicating a certain enjoyment. His easy, relaxed expression had none of the compulsion or desperation of their earlier kisses. His eyes seemed to say, "I'll miss you."

Diana didn't know what to think. "Thanks, Cleve, for your help with Elena," she said vaguely.

"Don't thank me yet. Nothing may come of it, you know." He pinched her cheek.

She felt shy. "I know that. But the fact that you've tried is important. I'd like to think you care about something like that."

"I do and have all along, though admittedly with less urgency than you."

She smiled. "I just wanted to let you know I appreciate it."

He lifted her chin with his fingers, then touched her lips with his. "Thanks for saying that."

When he finally turned to go, Diana felt her heart lurch. She didn't want him to leave. Only now did she realize it.

She stood quietly as he walked away, wondering whether he wanted to stay with her as badly as she wished it herself. Just then he glanced back and waved. Diana decided that he did.

After he had gone she went inside and paced the villa, thinking about what had happened, so worked up that she was unable to sit calmly and relax. The atmosphere between them had become so pleasant, but Diana recognized immediately that the situation was fraught with peril.

On the one hand, it was desirable that they get along better, on the other, she ought not let the new development in their relationship lead to anything more serious. Even kissing him involved risks, yet it was so clearly consequent from her feelings for him.

Diana decided to occupy herself with tasks that needed doing. First she got out her stationery, sat at the table and wrote to her boss, explaining her decision to stay an additional week or so. Then she wrote letters to friends, hoping the act of communication would put her in a more positive frame of mind.

The letter she wrote to Tom telling him she wouldn't be able to go to Philadelphia with him for Christmas was particularly difficult. Everything she thought to say by way of explanation seemed hypocritical or ungenuine, and she even had trouble summoning up feelings for him.

Nevertheless, she persevered. When she finished the letter, she set her correspondence aside to give to Cleve to put in the armed forces mail. Looking at Tom's letter, she realized that she really had no desire to see him at all.

Instead, her mind kept conjuring up images of Cleve. Her brain insisted on a dialogue with *him*, bedeviling her every attempt to put him from her thoughts.

The obsession she was developing was disquieting because it indicated something she didn't want to acknowledge—that she cared for Cleve Emerson. If he could so easily displace an old friend like Tom, what effect would he have once they had parted?

Diana knew she would have to forget him, for there was no other option. But the ensuing days would determine how difficult that task would be. It was within her power now to make sure the process was not too painful. Diana knew she had to be strong and wise.

LUPE CAME TO THE HOUSE early Monday morning, but Diana was already up. Not wanting to preempt the housekeeper, she had waited for breakfast. They were in the kitchen together, Lupe full of energy and enthusiasm.

"How was the visit to your friend, *señorita*?"

"Very nice. It was good to see Marta."

"And the colonel came for you?"

"Yes, Saturday morning."

"He was very unhappy when I told to him you had gone, *señorita*. Very unhappy."

"He seemed to be a little upset about it."

Lupe looked at her thoughtfully. "I hope you know it, but Colonel Emerson, he loves you, *señorita*."

Diana was surprised at the forthrightness of Lupe's statement. "Why would you say that?"

"I know it. Only a woman can make a strong heart weak."

"You don't think I make Colonel Emerson weak, Lupe."

"Weak—how you say it?—for desire."

"That's silly."

"You don't know thees man so long as I do, *señorita*."

"Colonel Emerson and I are fond of each other, Lupe, that's true. I consider him a friend…someone I care for very much. But that's all."

"I do not understand thees. Why only a friend?"

"Because it can never be more."

"You mean you don't love him?"

"No, I mean I would never let it get to that point because we are two very different people, with different lives. He is a soldier who roams the world in the service of his country. My home and my job are in Washington."

The housekeeper looked at Diana as though she had dashed her fondest dreams.

"If I should marry, Lupe, it will be to a man whose life is like mine. It's one thing to care for a person; it's a very different thing to share your life with him."

"I think, *señorita*, that to you the boots are so important that you must find a man who will share them."

Diana laughed. "That's a rather novel way of putting it, but actually not far wrong. To share is very important."

"To thees, I agree. But there es sharing and there es sharing. I can see that for you it es like a pie. You are one half, and the man es the other half. For me, *señorita*, it es also like the pie. But I believe the man es the crust, and the woman es the filling. He holds her, he faces the world, but she es the heart. Neither he or thees pie es anything without her. But without the man, she cannot exist."

Diana stared at Lupe, marveling at her wisdom, her insight. "That's a very interesting way to look at it, Lupe, but I personally cannot believe that a woman exists only by the grace of a man."

"Without love, no, you are right, *señorita*. It es then a tragedy. With love, however, it es neither crust nor filling. It es a pie!"

"Lupe," Diana said, placing her hand on the woman's shoulder, "if you are ever interested in a chair of philosophy at the university, let me know. I have some friends at George Washington."

"*Jesús, María, señorita*. Who would cook for my husband and my children?" She grinned knowingly. "And love them?"

The rest of the day Diana thought a lot about Lupe's pies, about Cleve Emerson, about her life in Washington and about the rift he had created in her heart. There could be no compromise, and yet how could she ever hope to organize her life without it?

The truth was, a life with Cleve would require too great a sacrifice—she needed a man whose life-style was much more like her own. If she married anyone, it should be Tom or a man like him. It was not her place in life to be the filling of a pie; her lot was to be self-sufficient and self-reliant. She wanted it that way.

Lupe left that evening after putting a light supper on the table. She had offered to stay, but Diana sent her home to be with her family. Diana would spend the evening reading, waiting for Cleve to return.

By eleven he was still not home, and she began to grow tired. His flight from Panama might have been delayed or even put off until the next day. She wanted very badly to see him, but decided to go to bed. After undressing, she slipped into a sleeveless cotton nightgown and crawled between the sheets.

Though Diana was ready for sleep, it would not come. She kept seeing Cleve in her mind's eye, seeing him in the various contexts in which she had encountered him. More and more, she thought of their lovemaking. At first, the recollection of it had been disconcerting—even embarrassing—but since her return to Palmerola the memory of their intimacy, just as her feelings for him, had changed. Now the thought of him aroused her.

Diana wondered whether Cleve was hopeful of being intimate with her again or whether he had seen the futility of their relationship. Other than the kisses, he had made no overtures, but she had sensed desire in him—a desire that seemed destined to end in lovemaking, unless . . . unless she made certain it didn't happen.

Far off in the night, Diana heard the sound of aircraft and her heart quickened. The sound drew nearer, and she could tell that it was a large plane, perhaps a transport. If so, it would be Cleve's flight from Panama.

Apart from the pulsing of the large engines in the sky, Diana heard vehicles moving around the base—probably preparing to unload cargo. It must be a very large plane, she thought, because the vehicle traffic seemed heavy.

She listened for the sounds of the approach, the changing pitch of the engines, but she didn't hear them. There was only the steady rhythm of the large airplane in flight. It seemed to be circling. But *why* was it circling? Could something be wrong?

Diana got up and went to the window, pulling back the curtain. Over the tops of the trees she saw the lights of the plane as it flew by, a mile or two beyond the field. It seemed to be going slowly, but planes always did in their final approach. Soon it had moved out of sight, though the throb of its engines could still be heard.

Feeling uneasy, Diana left her room and walked through the dark house to the living room. There she peered out the window and, after several moments, she again saw the aircraft over the roofs of the buildings across the compound. The plane continued on around the field so she returned to her room, where it soon reappeared in the sky over the trees.

Diana decided that something must be wrong. Planes did not circle a low-traffic airfield for an extended period unless there was a problem. The aircraft had moved on around to the side of the house Cleve's room was on, so Diana went into it and pulled back the curtain. She saw the runway flooded with light. A number of vehicles had been lined up, their headlights on, illuminating the pavement for a distance of a quarter mile or more.

Diana's stomach clinched. It was obviously an emergency, and she was sure the plane was Cleve's. Her first impulse was to run out to help, but she realized there was nothing she could do. She immediately feared the worst.

For the next ten minutes Diana moved from room to room, following the progress of the plane as it circled the field. With each trip around the house, Diana's anxiety mounted. There was absolutely no doubt in her mind that Cleve was on that airplane. Would she ever see him again? The thought of it ending like this—the poignancy of it—was more than she could bear.

Still the plane hung in the sky, seemingly afraid to land. Diana, too, was afraid. It couldn't go on forever. And she had to know.

At last the aircraft broke its pattern and moved far out to the west for a straight approach to the runway. More vehicles had arrived on the scene, and the illuminated area now seemed at least a half a mile long. Interspersed among the trucks, jeeps and cars were emergency vehicles, bright yellow in color—except for the ambulances with their white sides and red crosses.

The aircraft was nearing the field, its wings waving slightly from time to time to correct its course. Diana clutched her hands to her breast and bit at her lip, her heart pounding steadily in her chest. Her breathing slowed.

Finally she saw the large plane slipping out of the black sky into the pool of light flooding the runway. Then, its landing gear touched the pavement, sending a cloud of smoke up from beneath its lumbersome body. The large metal bird streaked down the corridor of vehicles until it finally rolled to a stop. Diana let out a sigh of relief, hardly having breathed during the past minute or so.

Several hundred yards from her, the plane, still bathed in light, sat immobile, as though it, too, were catching its breath. At that instant Diana felt joyful, happy for Cleve, happy he was safe. She was relieved for everyone aboard, glad they had made it.

She continued watching as the vehicles dispersed and the plane turned around on the runway. After a few minutes it began rolling toward the taxi strip and out of sight.

The excitement of the emergency landing had been so great that Diana knew there was no way she could go to sleep. Cleve would probably be home soon, and she wanted to see him, so she went to the living room to wait.

A few minutes later she saw a jeep approaching the villa, moving briskly across the compound. With the headlights glaring, Diana wasn't able to see who was in it, but it had to be Cleve. Staying in the shadows of the darkened house, she listened to the voices outside, recognizing Cleve's after a moment. He said good-night, then stepped to the house as the jeep drove off.

Diana watched the door open, and she saw his silhouette appear. "Cleve?"

He stopped. "Diana? Is that you?"

"Yes...you're all right?" She moved toward him across the darkened room without waiting for a reply. He dropped his bag, accepting her into his arms.

"Diana, what is it?"

She squeezed him fiercely, her face buried in his neck. "I saw the plane. I'm so glad you're safe."

Cleve stroked her hair as she clung to him. "It wasn't that big a deal."

"I saw how they lit up the runway, the fire trucks and ambulances. They thought you'd crash."

"We lost an engine a hundred miles out. They just took precautions. That's all."

"I was so scared," she murmured. "I knew you were on the plane."

He kissed the top of her head. "I didn't even know about it until just before we landed. Most of us were asleep. They woke us up just in case we had to use emergency procedures after touching down."

"Weren't you afraid?"

Cleve chuckled. "Apparently not as much as you." He lifted her chin. The light of some distant lamp flickered dimly on his face. She saw him smile just before he kissed her.

His scent was familiar. And there was a hint of aviation fuel as there had been that first night. Cleve ran his hand down her bare arm. In the excitement, she had forgotten that she was in her nightgown. Diana trembled under his touch, her face against his neck.

"I'm not accustomed to this kind of a reception," he murmured into her hair.

"I was afraid for you."

He let her words linger, savoring the implications of her feelings. Cleve thought how wonderful and strange Diana's reception was. He simply wasn't used to having someone care whether he made it home safely or not.

He lifted her face again, taking pleasure in the shadowed contours of it, loving her beauty, her concern. She blinked up at him, searching his face even as he searched hers. "Oh, Diana," he whispered.

And they kissed, a long, deep kiss full of emotion.

When their lips parted, she stared at him. In the faint light he saw both awe and distress in her eyes.

"Oh, Cleve . . ."

"No," he said, touching her lip, knowing her concern. "I don't want to lose this moment, there's magic in it. Don't spoil it . . . please." And he kissed her again, hoping she was feeling what he felt, hoping she was caught up in what was happening as much as he.

Diana accepted his kiss, pulling him against her, inviting his affection. He caressed her flesh through the gown, letting his hands run over her bottom, reveling at its firmness and the soft feminine curve of it.

Her hand trailed up the back of his neck and her fingers dug hungrily into his hair, taking what she could of him, betraying her own growing desire. The kiss deepened, their tongues intertwining and probing, their heads pivoting around the exquisite union of their mouths.

What had begun with tenderness flared with passion, and Cleve felt even more urgently his desire. Diana ran her hands down his torso to his thighs, laying the flat of her palms against the corded muscle. He clamped his pelvis more firmly against her in response, feeling fire in his loins, wanting her desperately now. Their mouths broke inches apart, their breathing intermixed and urgent.

She moaned, stopping short of the words of protest he knew were struggling to emerge from the back of her mind.

"Diana, my Diana," he mumbled into her lips, nibbling the soft flesh of them, his breathing, his words, his hunger a single, dizzy swirl of desire.

She was caught between the yearning within her and Cleve's ardent passion. She was trapped, buffeted, a twig adrift in a roiling sea of emotion, wanting him, craving him irrationally. She returned his kisses as eagerly as he gave them, unable to do otherwise, too caught up in what was happening to resist.

Before she knew what had happened, Cleve lifted her into his arms and carried her into his room. Standing over his bed, he peered at her in the darkness, his expression reassuring, though she could barely see him. Her arms were around his neck and she clung to him, waiting until his mouth found hers and he had kissed her again.

Then he laid her down gently on the bed and sat beside her, his hip against her side, his fingers finding her face in the obscurity. "I can't keep my hands off you, Diana. I can't."

She felt a surge of emotion and touched his cheek to tell him that she couldn't resist him, either, for she couldn't. And when her fingers grazed his lips, he kissed them and took them gently into his mouth, brushing the tips with his tongue, sending tremors down her spine. Then Cleve leaned down and lightly kissed her nose and cheek.

"You can't know how wonderful it was to get off that plane and come home and find you waiting for me." He ran his fingers under the neckline of her gown, tracing the swell of her breasts.

"I missed you," she whispered, expressing her feeling honestly. "I'm glad you're home."

His moist, full lips covered hers, gently and sensuously caressing them. She luxuriated in the sensation. Then, as she watched, he stood up, his eyes not leaving her. He began unbuttoning his shirt.

A moment later when Cleve turned away to empty his pockets onto the dresser, Diana slipped her nightgown over her head, pulled back the covers and slid between the sheets. When he returned to the bed, he saw her snuggled down and hidden from him, except for her face. He laughed softly. "You look nice and cozy," he said, and sat down beside her. He caressed her cheek.

"I am," she whispered.

After a long, torpid look, he turned away and quickly removed his boots, trousers and shorts. Then he pulled back the covers, exposing her naked body to his. For a moment he simply looked at her in wonder, his sigh indicating how taken he was by the comely vision.

Then instantly he was beside her, his arm around her, pulling her close against him. Diana's full breasts were hard against his downy chest, and his large body seemed to envelop her.

Cleve was smothering her with kisses now, his mouth roaming her face and neck, his mustache tickling the sensitive place below her ear. The warmth of their bodies mingled and their limbs intertwined.

Cleve kissed her eagerly, feeling a desperate hunger for her, a desire to possess her. As his excitement vaulted, Diana's hand began coursing his chest and stomach, her touch arousing him still more. Then the fever of their kiss abated, their tongues slowed their fiery dance, and Diana's mouth slipped from his and settled in the crook of his neck, where she teased him with her tongue.

Cleve moved his fingers across her soft, ivory skin to her breast, cupping it in his hand. Diana responded by lowering her face to his chest and taking his nipple gently between her lips, kissing and caressing it to erection.

He moaned softly at the sensation, marveling at her willingness to give him pleasure. The mutuality that had been lacking the first time was evident now, her affection ardent, enthusiastic.

Diana reached up and kissed him softly on the lips, then her hand, which had been resting on his torso, began gradually moving downward, over his belly to the dense tangle at the apex of his loins. Cleve froze, his masculinity aching with the nearness of her touch. Then, as she inched lower, he felt himself harden even more in anticipation of her. The throbbing in him was at once exquisite and painful—pulsing with eagerness, straining for relief.

The cool tips of her fingers lightly touched the shank of him, pausing uncertainly at the encounter. Then her hand moved with experimental caution up the proud arch of his being, finally encircling it, taking it, grasping it gently, unsurely. Cleve moaned at the tender sweetness of her touch, his heart racing, his groin throbbing.

Slowing, Diana began stroking him, not certain what would please him, knowing only that her intimate touch aroused him. She quickened the pace, her own excitement driving her on as much as the sounds of pleasure emanating from Cleve's throat.

Once or twice his pelvis heaved spontaneously, and Diana felt his body tense, the light friction of her fingers working magic. His excitement, the unfamiliar feel of him in her hand, sent fire into her, swelling her with desire, flooding her with anxious yearning for him.

She wanted him now, wanted him in her, desperately. "Oh now, please now."

Instantly he moved on top of her, large, warm, eager. At that moment Diana had a sense of his power over her, the strength to do his will. For an instant she felt trapped. Then, when it was apparent that he intended to be as tender as he was forceful, she lost herself in the pleasure he gave her.

Her willpower had already been numbed by affection but now, with her excitement mounting, she started giving herself up—first to Cleve and then to her own feelings. Her mind, her immediate consciousness of self, dissolved gradually into pure sensation.

Diana opened her legs to him and he took her, sweetly easing into her, his enormity startling at first. His mouth found hers then, the kiss more intimate than before, the exquisite union of their bodies complete. They were melded together, locked in an embrace that had force and life of its own, their undulations a ribbon of motion. From the single body that together with him she made, Diana began drifting off—all reality pleasure, an overpowering sea of sensation surrounding her, sweeping her away.

Then orgasm gripped her, lifting her, pitching her to greater heights. And she exploded, each particle and fiber of her being united with every other. She cried out, her pleasure transformed into sound, her voice echoing, uniting spirit, body, place. And she was spent. Completely.

Diana lay beneath him, her chest heaving under his weight. Cleve seemed dead from pleasure, given up to her, lost in her, drained of his powers.

She stroked his head, possessing him, the conquering female, her body aglow, electric. Joy filled her. She held Cleve, knowing him better at that moment than she had known any man. Sharing more than she had ever shared. Being more than she had ever been.

As she lay in the miraculous glow of their lovemaking, Diana slowly drifted back to the real world, and the ethereal realm of pleasure they had shared faded like the poignant moments of a dream. Cleve became the man for whose safety she had feared, the man she had come to care for.

She pressed her hand against the hot, moist flesh of his back, wanting to preserve the intimacy of the moment, touched profoundly by what they had together. His neck was near her face and she kissed it, feeling tenderness for him, wanting to share emotion with him as she had physical pleasure.

Cleve stirred at her kiss, lifting his weight from her somewhat, permitting the cool air between the steamy surfaces of their bodies. For the past minutes he had lain quiescent in her core, and as he withdrew from her Diana felt suddenly bereft.

He eased beside her, his lips finding her cheek, his soft moan telling her of his pleasure. "Diana..." he murmured, but said no more.

CHAPTER NINE

IN HIS DREAMS the plane made pass after pass at the runway but never managed to descend to earth, pulling up repeatedly just before the landing gear touched down. Each time Diana stood waiting, but each time he failed. Cleve knew it couldn't go on forever, because the fuel would eventually run out, but for some reason they just couldn't land.

Anxiety gripped him, his heart pounded in his chest, and then he heard the clock ticking. Cleve lifted his head from the pillow and, blinking against the early morning light, peered at the alarm clock beside him. It was five till six. The alarm would sound in a few minutes. Reaching over, he turned it off.

Beside him Diana lay asleep, her face turned partially toward him, wisps of her dark hair strewn across her cheeks and forehead. He looked at her for a moment, admiring the vision, never tiring of her beauty. Cleve wanted to kiss her just then. It wasn't his normal reaction to a woman the morning after he had slept with her—usually he just wanted to get away.

Carefully he got out of bed so as not to awaken her. Slipping on his robe, he looked down at her again. The sight of Diana in his bed—the intimacy of it—gave him a warm feeling inside, a proprietary, protective feeling toward her. And he remembered their lovemaking the night before. Unlike the first time, she had loved him as much as he had loved her. It had been a mutual experience.

Unable to resist, he leaned over her and kissed her softly on the forehead. Diana moaned slightly and turned onto her side, but didn't wake up. Cleve smiled and retreated to the dresser. Taking some clean underwear from a drawer, he went into the bath to shave and shower, a happiness in his heart.

After he had dressed, Cleve checked Diana again. She was still fast asleep, so he quietly left the bedroom. Lupe was just entering the villa as he came out, closing the door behind him.

"*Buenos días*, Lupe."

"Oh, good morning, Colonel," she said in Spanish. They hardly ever conversed in his language unless another English-speaking person was present. "When did you get back?"

"I flew in late last night."

"Were you on that plane last night? The one that nearly crashed? It was the talk of the village this morning."

"It didn't nearly crash, Lupe. We just had an engine go out. They took precautions, that's all."

"Poor Señorita Hillyer. Did she know about it?"

"Unfortunately she saw us land."

"Ay! She must have been worried to death."

"She was upset, yes."

"The poor darling." Lupe looked at Cleve, pondering. "I know that you do not like for me to speak of it, Colonel, but I am worried about her."

"What for, Lupe?" He followed her into the kitchen.

"She doesn't fully know it herself yet, but she loves you, Colonel. I am worried for her when she leaves you. She'll be very unhappy. I'm certain of it."

"Loves me? What makes you say that, Lupe?" Cleve found the suggestion surprising, though he hadn't yet characterized Diana's feelings for him. And, after the previous night, he wasn't at all sure what her feelings might be.

"It is my intuition, not her words, to be sure. But despite her silly ideas, I am sure she loves you. And you must open her eyes before it is too late."

"Wait a minute, Lupe. You're jumping the gun a little, aren't you? What makes you so sure I'm interested in her?"

Lupe dropped her eyes, embarrassed. She turned to the stove.

"Eh, Lupe? What makes you so sure?" He sat at the table.

"I have eyes, Colonel," she said over her shoulder. "I can see, can I not?"

"It's not what you see that concerns me; it's what you say. Tell me, what have you been saying to Señorita Hillyer?"

"Only the things that women say to each other."

Cleve could tell by the ambiguity of the response that it was something she would never admit, so he decided to drop the subject. Obviously Lupe was hard at work matchmaking, despite his admonition. Whereas it would have been a little annoying at first, the notion was less troubling now. Why?

He thought of Diana asleep in his bed, their intimacy the night before, the tenderness, the excitement, the depth of feeling on both sides. It had been wonderful. Too wonderful, though, because it wasn't at all clear where it was leading.

That was the part he had been ignoring, trying to forget. He had no idea, no plan, just a conviction that he wanted her. It was like that night at Jack Dawson's party—he saw her, was drawn to her and wanted her even though in a matter of hours he was to leave the country. What was it, if it wasn't just blind compulsion?

Cleve's mind returned to the housekeeper, who had been chattering away about American women and their misguided attitudes toward men, and something about pies? Pies? He'd only heard bits and pieces of what she was saying, but he heard enough to know that Diana and Lupe had talked a lot about the subject. Diana's "silly ideas," Lupe had said. What did she mean? And what did all this have to do with pies?

Lupe turned from the stove to face Cleve. "Forgive me, Colonel, for saying this to you, but with this American woman, you are not yourself. I don't know what it is, but your character seems to me different with her than with other people. Perhaps it is nothing more than your feelings for her, but…forgive me…if you love her, you must tell her so. It is not for you to be half a pie."

"Lupe, I don't understand what you mean by this pie business, but I think that we've discussed my relationship with Miss Hillyer enough. I know your intentions are good, and I appreciate your concern, but enough is enough."

"I am sorry, Colonel Emerson. I know this is not my business, but I care very much for her, as I do for you."

Cleve looked at her, feeling now that he had been a little heavy-handed. Perhaps it was his own frustration coming through. "Don't worry about it, Lupe. Let's just forget it."

In a few minutes Lupe put Cleve's breakfast before him. "Perhaps, Colonel, I should knock on Señorita Hillyer's door to wake her. She may wish to have breakfast with you."

Cleve remembered that Diana was in his bed, and he didn't know if Lupe finding her there would be an embarrassment. "No, don't bother her. Let her sleep." He decided that he had better go in and wake her himself, just in case.

As Cleve ate his breakfast, Lupe bustled around the kitchen. When he had finished, he slipped back into his bedroom, but found Diana already awake and heard her in the bath. Sticking his head in the open door to her room, he saw that she had rumpled her bed to make it appear that she had slept in it. Smiling to himself, he got his beret from his room and went back to the kitchen.

"I see that Señorita Hillyer is already up, Lupe. Will you tell her I'll be home for lunch?"

"Certainly, Colonel. And do you remember that I am going for a few days to visit my relatives after this morning? Earlier in the month we discussed it, and you said it was all right."

"Oh yes, that's right, I'd forgotten. But it doesn't matter. Diana and I will get along just fine." He bid the housekeeper farewell and headed out the door and across the compound.

DIANA HEARD the front door close and came out of the bath, having showered and dressed. She hadn't wanted to see Cleve that morning because when she awoke in his bed the world seemed a very different place than when she had fallen asleep in his arms.

She remembered the previous night with total clarity—it had been an incredible experience—but she hadn't been herself. It was as though she had been drugged, drugged by feelings over which she had no control.

Diana knew that things always looked different by the light of day, but this morning in particular found her in a state of confusion. She had to think things through, get a grip on what was happening.

Lupe was a little more circumspect than usual, though she was full of gossip about the incident involving Cleve's plane. As Diana ate they exchanged impressions of the event, but there was still a touch of reserve in Lupe's manner. The subject of her relationship with Cleve didn't come up. Diana wondered if something had been said.

"Oh, *señorita*," Lupe said as she washed the breakfast dishes, "I nearly forgot it, but the colonel said to me to tell you he will be home for lunch."

"Oh, fine. Thank you, Lupe." She sipped her coffee, wondering what it would be like when she saw Cleve. But she quickly decided that brooding over it would be unproductive. Better that she occupy her mind with other things, such as Elena. She thought about the upcoming trip to Tegucigalpa to visit the Esparzas. Though her purpose in going was to lobby on Elena's behalf, Cleve had said the occasion would be a social one, and she had to plan for that aspect.

"Perhaps the colonel did not tell you, *señorita*," Lupe said as she dried a cup with a tea towel, "but this afternoon I am leaving for a few days to visit some relatives of mine."

"No, I wasn't aware, Lupe. But that will be nice for you, I'm sure."

"Yes, it es my sister and her family. I like very much to see them."

"When do you go?"

"Not until late. But thees morning I am going into Comayagua with Ernesto and Maria to buy some presents."

Presents. It occurred to Diana that it might be a nice idea to take something to the Esparzas. She wondered if the idea had occurred to Cleve and guessed that it hadn't. Men tended not to think in those terms. But, even if he had, it would be nice for her to have some sort of a little gift for them, as well.

"Lupe, I haven't had a chance to do any shopping since I've been in Honduras. Do you suppose it would be possible for me to go into town with you and Ernesto and Maria?"

"But of course, *señorita*, it would be a pleasure for us. I am to meet them at the gate of the air base at half-past eight. We will go together."

THE FOUR OF THEM rode in the cab of Ernesto's pickup, but Diana had the window seat, and so, apart from the bumpy ride, it was not an unpleasant trip. For Lupe she had worn a teal-blue skirt and sweater, rather than pants, which pleased the housekeeper enormously.

Maria and Lupe chatted away during the ride into town, enabling Diana to be alone with her thoughts. A strange feeling of uncertainty and foreboding hung over her, and she knew it was because of Cleve and the fact that she was beginning to care for him deeply. And it frightened her.

When they arrived in Comayagua they decided to split up, since Diana was interested in a different type of merchandise than the other women. Ernesto led her to the street where the nicest shops were located. They browsed for a while, until Diana found a beautiful, handcrafted leather stamp box, which she thought would make a suitable gift for the Esparzas. For her friends in Washington she bought some hand-painted ceramic tiles that could be used as trivets.

When Diana had pretty well gone through her list, she and Ernesto headed off to where they planned to meet

Maria and Lupe. Walking along the street, they passed the El Presidente Hotel.

"It's a shame they don't have a reputable hotel in this town," Diana said in an offhand manner. "They might get a little tourist business if they did."

"But Señorita Hillyer, the El Presidente is a wonderful hotel. Not so big as some in the capital or those in your country, but an excellent hotel still."

Diana looked at him, perplexed. "Colonel Emerson told me it had a very poor reputation and that there was prostitution going on in it. He said it wasn't a safe place for a woman alone."

"But no, *señorita*, this is not true. I don't know why the colonel would say this. I am sure he knows."

Diana realized immediately what had happened. That first night Cleve had wanted her to stay at the air base with him, and it was convenient that she think there were no suitable accommodations in town. She realized she had been naive, far too trusting of Cleve. "Perhaps, I misunderstood what Colonel Emerson said, Ernesto."

"Yes, perhaps *señorita*, for the hotel is a good one. I would let my own daughter stay in it."

On the ride back to Palmerola, Diana thought about Cleve's little deception and the seduction that had followed that evening. It was obvious that he had had the whole scenario in mind from the beginning, and that it had worked out just as he had planned. Of course, he couldn't have anticipated finding her in his room, but there was little doubt he wanted her in his house so that an opportunity would present itself.

It was nearly noon by the time they dropped her off at the gates of Palmerola. Diana said goodbye to her friends, wished Lupe a pleasant trip and headed across the base toward the American compound.

Walking near the edge of the field, Diana saw a large transport plane being unloaded. In addition to the air force personnel, there were a number of Army Rangers with their distinctive red berets moving amid the pallets of materiel. She stopped for a moment under a large tree and watched the men working, wondering if Cleve might be among them.

After a few minutes Diana saw a jeep approaching the work party. There were a couple of rangers in the vehicle and, as it pulled up near the plane, Diana saw a tall officer, erect and authoritative in manner, dismount the jeep and move among the troops. She recognized immediately that it was Cleve.

Fascinated at seeing him in his environment, she observed his manner with the men, noting the deference and respect he commanded. Cleve Emerson struck her as the consummate officer—Old Pain and Pleasure—doubtless as effective a leader as he was impressive to observe. It was obvious to Diana that the man was in his element.

Lupe's term for him, *caudillo*, made more sense now than it ever had. He was a military man, a leader of men through and through. How could he ever be anything else?

Studying him, Diana had a profound sense of how different they were, how different their worlds were. To imagine them together seemed so unlikely at that moment. It saddened her, but she knew it was true.

She was about to turn away when Cleve returned to his jeep alone, climbed in and headed off across the tarmac toward the villa. Hurrying on herself, Diana felt a sense of conviction about what she had to do.

Cleve was waiting for her in the living room when she arrived.

"Well, there you are!" he said with a broad grin. "I was afraid you'd run off on me again."

Diana stood in the doorway, her turquoise eyes narrowing. She just stared at him. He realized something was wrong. "Where've you been?"

"At the El Presidente in Comayagua."

"The El Presidente?"

"Yes, that den of iniquity you wouldn't consider letting me stay in."

Cleve blinked, regaining his composure after a brief lapse. "Well, I may have exaggerated the problems there a little...."

Diana walked to the table and put her packages down. "Your knack for understatement is matched only by your candor, Colonel Emerson."

"Are you upset, Diana?"

"I would be, but considering the way things have turned out, I guess I won't throw any dishes at you. Your credibility has suffered a major reversal, however."

Cleve smiled and walked over to her. He took her by the shoulders. "I can handle that, I suppose. It's friendship that really counts." He kissed her on the cheek.

Diana lowered her head. "I want to talk to you about that, too."

"About what?"

"About last night. I've been thinking about it all morning."

"And?"

She looked up at him, seeing his soft brown eyes waiting. There was unhappiness in them. He knew what was coming, she could tell. "I've started caring for you very much, Cleve."

"And that's bad?"

"Yes. I wish it weren't, but it is."

His expression grew somber. "What are you saying? That you're moving into the El Presidente?"

"I considered it, but no. I think I'll go back to Marta's."

His lips drew into a thin line, his brows furrowed. "What about Tegucigalpa?"

"I'd like to go—for Elena's sake—if you'll let me."

"Certainly I'll let you. Why wouldn't I?"

"I thought you might be angry with me. This is becoming a habit, I know. I wouldn't blame you."

He sighed deeply. "I'm not angry, no. Disappointed, but not angry—at least not with you."

"Well, it's my fault. If I hadn't slipped last night—"

"No, Diana, don't sully it by talking that way. Please."

"I didn't mean it that way, Cleve. Honestly. I wanted to be with you, make love with you. I've come to be very fond of you. But it's unfair to be with you when I know very well what I've got to do."

"If it's my feelings you're concerned about, don't be."

"But I am."

"The truth, Diana, is that it's yourself you're protecting . . . against me."

"I don't want to be hurt, no."

"Do you think I want to hurt you?"

"Not intentionally."

"All I know is that I want to be with you. That's all that matters."

"And I want to be with you, Cleve, but maybe I don't have as thick skin as you do. Maybe I can't just live for the moment, spend a couple of glorious weeks with someone, cry over it for a few days, then move on to something else."

"You think that's what I do?"

"Don't you? I mean, what do you have in mind if it's not that? Are you going to pack up and come back to Washington with me? Every time you meet a woman you care for, do you just tell the army to go to hell? No, I know how it is. It's your life. You'd resent me or any woman who came between you and your goals. And I'd feel resentment, too, if the situation was reversed, so I can't blame you. You're dealing with the problem at hand the best way you can."

"And it's selfish of me to expect you to do the same?"

"I'm not saying that. I told you, I don't blame you. You haven't made me any promises, misled me. You've played it straight. Instead of saying, 'Thanks, but no thanks,' I went to bed with you, I lived for the moment."

"So now you regret it."

"I wish I hadn't even met you, in a way. I have a nice comfortable life in Washington and a career I love. It would have been so much easier if you hadn't come along." She touched his arm. "But on the other hand, I've never known a man like you. I've never experienced what we've had together. It's something I'll never forget."

As Cleve looked at her, his eyes developed a misty film, but he managed to smile. "You're saying that since that's the way it is, you may as well shorten our time together by a few days and move on now."

"I'm not trying to be cruel. I'm trying to protect myself . . . and you."

He turned away from her. "I don't need protecting."

"I do."

"What do you want me to do then?" he asked, glancing over his shoulder.

"Will you have someone take me into town so that I can catch a bus for La Esperanza?"

"I'll take you myself—in the morning."

"No, Cleve. This afternoon. I can't spend another night with you. I don't trust myself."

He gave a half laugh, turning back to her. "That's the damnedest compliment I've ever had."

"It *is* a compliment, in a way. At least it shows the effect you've had on me." She laughed ironically, avoiding his eyes. "It'll give you another chapter to put into your memoirs."

"You'd think I'm enjoying this by the way you talk."

"No, maybe it's just a case of misery loving company."

"For the record, *I'm* miserable, Diana. I'm not enjoying this in the least."

Diana's hands were clasped in front of her. She stood before him with her head bowed. After a moment a tear rolled down her cheek.

Cleve caught it with his finger. She looked up at him, her eyes flooded. Then she turned away. "I'll pack," she said in a barely audible voice, "while you have your lunch."

ALL THE WAY INTO TOWN neither of them spoke. After Cleve had parked the jeep near the bus station, he glanced at his watch, then at Diana. "We've got fifteen minutes."

She nodded.

"I doubt that Marta will get the message in time that you're coming, so you'll probably have to hire a car to take you to the village."

"Okay."

He stared at her. "I wish you'd wait until tomorrow. I could drive you directly to the Peace Corps station. It'd save you all this trouble."

"I can't, Cleve. I have to go now."

He got out of the vehicle, took Diana's bags and went around to help her down. She looked up at him when he didn't release her arm.

"This doesn't make sense to me," he said.

"It's being responsible."

They walked slowly toward the milling crowds of the bus station.

"Are you angry?" she asked.

"In a way, yes. But not with you. I understand it's no easier for you than it is for me. It just seems absurd—completely absurd—to shake hands with you and walk away."

"I don't expect that, Cleve."

"I feel guilty just wanting to kiss you."

"Don't." She stopped him, and they faced each other. Diana reached up and touched his lip with her finger. He kissed it, and she pulled her hand away. "This is just too hard."

He watched her, sensing her vacillation. "Stay with me, Diana."

She shook her head and began walking briskly toward the station. Cleve followed her into the ticket office and stood nearby as she tried unsuccessfully to communicate with the ticket agent behind a caged window. Finally he intervened, clarified the confusion in the man's mind as to whether she wanted a one-way or round-trip ticket.

They walked outside to where the buses loaded.

"I'll be glad to get back to Washington where I don't have to be led around by the hand," she said in a low voice. "You'd think I could do something simple like buy a bus ticket."

"You'd have gotten it straightened out eventually. I just didn't want to stand there and watch you struggle with it."

"What was that he said at the end?"

"He said that 'La Esperanza' won't be on the bus. You have to look for the one marked 'Siguatepeque.' They change the destination plaque to La Esperanza when they get there. Siguatepeque's the town you go through on the way."

"Well, if I don't show up on Friday, figure I'm somewhere in Honduras riding around in circles on a bus."

"I wish you'd let me come and get you."

"No, I've put you to enough trouble, Cleve. I prefer it this way. I'll be grateful if you'd just meet me here Friday."

They watched the peasants laden with baggage, children and an occasional chicken jostling about the buses. There was a lot of activity and noise, and people didn't pay much attention to them standing in the shadow of the building.

"Could I ask another favor of you, Cleve?"

"Sure."

"Would you call the airline in Tegucigalpa and make a reservation for me on the twenty-seventh? My ticket's open at the moment. I didn't know when I'd be returning to Washington."

"Okay, I'll call first thing in the morning."

Seeing that Cleve was sad, Diana took his hand. "I'm so sorry to have done this to you, to have come into your life like this and upset things."

He grimaced, but said nothing.

"Do you hate me for it?"

"No, to the contrary. But this isn't an easy thing to do."

"I know," she whispered, her voice cracking.

"Damn," he muttered, then stared out over the chaotic scene.

Diana's eyes glistened. "Will you just hold me? For one last time, hold me in your arms."

Cleve clutched her to him. He felt as though his heart were being torn out of him. He wanted to ask her to stay again, but he knew she wouldn't. It would only make it harder for her.

She glanced up at him, having regained her composure somewhat. "It's time, isn't it?"

He nodded.

At that moment leaving seemed desperately wrong, but she knew she had to go. Taking her bags, she turned and walked slowly toward the bus.

CHAPTER TEN

THE WIND MOANED softly in the pines outside the adobe house. It was a mournful sound, and Diana shifted uncomfortably on the cot Marta had set up in the bedroom, trying not to let her mood sink lower than it was. Cleve was ever present in her mind, and she sighed audibly without noticing it.

"You still awake, Diana?" Marta whispered from her bed.

"Yes, I can't sleep." She raised her head from the lumpy pillow and peered at her friend in the darkness. "Can't you sleep, either?"

"No."

"Why?"

"Between all your tossing and turning and that creaky cot, there haven't been so many sounds in here since I had rats."

"I'm sorry."

"It's all right, I'm just teasing. I've been thinking about you and Cleve."

"God, you too?"

"That guy's really gotten to you, hasn't he?"

"Yeah, and I hope I get over him as quickly as I fell for him."

"Maybe somebody's trying to tell you something. Maybe you're not supposed to get over him."

"Are you crazy?"

"What makes you so sure he's wrong for you? Is it because he's in the army?"

Diana thought. "That's part of it."

"What's the other part?"

"At first I thought we had absolutely nothing in common except a mutual attraction—just a physical thing. But then when I got to know him better, I saw things in his personality—his intellect and character—that appealed to me, things we shared or both understood."

"So, what's wrong with that?"

"Nothing. I suppose that's why I care for him. But it's not enough. Cleve is so different from every man I've ever known or cared for."

"Maybe that's good. He wouldn't be special otherwise."

"Oh, I don't mind that he's different from them. He's different from me, that's what I mean."

"Diana, I don't understand. Of course he's different from you. It'd be awfully dull if you were the same—unless you're saying that you're incompatible."

"No. We're not exactly incompatible, that's not what I mean, either."

"Pardon me for saying this, but you sound confused. I haven't heard a convincing argument other than the fact that he's in the military."

"Well, maybe that's the problem then. It's our lives that are incompatible."

"Do you love him?"

Diana was knocked a little off balance by the question, not because it hadn't occurred to her—it had. Marta's asking it, however, pointed out how terribly relevant it was. "I don't know, perhaps in a way I do."

The other's silence said a great deal.

Diana became defensive. "I don't know what difference that makes, though."

"Have you discussed your feelings for each other?"

"Yes, I told Cleve that I care for him. He said the same."

"Did he tell you that he loved you?"

"No. I'm not sure that he does."

"But he cares for you?"

"Yes, I think his feelings for me are special. I don't have the impression that I'm just another woman to him. But to tell you the truth, I don't think Cleve wants to love anyone. I think he'd be afraid to admit it if it was true."

"Why?"

"Because it would only make things worse. He can't do anything about it, not as a soldier."

"That's silly. Soldiers marry just like anyone else."

"Yes, but it's not a normal existence. It takes a special sort of woman—someone who knows and wants that kind of life. His career ruined his first marriage, and now he's gun-shy. I can't blame him. Besides, he knows I'm not the kind of woman who could be happily married to a military man."

"Have you discussed it?"

"Marriage? No, of course not. It's too early to tell if our feelings for each other are anywhere close to that. The point is, if nothing could possibly work out between us, why get involved?"

"I'm just wondering if you aren't being premature in dismissing the possibility."

"Marta, that's absurd. If I was to marry Cleve—hypothetically speaking—I couldn't even be with him. Dependents aren't allowed in Honduras. And I'm not a camp follower, anyway. I've got my own life and career."

"Well, he won't be in Honduras forever. Do you know where he's going next? Maybe he'll have assignments in the future that you can live with. Maybe a compromise is possible—a middle ground worth considering and talking about."

"No, Marta. It'd never work, and Cleve knows it as well as I do. He loves the army. You ought to see him with his troops. This afternoon I saw him at the air base with some of his men. He's a soldier through and through. He wants to be a general like his uncle, like his father would have been. There's no place for me in his life."

Again, Marta let the silence hang between them. "Well, if you're both convinced, I suppose there's no point in pursuing it."

"That's why I left."

"But Cleve didn't want you to leave; he wanted you to stay."

"He wants me for as long as he can have me. He isn't thinking of the future, though he knows very well what lies ahead."

"Maybe he loves you more than you think."

"No, short-term relationships are a way of life with him—out of necessity, if not choice."

"If you're so sure, Diana, I guess there's nothing left for me to do but support you."

"That means a great deal to me, Marta."

"Is there anything I can do?"

"I wish there were, but no, I just have to see things through and do what I can for Elena. I've come this far, I should finish the job."

"Maybe I could meet with these people in Tegucigalpa for you. As long as the Peace Corps didn't get wind of it—"

"No, Marta. That's why I came down here in the first place. Your hands are tied, and you can't afford to take the chance. Besides, it would be unfair to Cleve, considering the trouble he's gone to. Even though it will be tough, I owe it to him to go to Tegucigalpa."

"What happens after that?"

"I've got reservations for a flight back to Washington on the twenty-seventh."

"Will you ever see him again?"

Diana was staring into the darkness. "I doubt it." She felt uncertainty well up inside her. "I...I don't think I'd want to go through this again."

THE FOLLOWING DAYS were quiet ones for Diana. The sleepy pace of village life made her brief stay with Cleve at Palmerola seem like a glittering holiday.

Part of the time she followed Marta around as she performed her tasks at the station. When Marta was busy with paperwork, Diana sat outside, amusing herself with the children—who she managed to exchange a few words with—and watching life in the village. More than ever she became aware of the passing of the hours of the day by the movement of the sun.

Evenings were brief once dinner had been eaten, because there was no electricity. Any activity after dark was done by the light of kerosene lanterns or pine torches. Most people, including Marta, retired early.

The night before Diana was to return to Comayagua, she and Marta were invited to a wedding in the village. The young couple was poor and, as Marta explained to Diana, the marriage was to be a free union or common-law marriage, solemnized by hardly more ceremony than a special dinner between the two families and a few friends.

Marta was invariably invited to weddings in the area for two reasons: she was well liked and respected, and she always brought along a bottle of wine, a commodity not readily available to most of the people in the poor mountain villages.

"But Marta," Diana asked, "don't you feel the hospitality is insincere?"

"Not at all. Forgive the immodesty, but I've managed to become a minor celebrity in these mountains. I think it's important to promote my status so that I can have influence where it counts."

"You sound like a politician."

"Hey, kid, don't knock it. This is a traditional society, and you have influence only if your status is recognized. When I'm trying to promote good sanitation and health practices, I'm up against a lot of folk wisdom that's totally at odds with what I'm preaching. Medical doctors are a rarity, so people are used to cures based on folk beliefs."

"Folk beliefs?"

"Yes, the people listen to the advice of a person who has a reputation for knowing how to cure. They're called 'intelligent,' and they are consulted when there's an illness. Some of my ideas about basic hygiene strike these people as mighty curious, and scientific credentials don't count for much. That's why my 'politics,' as you call it, is important. Whatever I can do to gain influence, I do. Weddings are good, because they give me a chance to get in on the ground floor of a new household."

"Marta, you're a cross between a ward politician and a witch doctor."

"There are certain similarities, believe me."

"You're sure there won't be a problem with my going tonight?"

"No, your association with me makes you welcome. Besides, you've become a curiosity in the village and that means you're good luck."

"God, if they knew my track record in romance, they'd probably shun me for fear it'd rub off."

"The only thing that makes you suspect is the same liability I have—being unmarried past the ripe old age of twenty."

Diana laughed. "*Well* past the ripe old age of twenty."

"The bride tonight, Concha, is sixteen."

"Lord, I was a sophomore in high school at sixteen."

"If you think that's bad, Concha's mother, Manuela, is thirty-three, and she could be a grandmother in less than a year."

"Don't tell me more, I'm feeling like a spinster already. No wonder Lupe is frantic to get me married." Diana laughed. "The bride will undoubtedly take pity on us and aim the bouquet in our direction."

"That's not part of the custom here, I'm afraid."

"From what you say, it doesn't sound like much of a wedding at all. Doesn't anybody ever 'do it up right'?"

"Formal weddings are impractical, even a civil one. Besides the expense, it means trooping everybody down to La Esperanza. It's a kind of status thing. When Concha and Fernando are older and richer, they may have a formal wedding. A few couples in the village have had one. It's the rough equivalent of what getting a color television set was when we were kids. It's a lot more practical just to declare yourself married."

"You know, the simplicity of it is rather appealing."

Marta smiled. "In light of things, are you sure you're up to a wedding?"

Diana gave a half laugh. "Don't worry about me. I think I'm safely, if not happily, in my spinsterhood."

But even as she said it, Diana thought of Cleve Emerson and the fact that she would be seeing him at the bus station in Comayagua the next day. Cleve Emerson. He had haunted her day and night since they had parted, a determined specter roaming her mind, continually challenging her resolve, drawing her conviction into question.

EARLY THE NEXT AFTERNOON, Diana was in La Esperanza boarding the bus for Comayagua. In her arms were presents for Elena from Marta, Raul and some of the other villagers. She would ask Cleve to take her to the cantina so she could deliver the gifts.

Cleve. His image drifted back into her mind. Sitting on the bus, Diana felt nervous, not knowing what sort of a reception would be waiting for her or how she would react. With each day that had passed since leaving Cleve, her determination to keep him at bay waned. She could no longer deny that she was desperately anxious to see him again.

Until the wedding party the night before, she had accepted her feelings for Cleve, but felt confident she could handle them, confident she could keep everything in perspective—at least until she was safely home in Washington. But seeing the young couple together, Diana's yearning to be in the arms of her lover overwhelmed her. Memories of her times with Cleve flooded her mind, and she thought of the joys of being with him, rather than the pain of their ultimate separation.

The bus ride back seemed to take forever. The parched valleys and plains seemed endless. Time moved incrementally, as it had in the village, though Diana's mind raced ahead to the man waiting for her. How could she resist him?

She knew that the issues and problems were unchanged. And she knew that their separation was imminent and unavoidable. What had changed was the way she had come to view the days they would have together until they parted.

If it was to be nothing but an interlude, why not make the most of it? What had taken her from him in the first place was fear, and now Diana regretted that she had been so weak. She only hoped that he would forgive her and that they could happily share their last few days together.

Finally they reached the outskirts of Comayagua. Diana's heart began racing in anticipation. Then, momentarily, a sinking feeling overcame her. What if he was angry? What if he wasn't even there? Maybe he had sent someone else to pick her up.

The bus pulled up to the station, and Diana scanned the crowd anxiously. There, against the building where she had stood with him just days ago—aeons ago—was Cleve. He was tall and handsome in his jungle fatigues and beret. Though his bearing was that of a soldier, there was also a gentleness about him, a sensitivity and tenderness that Diana felt she alone knew.

She waited for most of the other passengers to disembark to avoid the jostling and pushing, then descended, her arms full of packages. When she stepped down onto the street, Diana saw him, looking at her as she looked at him, each of them frozen amid the swirl of passengers and baggage.

For several moments neither of them moved. They were each savoring the image of the other, taking in the cherished vision that had tormented them during their separation. From the silent communication that followed, Diana understood that everything was well between them. Cleve's eyes told her that it was okay.

An instant later she had thrown herself into his arms. Cleve's face felt cool against her fevered cheeks, and she sighed at the wonderful feeling of his strong arms around her, remembering how exquisite it was to be held by him.

"Oh, Diana," he whispered into her hair, "how I missed you."

Then he pulled back, looked into her eyes and kissed her hungrily. Diana melted into his embrace, overcome by him, wanting him as badly as he wanted her.

"I was sure you were upset with me," she mumbled into his lips.

He gave a little laugh and kissed her again. "It doesn't matter. You're back." Cleve looked at her, his soft brown eyes filled with emotion, his lips gradually curling into a smile under his mustache. He glanced down at the parcels she had clutched in her arms.

"Some of these are for Elena. Could we go by the cantina and drop them off? I'm sure they would mean a lot to her."

He nodded. "Sure, if you'd like."

When he had retrieved her luggage, they headed off to the jeep, Diana taking Cleve's arm, feeling incredibly happy.

"How is everything at Marta's?"

"Fine, just fine." She wanted to say she'd hardly noticed, not having thought of a thing except him since she'd left, but she didn't. "How are things at Palmerola?"

"I've been busy with getting Chaparral organized but, to be honest, I haven't done a very good job of keeping my mind on my work."

"Why not?"

"Thinking about the army-navy game, of course."

Diana laughed. They came to the jeep, and he tossed her things in the back and helped her onto the seat. Then he leaned over and kissed her again, this time tenderly, lovingly.

Cleve climbed in and they headed through the streets of town toward the cantina district.

"It'd probably be best if I took the packages in to her, Diana."

She turned to him. "I was thinking I'd like to. I've never met Elena, and this will probably be my only chance."

"It's not a place for you."

"I know. And I didn't handle it very well last time, but it's important to me. I really want to see her, know what she's like."

"It may not be very pleasant."

"I realize that."

In a few minutes they had come to the sleazy area where the cantinas were located. It was late afternoon, and the shadows of the winter sun were long. The pigs still rooted in the dust, and several small boys—the children of the prostitutes—were throwing rocks at an old barrel in a field. Cleve stopped the jeep in front of My Glorious Night.

She turned to him. "Let me go in, please."

"I think I should go with you."

"No, Cleve. I want to do this."

His expression was pained. "Well, be careful, and don't stay too long." He reached back, gathered the packages and handed them to Diana.

Cleve watched her walk across the road, her slender, shapely body so familiar and dear to him. It was good to have her back. The past days had been hell; the fifty or sixty miles separating them had felt like a million.

He sat in the jeep impatiently, his fingers drumming the steering wheel, an uneasiness settling over him. Cleve surveyed the building, his ears alert for any sounds of distress. He knew he probably shouldn't have let her go in alone, but he didn't want to begin their reunion with a spat.

After several long, agonizing minutes, Diana reappeared at the door of the cantina. The packages were still in her arms. She walked with brisk, angry strides toward the jeep, her face red with rage.

"They won't let me see her!" she exclaimed.

"Dammit!" Cleve climbed out and, taking Diana's arm, led her back to the cantina.

She glanced up and saw that his anger matched her own. The allegiance was heartening, and she felt better.

When they had just about reached the door, a guard with a carbine on his shoulder stepped out, greeting them with a wary look. Cleve brushed past him, and Diana followed him inside.

The proprietor, a heavyset woman in her fifties with bright orange hair, left her place at the corner of the bar and walked slowly to the couple. Cleve greeted her in Spanish, and the woman broke into a broad smile.

Diana listened as they conversed for a minute or so, noticing that the woman's attitude was markedly different with Cleve than it had been with her. There was a solicitousness that Diana found annoying.

After some more discussion, the woman led them to a small room just off the bar, containing a table and half a dozen straight-back wooden chairs. Cleve and Diana went inside, and the woman closed the door behind them.

"She said she would get Elena," he told her, gesturing for her to sit down. "Her excuse was that the girl was sleeping. I don't know whether it's true or not."

They waited in the austere room, which Diana assumed must be used for playing cards. There was the stale smell of cigarette and cigar smoke about the place, no window, and only a single naked bulb for light. Diana shivered and was glad for Cleve's presence.

They had been waiting for nearly ten minutes when the door opened again. The proprietor looked in, smiling at Cleve, then stepped aside and ushered in a slender girl wearing a simple cotton dress. Her eyes were doleful and distrusting, glancing first at Cleve, then at Diana.

Her long dark hair had been hastily brushed and her face washed, but she did look as though she may have been sleeping. Diana's heart went out to the girl who, in addition to all the other indignities she had been subjected to, had just been dragged from her bed to meet a couple of foreigners for a purpose she couldn't possibly imagine.

Cleve stood, greeting the girl in Spanish. She looked up with uncertainty at the man towering over her. He introduced Diana who smiled, trying to reassure and comfort her, but knowing that first they had to gain her trust.

The cantina proprietor had lingered in the doorway. As Elena sat down, the woman withdrew and closed the door. Cleve was talking in a soft, reassuring tone, apparently explaining the purpose of their visit. When Elena had comprehended who they were and the reason for their presence, she visibly relaxed, then asked a question in her small voice.

Looking at Diana, she said something that sounded very warm and friendly.

"She thanked you for trying to help her and Raul," Cleve explained.

"Thank you, *señora*," Elena said, smiling at her.

"I'm so sorry we didn't succeed, Elena. But we'll get you out of here, don't worry."

Cleve translated.

The girl nodded, mumbling her thanks.

Diana took the presents that she had placed on a chair and handed them to Elena. Cleve explained that Diana had brought them from the village.

The couple watched as the girl shyly began opening the packages. Diana felt her eyes swell with tears. The night before she had watched Concha—a girl of about the same age—opening her presents, but how different the circumstances were.

Elena unwrapped each gift carefully, her slender little fingers nervously removing the twine and pulling away the simple paper. Diana saw tears streaking down the girl's cheeks, and her heart wrenched.

When Elena had placed each item carefully on the floor beside her, she looked up at the couple, thanking them emotionally. She seemed so slender and vulnerable and deprived. Diana couldn't stand it any longer, just sitting there and watching. A maternal instinct filled her, and she got to her feet and went to Elena. The girl rose and they embraced, both weeping silently.

Cleve watched the woman and the girl, a lump forming in his throat. He, too, got to his feet, wanting to do something, wanting to comfort and embrace them both. He felt so helpless, so angry at the circumstances that brought on this suffering.

Just then the door to the room opened again and the proprietor appeared. She smiled at Cleve as she had before, but looked disconcerted at the scene taking place in her establishment.

"Please, Colonel," she said in Spanish, "I permitted this as a courtesy, but now you must go."

Diana and Elena had turned at the sound of the woman's voice, their arms still around each other. Cleve saw the expression on the girl's face and felt a twinge deep in his gut. He shot the proprietor a glance, feeling his bile rising, but knowing this wasn't the time or place to take action.

"We'd better go, Diana," he said softly.

Her eyes were imploring at first, but she too knew that there was nothing that could be done. Cleve's expression was solemn, stony; the proprietor's adamant, unrelenting.

The woman uttered a few commanding words to Elena, and the girl gathered her gifts. Mumbling her thanks to Diana and Cleve, she went to the door looking back once before disappearing.

The corpulent woman in the doorway grinned. "Can I offer something to drink?" she asked in halting English. "A beer, perhaps?"

"No, we don't want anything," Cleve replied, taking Diana's arm. "Come on," he said to her, "let's get out of here."

They walked through the dank bar, past the guard and into the street. Cleve's hand was clamped on Diana's elbow, but he said nothing. She could feel the emotion in him, a silent rage that seemed more awesome than her own.

Diana stopped at the jeep and looked back at the cantina. It was as though she had left her own daughter there, her own child. Obediently she climbed into the vehicle, but her eyes never left the building. Not far from them a pig snorted, and a shiver coursed up and down Diana's back. How could they just drive away and leave that young girl in that godforsaken place?

She turned to Cleve imploringly, but he was sitting motionless, staring straight ahead, his breathing heavy, forced. The muscles twitched in his jaw. Diana looked back at the cantina, her stomach clenched in a knot, Elena's face burned immutably into her consciousness.

Then Cleve turned and looked at her. For a long moment their eyes were frozen in a painful union, two human beings sharing common agony. "Oh, Cleve, she's just a baby, a young girl."

Her own words overwhelmed her, and Diana began crying softly in sorrow. An instant later, Cleve jumped from the jeep and Diana saw him marching with quick, determined strides toward the cantina. Her heart leaped, not knowing what he intended, but she saw in him a determination that couldn't be denied.

The guard, who was lingering still at the door, must also have read purposefulness in Cleve's manner, for he swung the carbine off his shoulder. Though the American was unarmed, he was not deterred by the show of force. The Honduran blocked the doorway, then called anxiously inside. Apparently seeing that the guard wouldn't yield, Cleve stopped in front of him.

Forceful words were being uttered on both sides, but Diana couldn't tell what was happening. Watching anxiously, she saw another guard appear behind the first. There was more talking, then the men stepped aside, admitting Cleve into the bar. The guards disappeared inside after him.

Diana stared at the doorway, her heart beating wildly in her chest, her anguish turned to fear. What could he be doing?

After a moment or two she heard loud voices, shouting from the building. It went on for at least a minute. People passing by stopped and looked.

Finally, Cleve came stomping out of the cantina, his face nearly as red as his beret. He walked directly to the jeep and climbed in. The veins at the side of his head were bulging.

"What happened, Cleve?"

"That bitch wants five thousand dollars for Elena."

"Five thousand? What do you mean?"

"I told her I would buy the girl out. I asked what the debt was, and she told me it was five thousand dollars! It's extortion, that's what it is. Extortion!"

Diana felt her heart sink. After seeing Elena, her compassion for the girl was stronger than ever, but Cleve's news dashed what hope she had. "Oh, no! How can they do this?"

But Cleve was still steaming. He started the engine, jammed the jeep in gear and popped the clutch, spinning the wheels and sending the vehicle lurching down the street. "It won't end like this," he said over the roar of the wind. "I promise you that!"

CHAPTER ELEVEN

THE DRIVE BACK to the air base was a somber and unhappy one. It was nearly dark by the time they reached the villa. Cleve's anger had tempered, but neither of them was in a very positive state of mind. Diana felt a closeness between them, but it was the sort forged by adversity. Still, she was glad for once that they were on the same side of the issue. He put his arm around her shoulders as they entered the house.

"I had a little surprise prepared for your return home," he said sadly, "but a celebration seems inappropriate under the circumstances." He turned on the light, revealing a room decorated with Christmas ornaments.

On the table was a small plastic tree covered with colored bulbs and tinsel. Strings of plastic holly were strung all around the room, and poster-size pictures of snowmen, carolers and Santas adorned the walls.

"It's not very elegant, I know, but considering the only place I had to shop was the PX in Panama, it's the best I could do."

"It's lovely, Cleve. And sweet of you to try to make it festive."

"Since I kept you from being home for Christmas, I thought it was the least I could do."

Diana put her arms around him and held him tightly. "You're really thoughtful."

He squeezed her, but said nothing.

"And you were wonderful with Elena. I was very proud of you."

"I wanted to take her with us," he said solemnly.

"So did I. It about killed me to leave her there." She glanced up, studying his face. "Cleve, why did you change your mind about Elena?"

He took a deep breath, then slowly exhaled. "I guess I let myself get sucked into it, that's all."

"What do you mean?"

"Sometimes your emotions can be your worst enemy, at least if you've got a job that calls for toughness. All those reasons I gave you why I can't help Elena are still valid. None of that has changed. But seeing the two of you like that—your arms around each other, crying—has made it a personal thing. Whether I like it or not, whether I want it or not, I'm involved."

"Is that bad?"

"It can be if you want to do your job." He smiled benevolently. "I'm a professional soldier, and my life is full of this kind of conflict—duty versus feelings. When you're leading men in combat, you constantly face difficult decisions affecting lives.

"Sometimes you have to do the hard thing—sacrifice the few for the many, for example. It's not easy, but you're trained to do it. You block out the immediate human issue for the sake of some larger goal."

"But why must you choose? Can't there be compromise?"

"Sometimes, but the price of compassion can be pretty high."

"What do you mean?"

"Let me give you an example. Say my intervention with Elena today gets back to Lopez and his superiors in Tegucigalpa. Say they decide I'm getting to be a pain in the neck, and a few words are whispered to the American ambassador or my own superior officer. If it's bad enough, I could get bounced right out of here, and then they'd send somebody in to replace me who can do what he's supposed to do."

"Do you think that will happen? Are you going to get in trouble over this?"

"Hopefully not. I don't think I've gotten so far out of line that anyone will squawk . . . yet. But we've got to be careful. My problem is that I've bought into it emotionally, and it won't be easy to pull back. That's the danger in a situation like this. Once you open the lid, it's hard to get it closed again."

"If that's the worst that can be said of you, Cleve—that you've got too much compassion bottled up in you—then you have nothing to be ashamed of. I respect your humanity, the fact that you care."

He laughed. "Now if I could just get you assigned to the promotion board, my problem would be solved."

"It's important to you, isn't it? Becoming a general, I mean."

"Well, I've devoted my adult life to it, and half my childhood for that matter. It's not easy to abandon the goals and values you've always lived for."

Diana realized he had just uttered the words to justify himself. He hadn't intended it as a comment on their relationship, but it amounted to that. Cleve was a soldier—a good one, obviously—but he was also gentle, and that was the side of him she loved best.

He had fallen silent and Diana hugged him fiercely, first because of the man he was, and secondly because the hours were ticking away, and soon he would be in her arms no more.

They went to the couch and sat down. The room was quiet, and the decorations somehow looked sad rather than festive. Cleve put his arm around her, and Diana let her head rest on his shoulder.

"I was going to borrow a tape deck and some Christmas music for your homecoming, but the men are having a party tonight and needed their equipment, so we'll have to do without." He looked at the tree. "I wanted to buy a string of lights, but there's really no place to plug it in here."

"It doesn't matter."

"Oh, I almost forgot," Cleve said, getting up. "I did get some Christmas candles."

He went to the table and slid a couple of candles around in front of the tree, lighting them with a match. Then he turned off the light. A mellow glow filled the room. Cleve returned to the couch.

"That's a little better, isn't it?"

Diana hugged him. "Yes, that's very nice."

They sat watching the flickering flames and the shimmering light on the tinsel. The mood was warmer than before, but there was a pathos that persisted. Elena was never far from either of their minds.

"When's our flight?" she asked.

"Late. Departure is scheduled for ten-thirty. It's a Honduran Air Force flight. I managed to get approval for you through the base commander. It saves a long drive."

Diana stared at the flames, liking the feel of Cleve's arm around her. She had been so upset over Elena that she hadn't really thought about herself and Cleve. This would be their last evening alone together. The next day was Christmas Eve. There would be social functions at the Esparza's, lobbying on behalf of Elena for a couple of days, and then, on the twenty-seventh, her return flight home.

If she hadn't gone to Marta's, they would have had more time together. In retrospect it seemed like a terrible mistake, but then other problems might have arisen, and she probably wouldn't have seen Elena. The experience had been an upsetting one, but it was something she had to do. If nothing else, it justified the sacrifice she had made in coming to Central America.

"Bet you've never had a Christmas like this before," Cleve said. He ran his finger lightly over the shell of her ear.

"Have you?"

"Whenever you're away from home they're always a little bittersweet. But I've gotten used to it. I've had enough of them."

Diana rolled his words over in her mind. "Where is home to you, Cleve?"

"I suppose with my uncle and aunt. Not having parents, or a wife and children, Paul and Sarah are all I have—though I haven't spent more than a couple of holidays with them. How about you?"

"I usually spend the holidays with my mother, though we've missed a few in the past five years. Since I'm older now and have my own life, and since she's remarried and lives in California, it takes more of an effort for us to get together."

"Maybe we belong together this Christmas, Diana." He squeezed her, and she wondered at his words.

Diana thought of Washington and the way it would be if the situation was reversed, if Cleve was *her* guest for the holidays. "You know what would be nice?" she said, musing. "If I could make you a big turkey dinner with all the trimmings. That'd make it like Christmas at home, wouldn't it?''

He stroked her cheek with the back of his fingers. ''Maybe another time, Diana. Another Christmas.''

The timbre of Cleve's voice left her with a strange feeling in the pit of her stomach, and she looked at him. His expression was wistful and dreamy. Then his mouth twisted slowly into a smile.

''You know what? You're awfully special to me . . . magical.''

His tone struck her as oddly sentimental. ''That's a really sweet thing to say.''

''Ever since Jack's, I've been carrying an extra burden I hadn't counted on, living with this terrible and wonderful feeling.''

She saw emotion deep in his eyes. ''What do you mean?''

''I'm obsessed with you.''

His words covered her like a blanket. They were frank, to the point, unabashed. It was like another thread in their growing web of intimacy.

Cleve slid his fingers up the back of her neck, playfully squeezing it. ''I never want to let you go.''

''Oh, Cleve.'' And she dropped her head against his chest.

BY TEN-FIFTEEN THE AIR had cooled considerably and there was a wind blowing across the plain. O'Malley came to the villa with a jeep to pick them up and Cleve, wearing civilian clothes, carried their bags to the door. Hardly anything was said during the short drive to the hangar on the Honduran side of the base, where they were to wait for their flight.

Diana tied a scarf around her head for protection against the wind and held her suede jacket close about her neck during the breezy ride. At the hangar, Cleve helped her from the vehicle and took their bags from the back. They bid O'Malley goodbye and went into the building.

A Honduran airman showed them to a small waiting room with cracked leather furniture. They sat down on a couch, and Diana looked around the rather Spartan surroundings.

There was a small window, the ubiquitous hanging light bulb, nothing on the walls and a few Spanish magazines on a small table. Cleve smiled on seeing Diana's rather forlorn expression.

"Not exactly Dulles International, is it?"

She shook her head. "Are military installations always this dreary?"

"I'm rather used to them, but I guess they are, yes."

Diana eased closer to him, liking the warmth of his body and the comfort of his presence. Cleve took her hand and held it in his. After a few minutes the airman reentered the room, spoke briefly to Cleve in Spanish, then left.

"He said the flight is delayed from San Pedro Sula, we'll have to wait a while," Cleve explained.

She really didn't care—in a way, the news was like a reprieve. Despite the fact she was leaving Palmerola with Cleve, her departure was clearly the end of a wondrous chapter of her life.

Even without a ticking clock, Diana felt the time slipping away. A few days together in Tegucigalpa, then they would part. Outside the metal building the wind had come up, making her mood and the night seem all the more forlorn.

Eventually they heard the sound of an airplane approaching, and moments later, the airman came to inform them that it was time to board. Cleve and Diana glanced at each other, gathered their things and followed the man out into the night.

The plane, a tail dragger, sat on the tarmac near the hangar, its starboard engine running, the passenger door open and waiting. The airman took the bags and led the way. Cleve helped Diana to the top of the ladderlike steps.

The interior of the plane was dimly lit by several weak overhead lights, and Diana nearly stumbled on the rough, sloping flooring. There was a single row of fold-down seats around the cargo bay, and she followed Cleve to two of them near the front. There were four other passengers, all Honduran military personnel. Three were sitting on the other side of the cabin, opposite them, all but one were asleep. The fourth, an officer, was sitting farther down on their side, reading a book in the dim light.

Cleve helped Diana with the worn seat belt, and they sat quietly as the door was closed. She glanced up toward the cockpit and saw the face of the pilot and co-pilot, who were looking back at her with interest and curiosity. Edging closer to Cleve, she felt the eyes of the two men and was more conscious now of the stark, utilitarian ambience of the military aircraft.

Cleve's hand was resting on his knee, and Diana reached over and covered it with both of hers. He smiled at her in a relaxed sort of way that seemed characteristic of his mood. To him this was all so routine; only her presence must have seemed out of the ordinary.

"You okay?" he asked.

"Yes, this is sort of a strange experience for me. I feel a little funny."

"The ride will probably be a little bumpier than what you're used to, but aside from the lack of creature comforts in these old C-47's, it's pretty much the same as a commercial flight." He grinned. "No strafings by enemy fighters, I promise you."

"You know, it does seem like a war situation. I hadn't realized it until now, but I almost feel like a refugee escaping from the front."

"I think you've seen too many war movies. I don't know these Honduran fly-boys," he said, gesturing toward the cockpit, "but from what I hear they're okay. Chances are you're safer here than on the Capital Beltway during rush hour."

She smiled up at him. "I'm not afraid, Cleve. Not when I'm with you."

DIANA NEVER really went to sleep, but she drifted for long moments, her head on Cleve's shoulder, her hands in his. The flight was fairly brief, but because of the earlier delay, it was almost midnight by the time they touched down in the capital.

"Bet it will be a while before you have another Christmas Eve that begins this way," Cleve said as they deplaned.

The air in Tegucigalpa was even cooler than in Palmerola. Diana shivered as they walked across the tarmac toward the well-lit building that served as a passenger terminal for military aircraft. The air inside was hot and dry, a welcome change.

Cleve went to speak with the clerk on duty, and they were directed to an adjoining lobby area where a civilian, the Esparza's chauffeur, was waiting. The man greeted them with polite cordiality and led them to a somewhat aged, but well-maintained, American-made limousine. Diana climbed inside while Cleve supervised the loading of the luggage. The plush interior of the vehicle, though dated, had the feel of civilization.

Cleve seemed delighted with the sight of her as he got in. "Sitting in a limousine suits you, Diana."

She ran her fingers over the velour seat next to her. "Isn't civilization wonderful?"

He leaned over and kissed her smiling lips. "You're as beautiful a princess as you were a peasant girl. I find you irresistible every which way."

She cuddled close to him as the driver put the car in motion. "I'm so glad we're together."

The drive to the Esparza's estate was nearly as long as the flight from Palmerola. The route they took skirted the capital city, but Diana had a glimpse of the lights on the hills in the distance. They drove for a long time through the dark countryside, revealed minutely by the headlights of the car and punctuated with an occasional lighted window in the dwellings along the road. To either side was the dark silhouette of mountain ridges, much nearer than they were on the broad plain of Comayagua.

At last they entered the gates of the estate, which was actually a large ranch. The drive from the road to the house ran for nearly a mile through open pasture to some woods. There, a Spanish mansion stood proudly at the base of the mountain. The entry was well lit, but except for several lamps shining through the windows of what were undoubtedly the public rooms, most of the house was dark. But even in the small hours of the morning the elegance and grandeur of the estate was apparent.

Almost before the limousine had stopped at the entrance, the large wooden door to the house opened and, behind a servant in white livery, a dignified and genteel man in his fifties appeared, wearing a smoking jacket. He strode to the head of the steps and waited.

The servant had descended to the limousine and opened the door, helping Diana out. As Cleve followed her, Alberto Esparza-Padilla slowly walked down the steps, his smile broadening until he reached the couple. The men shook hands warmly, greeting each other in Spanish.

They turned to Diana immediately, the Honduran's eyes twinkling with courtly cordiality.

"Diana," Cleve said in a refined manner, "may I present my dear friend, Señor Esparza-Padilla. Alberto, this is Miss Diana Hillyer from Washington."

The man took Diana's hand and kissed it perfunctorily, but with exaggerated courtesy. "Miss Hillyer, welcome to my humble home." He stepped back and extended his hand toward the open door. "Please come inside where it is warm."

They mounted the steps and entered a spacious vestibule with a high ceiling, a wrought-iron chandelier and polished tile floors. Beyond it was a large salon with an enormous fireplace against one wall. There was a cheerful blaze burning in it.

"How pleasant," Diana exclaimed.

Señor Esparza nodded graciously. "I would be pleased to offer you a drink. Perhaps a cognac before you retire?"

Diana looked at Cleve.

"I'm very sorry, Miss Hillyer, that my wife is not here to greet you, but she retired early, leaving me with the agreeable task of welcoming you to our home."

"It's most understandable, Señor Esparza. I'm sorry that we are so late in arriving." Diana could tell that the offer of cognac was primarily directed at Cleve. She also understood that the reference to his wife having retired was intended to give her a gracious way to decline. "I am tired from the trip," she said. "Perhaps I'll go to bed, as well. Will you forgive me for not joining you?"

Esparza inclined his head slightly in acknowledgment, and Cleve smiled at her warmly. As their host turned to a woman servant standing in the background, Cleve secretly slipped his fingers around Diana's hand and squeezed it affectionately.

"Teresa will show you your room, Miss Hillyer, if you'd be good enough to follow her."

"Thank you," Diana said, extending her hand to Señor Esparza. "Thank you so much for your hospitality." She glanced at Cleve. "Good night."

His smile was full of affection. "See you in the morning, Diana."

"Sleep well, *señorita,*" their host called after her.

Following the maid, Diana ascended the broad sweep of dark, polished wood stairs to her room.

THE NEXT MORNING Diana was vaguely aware of someone entering her room. She blinked into the sunlight streaming in the window and turned to see Cleve just as he sat next to her on the bed. He reached down and brushed strands of dark hair from her eyes.

"Good morning, princess. How'd you sleep?"

Rubbing her eyes, she saw that he was dressed in riding clothes. "How long have you been up?" she mumbled, stretching under the sheets.

"A couple of hours."

"Heavens. What time is it?"

"About nine."

"Oh...I'd better get up." She looked again at Cleve's clothes. "Have you been riding?"

"I was planning on it. Alberto has some wonderful horses. Would you like to come with me? That's why I woke you."

"Yes, I suppose so. I'm not the world's most accomplished horsewoman, but I enjoy riding."

"Good. I've convinced Alberto and Isabel that they should have a Christmas tree, so they suggested that I ride up into the mountains and find one. It would be a nice way to spend Christmas Eve morning, don't you think?"

Diana beamed. "It'd be wonderful."

"Hurry and get ready. There's a big breakfast waiting for you downstairs. Isabel is dying to meet you."

Diana reached up and ran her finger along Cleve's mustache, feeling childlike. She giggled happily.

Cleve caught the finger between his teeth. "Hmm," he said, grasping her wrist and examining her finger. "I think I'll have to fatten you up a bit."

"I'm fat enough," she protested.

"Let me see." He moved his mouth down her arm, nibbling as he went. "Getting better," he mumbled into the fleshy part of her arm.

She laughed gleefully. "That tickles!"

He lifted the covers and peeked under them. "Anything else to nibble on?"

Diana jerked the bedding from his hand, pulling it tightly around her chin. "Just me."

"What could be better?" He started to lift the covers again, but Diana held them firmly against her.

"We're in polite society now. No more scandalous behavior!"

"But Diana, the more refined the gentleman, the more scandalous he has an obligation to be!"

"Now you tell me!"

They laughed, and Diana sent him from the room.

ISABEL ESPARZA WAS an exquisite, patrician woman in
her early forties. Her hair and eyes were coal black, her
features, her figure, her hands, all thin, elegant, refined.
The *señora* seemed positively delighted to have Diana as
a houseguest. While Diana ate her breakfast, the two men
took their coffee into the library for a quiet chat, and Isabel stayed with her to drink her tea.

"I think it's marvelous that you've come to Honduras
for the sake of a young woman like that," Isabel said, her
English perfect, more British than American in accent.

"I confess to being a causist, Isabel."

"If no one is this country has bothered to thank you
for your efforts, Diana, I shall." She sipped her tea. "I
suspect your experience has been more akin to hostility
than gratitude."

Diana nodded. "I'm afraid you're right."

"Ours is a primitive country, I'm afraid. But we're
making progress, whether it looks like it or not."

"I must say I'm glad to have had the chance to meet
you, Isabel. Most of the women I've met here have not
been the type that I could really discuss the issues with.
Cleve's housekeeper, for example, is a wonderful woman
with tremendous spirit, but we really have no common
ground. It's very difficult for her to see where I'm coming from."

"I encounter the same problems. You see, I'm a bit of
a—what's the word?—maverick. Yes, that's it. I'm a
maverick in my own country. I'm a co-founder of the
Honduran Women's Organization. It's a rather modest
endeavor, I'm afraid, but we do address issues of particular interest to women."

"Isabel, you sound like a regular Carry Nation."

"Hardly that. It's scarcely a frontal assault against the
bastions of traditional society, but we do try to bring is-

sues to the attention of our decision makers. It's as much a social process as it is political, I'm afraid."

"Whatever works."

"We must discuss your young lady before the dinner party tomorrow night, Diana. From what Cleve has told us, that problem will doubtless be solved through social channels."

"Certainly."

"I know, though, that Cleve wants to take you riding this morning, so perhaps we can talk this afternoon. I'll be busy this morning with my staff finalizing plans for the party."

"Sounds like it's going to be quite an affair." Diana felt a little panicky at the prospect of anything too elegant, not having brought a thing to wear more formal than a knit dress. "Just how formal is the party, Isabel?"

"We tend to be a little extreme, I'm afraid. And I imagine you didn't pack for this sort of thing, did you?"

"No, not at all."

"I had anticipated that, and it's all planned. We'll go into Tegucigalpa this afternoon to my favorite dress shop. I'll buy you a dress."

"Oh no, Isabel, I couldn't accept anything like that."

"My husband is not a poor man, Diana, but that's not really the point. You have come all the way from the States to help one of my countrywomen at a substantial sacrifice to yourself. It would be a small token of my appreciation and, let's say, of all the people of Honduras."

"That's most generous of you, Isabel, but I couldn't accept."

"You not only will, you must! If I decide to have a formal party and invite a guest without giving ample warning, it is my duty to see that they are comfortable.

I'm afraid it is the Honduran way, my dear.'' She smiled graciously. '''When in Rome, do as the Romans do.' It is the law of international travel.''

Diana could see there was no denying Isabel Esparza. ''You are very kind.''

The woman patted Diana's hand. ''Well, I suspect that Colonel Emerson is anxious to get out in that wonderful air for a ride. I won't keep you any longer. We'll leave for town after lunch. That should give everyone ample time, don't you think?''

CHAPTER TWELVE

THE ESPARZA'S GROOM brought out several horses for Cleve to examine. Cleve looked over the animals, approaching a big strawberry roan that appealed to him in particular. He put his hand on the horse's shoulder, gauging his spirit and temperament.

"This is a fine animal," the groom said to Cleve in Spanish. "It is a favorite of Señor Esparza's brother. It has good heart and good strength."

"Excellent. Have the boy saddle him, then." Cleve looked at Diana, who stood watching him going through the ritual of selecting the horses. "For the young lady a gentle animal. A gentle horse that can run with the roan."

"I have a mare that would do well, Señor Emerson. A moment, please."

The man gave orders to the stable boy, and a bay mare was soon led out for inspection. Cleve turned to Diana.

"Does this one suit you?"

The groom commented to Cleve on the horse's favor with Isabel.

"He says that Isabel usually offers this one to her guests when she goes riding."

"I'm sure she'll be fine then."

He indicated their decision to take the mare, and the groom led the horse back inside to be saddled. Cleve walked over to Diana, noting her tight jeans and the comely shape of her legs. Because of the crisp air, Diana was wearing her suede jacket. Isabel had lent her a pair of gloves.

"Nice morning, isn't it?" he said, the faint vapors of his breath swirling between them.

"Wonderful air."

Cleve smiled at Diana, wanting to touch her, feeling cruelly restricted by the constraints of the public setting. He was anxious to get away from the house so he could be alone with her. Seeing the bare flesh of her throat, he tugged the zipper of her jacket up an inch or two, glad for an excuse to touch her. "Can't have you catching cold, can we?"

Diana blushed a little and took his hand, which still toyed at her zipper. "You're very protective."

"Too protective?"

She grinned. "I pity your poor daughter—if you ever have one. But no, not too protective. I like it."

Cleve threw caution to the winds and leaned over and kissed her softly on the lips. She smiled up at him. "Our hosts might get the wrong idea," she said demurely.

"Do you suppose it's too late then to go back to Palmerola for Christmas?"

"Why? Don't you like it here?"

"Yes, but it's so private there."

"I'm beginning to see there was method to your madness, Cleve Emerson."

"Yes, and I realize now this trip was a mistake. A mad and very unmethodical mistake."

"*I'm* enjoying it."

"I am, too, except for all the people around." He let a mischievous grin creep across his face. "Soon, though, we'll only have the horses to contend with."

"You didn't have any ulterior motive in volunteering to go after a Christmas tree, did you, Cleve?"

"Certainly not."

They both laughed.

The groom and his helper led the saddled horses out of the stable, as well as a packhorse for the tree. Cleve helped Diana mount the mare. Then, taking the reins of his roan, he swung into the saddle. The groom handed him the reins to the packhorse and stepped back.

"Wait, Señor Emerson," the man said. "You asked for an ax, let me get it for you." He went into the stable and returned with a long-handled ax. Stepping to the packhorse, he tied the tool to the animal. "There you are. It is ready. Have a good ride!"

Cleve thanked the man and boy, then turned and headed his horse around the stables toward the riding trail leading up the valley. Diana followed Cleve at first, but then pulled up alongside him.

"This is absolutely perfect," she said, taking in the crisp pungent air.

He nodded and looked around at the abundant nature surrounding them. The sun was well above the ridge on the eastern side of the valley. The sky was cloudless and crystalline, like a blue diamond. On the western slope, pines blanketed the mountain. The dampest air lay where they rode on the valley floor.

Cleve looked at the woman riding beside him, enjoying her beauty as much as the scenery. Again he felt impelled to touch her, so he extended his hand and she reached out to meet it, their fingers touching before the horses separated.

"This is definitely the way to spend Christmas Eve morning," he said, exalting in the great happiness he felt. What could be more perfect, he wondered, than being in a beautiful place, free to ride about it as you like, and having a magical creature at your side? Cleve's heart beat nicely at the thought.

"I'm so glad I had this opportunity to come with you," Diana said. "The Esparzas are so hospitable and nice. I just adore Isabel."

"She's a lovely woman...and very interesting, too."

"And her English is fantastic. Where'd she learn to speak like that?"

"Isabel is a Bay Islander, from the islands off the Caribbean coast, the Islas de la Bahía. It's part of Honduras, but the people are culturally British. They speak English and are Protestant."

"And yet she's Honduran?"

"Yes, her family is essentially ladino, meaning integrated into the Latin culture. Isabel herself is bicultural, equally Spanish and British."

"How fascinating. She did seem different to me, yet I couldn't quite put my finger on what it was."

"I believe Isabel was actually born in Tegucigalpa, where her father was a wealthy businessman, but the family maintained a place in the islands and traveled there regularly. I think Isabel spent some of her school years in England, too."

"I hope I have a chance to get to know her better. I feel a real rapport with her."

Cleve was pleased. "Good. I'm fond of Isabel myself—and Alberto. They're great people."

There was a glimmer in Diana's turquoise eyes and she laughed. "Shall we gallop?" she called out gleefully.

"If you'd like." But before he had said it she had taken off.

Cleve pressed his heels into the roan's sides, clicked into its ear, and the animal lurched ahead in pursuit of the mare, the packhorse dragging along behind. They galloped for about half a mile, the roan wanting to break away at full speed, but Cleve having to restrain him because of the packhorse. Still, they moved nicely. The wind was in their hair and stinging their eyes. Finally Diana reined in her horse.

"Whew!" she said when they had stopped, her breathing heavy. "I haven't done that in years."

"It's been a while for me, too."

Diana smiled, her cheeks bright pink from the exertion and the air, her white teeth and glossy hair glistening in the sun.

"You're beautiful," he said, unable to withhold comment.

Diana reached out to touch his hand, but the horses were still excited and stutter-stepped away, turning and tossing their heads.

"Let's walk them a bit," Cleve said, "and they'll calm down."

The valley had narrowed considerably, and the woods closed in on both sides. Before they had gone very far the trail entered the trees and began climbing. The scent of pine was heavy in the air.

"I love that smell," Diana said.

"Me, too. I think I could live in the woods, be a hermit or a mountain man or something."

"That's a long way from the hallowed halls of Oxford."

"So are the Army Rangers," he said with a grin.

The horses climbed steadily, the trail at times rocky and steep. Having left the protected valley bottom, and with the sun higher now in the sky, the air had warmed considerably. The riders had slipped off their jackets and were in shirt-sleeves.

"Where are we going to find this celebrated Christmas tree?" Diana asked after a while.

"Alberto said there are a number of stands of nice young pine up on this mountain. I thought we could find a good spot and rest the horses while I cut down a tree."

"Not to mention rest me!"

"Are you tired?"

Diana nodded.

"Let's find a spot then."

They came to a small stream running off into an ancillary valley, and Cleve turned the roan up the stream, leaving the trail. They had gone about a quarter mile to a point where the valley opened into a meadow. At the far end of it was a stand of young pine.

"There should be a tree for us in there," Cleve said, pointing.

Amid the pine was a small glen protected by larger trees and bordered by several fallen logs. Pulling up, Cleve dismounted and then helped Diana down from her horse.

"Feels good to be on the ground again," she said.

Cleve led the horses to the edge of the meadow and tied them to some saplings. He took the ax from the saddle horse, as well as a blanket that had been rolled and tied to the animal. Then he walked over to where Diana was sitting on a log in the sunshine, her face turned upward to the warming rays.

"Feels good, does it?" He put his hand on her slender shoulder, squeezing the tight muscles running from her neck.

"Hmm. And so does that." She touched the caressing hand.

Cleve put down the ax and blanket, stepped around behind her and firmly massaged the corded muscles with his thumbs.

"Oh, heaven."

He leaned over and kissed the side of her throat, the fragrant scent of her perfume combining pleasantly with the verdant smells of nature. Diana reached up and pressed his head against the side of her face, her fingers cool against his skin. Then Cleve stepped over the log and sat beside her, his arm around her as his mouth dropped to cover hers.

He kissed her deeply, tasting the sweetness of her, noticing more her fragile delicacy than her sensuous femininity. Finally, their lips parted and he looked into her face, feeling wonder at the vision he beheld. A low purr rose from his throat, a tribute to the woman and the awe in him she engendered.

"How about if I build us a cabin here, and we make this moment last a hundred years?"

Her eyes studied his, knowing the words were just his poetry, but also knowing that the emotions he felt were intense, like hers. "It *is* a dream, Cleve, and I don't want to wake up...ever."

He kissed her again. "Do you think the world would forget us and just let us be?"

"I wish." The sun and Cleve's affection had warmed her considerably.

He smiled, then turned and took the ax, which was leaning on the log beside him. "How many bedrooms would you like?" he asked, lifting it to his knees.

"I'd like a house like Isabel's," she replied matter-of-factly.

Cleve looked at her, then at the ax in his hand. "That may take a while."

"I don't have to be back till lunch."

"Maybe I'd better start with Alberto's tree, then." He took her hand. "Want to come and pick?"

Cleve grabbed the blanket and led the way into the copse of pines. They wandered among the trees, examining each for shape and size. Finally they selected one about eight feet tall, almost perfectly symmetrical.

"This one okay with you?" he asked.

"Yes, it's perfect."

"All right, princess," Cleve said, spreading out the blanket nearby on the carpet of pine needles, "you supervise."

Diana sat on the blanket and Cleve stood over her, looking down, bemused. He unbuttoned his shirt, stripped it off and tossed it on the blanket next to her. Diana's heart quickened with his show of masculinity.

Taking the ax, he strode to the tree. The sun felt warm on her shoulders as she watched Cleve, his powerful chest and arms naked, looking dashing in his high-topped riding boots. Gripping the tool, he glanced back at her and smiled under the brush of his mustache.

Then he lifted the ax over his shoulder and swung at the tree, the steel blade biting deeply into the trunk. Working the instrument free, he swung again, this time at a lower angle so that a wedge was opened in the pale wood. The next blow cut deeply into the tree. One more blow precipitated a loud crack, and the little tree toppled over at Cleve's feet.

He smiled at Diana, cupping his hand to his mouth. "Timmmberrr!"

Diana laughed. The whole process had scarcely taken half a minute. He walked back to the blanket and dropped down beside her, grinning.

"That was certainly a big build-up for a very modest show," she teased. Then she reached into her pocket, pulled out a tissue and began mopping Cleve's perfectly dry brow. "Are you tired?" she asked, unable to hold back her laughter.

He captured her hand in his, then pressed her fingers to his lips. She saw the same desperate hunger in his eyes that she felt. Wanting to be held by him, even as he wanted to hold her, Diana sank to the blanket and into his arms.

Cleve's face hovered over hers, his mouth descending now and then to nibble at the edges of her lips. The musk of his naked flesh surrounded her, intoxicating her, awakening her inner being to his presence.

Propped on one elbow, he began unbuttoning her blouse, his eyes never leaving hers, his intentions apparent. Diana unbuckled her belt and unzipped her pants as Cleve was releasing the clasp of her bra between her breasts. Her boots were preventing her from slipping off her jeans, but before she could reach down to remove them, Cleve's hand was under the cup of her bra, gently kneading her breast. His mouth descended to hers.

Diana eagerly accepted his probing tongue, wanting him in her. She felt his thumb lightly stroking her nipple to erection, the resulting path of excitement leading directly to the depths of her feminine core. He had aroused her almost instantly.

Breaking the kiss, Diana squirmed from his embrace, sat up and began taking off her boots, ignoring him in her eagerness. Beside her, Cleve, too, began to undress. Moments later they turned to each other, their bodies as primal as their surroundings. They fell instantly into each other's arms, Diana melting into him, the length of her covered by his warm flesh.

"Oh, Diana!" he whispered through his kisses.

"Cleve! Oh, God..." And she was smothered by his lips.

The kiss was long and deep. The friction of their skin, and Cleve's hand roaming over her, moistened the place between her legs, making it throb with desire. But then he pulled back, letting her hot, anxious breath caress his face, letting her breasts and pelvis arch toward him, unfulfilled. He permitted her near him, but not too close, choosing affection over passion, letting her ardor cool.

Cleve ran his fingertips over her fevered skin, his eyes more worshipful than ardent. Diana knew he wanted to calm her, his kisses trailing away until finally he eased onto his back beside her. She watched him, her head on his shoulder, her face just a few inches from his.

Feeling awed by the magical way he could arouse her, Diana cuddled closer, but acquiesced in the slower pace of their lovemaking. She touched his lip, tracing the line of his chin and jaw.

"Are you going to make love with me?" she whispered.

He was looking into the heavens above, nis expression calm and serene. "Yes, my darling. I want this to last . . . for a long, long time."

He cradled her against him, kissing her forehead lovingly, protectively.

Then, after long minutes under the warming glow of the sun, Cleve began their love dance. Gently he took her, his body a swirling poem of sensation. He enveloped her, mesmerized her, entreated and enticed, freeing her through conjugation. Feeling and awareness blended into a single pulsing union of body and spirit, man and woman.

Diana drank him in, relinquishing herself to him, giving herself up completely. The storm of their love took them both at once and together. He burst inside of her and she inside of herself, the conflagration racing across the surface of her body and throughout her core. And then, spent, it subsided, feeling slowly dwindling into nothing.

In the void that followed, Diana felt their common body becoming two. She stared past the man on top of her into the limitless sky, feeling overwhelmed by what she saw, yet so much a part of it. Cleve rolled to her side, his face, too, turned to the heavens.

As they lay together, he intertwined his fingers in hers, caressing her palm with his thumb. They stayed that way, their hands joined, their racing hearts slowing to a more normal rhythm.

Diana heard Cleve sigh, pleased by the peace and contentment in the sound. At that moment, she felt so fulfilled as a woman, so whole.

"This is as near to heaven as I've ever been," he murmured. "Undoubtedly as close as I'll ever be. I can't imagine more than this, Diana."

She rolled her head toward him, touching his dear face, the countenance that was so very special. "Cleve, I could only be happier if the rest of the world somehow dropped away, and we were left like this, together."

"It *is* our enemy, isn't it—the world? Our problems are out there, not here."

"I don't want to think about that—and I haven't been letting myself—but I know we must."

"I made myself forget, too."

She shook her head. "I guess that makes us both irresponsible and foolish."

"No, Diana, it's the wise thing to do. We can't change the world, so we may as well take what it gives us."

"You know, fatalism has always been contrary to my nature, but now, for the first time in my life, I understand it."

Cleve squeezed her hand. She smiled, and he rolled over and tenderly kissed her lips. "I'll never regret this."

"Nor I."

But Diana felt the sadness that she had so earnestly resisted start to creep in. She had managed since their reunion to live just for the moment. The magic of the hours since then had enabled it, but now the specter of their separation began looming over her. Reaching the pinnacle meant the only way to go was down.

"Will you stay in Tegucigalpa until my flight on the twenty-seventh?"

"I'd like to. Unfortunately, I can't. I've got a contingent of army and air force brass arriving the morning of the twenty-sixth to look over our preparations for Chaparral, the joint maneuvers coming up after the first. I'll have to be back at Palmerola bright and early. It means leaving Christmas night, I'm afraid."

"Oh Cleve, that's tomorrow night!"

"I know. The world seems to give, but it also takes away." He pressed his cheek against hers, holding it there. "That's why I treasure this so."

He felt the emotion in her silence, worried that the mood had been broken and wished with all his heart that it hadn't, that the moment could last forever.

Cleve still held his face to hers. "Can we forget tomorrow night, Diana," he whispered into her hair, "pretend it will never come?"

"Yes," she said, but the tears had already brimmed her eyes, and she knew it was a promise she wouldn't be able to keep.

THEY RETURNED to the house after lunch, and Diana had to hurry so as not to keep Isabel waiting. While Cleve showed Alberto the tree, she slipped upstairs to bathe and dress for the trip into town.

Half an hour later, she descended the stairs wearing her teal-blue skirt and sweater, with gray heels and a gray purse. "I'm so sorry we were late, Isabel," she said apologetically to her hostess.

"Don't worry, my dear, our appointment is not until three. We have plenty of time. But you must have some lunch, or you'll be famished before tonight. Come on," she said, taking her by the hand, "Constanza has made you a salad and some soup."

Isabel had a cup of tea with Diana while she ate. The men were busy with the handyman in the shop, designing a stand for the tree. When the women had finished, the chauffeur brought the car around to the front of the house, and Diana and Isabel set off for town.

"Francisca Ramos has the nicest dress shop in Tegucigalpa," Isabel said, "and whenever I shop locally I get my things from her. But she has a tendency, as you'll see, to put on airs. She likes to be called Francoise—that's the name of her shop—but, much to her chagrin, I call her Francisca." Isabel's laugh was devilish. "If I am plain and simple Isabel, she can be plain and simple Francisca."

"I'm sure it will be a lovely shop. Certainly adequate for plain and simple Diana."

Isabel laughed. "We think alike, Diana. I like that."

For a while Diana looked out at the countryside, not having seen much of it on the drive from the airport the night before. Isabel pointed out places of interest from time to time. Diana enjoyed the woman's company.

"So," Isabel said, touching Diana's arm, "perhaps we should talk about your young woman in Comayagua. I have some ideas, so perhaps it would be well to coordinate our strategies.''

"Yes, certainly.''

"After Cleve called with the story, Alberto and I talked about how we might help. As it turns out we are socially acquainted with Colonel Victor Molina-Delgado, the commander of the armed forces. Unfortunately, we are not so close that a favor could be asked directly. Instead, the way must be prepared.''

"It's beginning to sound complicated.''

"Not really, Diana, but in Latin America we are not so . . . direct as you are in the north. To ask a favor without the personal standing to do so creates an embarrassment for both parties. The situation must be . . . nurtured to the point where the favor is freely offered. It's a fairly simple process, but one that should, in all propriety, be undertaken. I think you can be helpful.''

"How, Isabel?''

"We will create a situation in which Colonel Molina finds himself wanting to help you with your little problem. We will make it his idea.''

"I see. This Colonel Molina apparently has it in his power to order Elena freed?''

"I'm sure he knows nothing of her. But he is the commander, and all the military men in the country are in his service—including the local police and military officials in Comayagua. If he wishes it, it will happen.''

"And I'm to ask him?''

"Not exactly. Tomorrow night at the party, you and I will talk to Molina about your interest in this girl. Without accusation, you will express your frustration, Molina will take pity on you and do what he can to influence the situation.''

"But in point of fact, he's involved in this terrible situation—the cantina system—isn't he, Isabel?"

"The power structure of our country is involved in everything that goes on. To that extent you are right, yes. People at various levels owe allegiance to their superiors, and conversely, the *patrón* must protect those under him."

"Yes, I've heard of the *patrón*."

"The cantina system is not Molina's invention, however. It is a product of the marketplace. There are commercial interests involved. These interests are protected by those in authority at the local level. People like Molina are rather removed from it all, involved only to the extent that they protect the local authorities and ensure their freedom of action. It is a passive corruption, Diana. That does not make it right. It merely explains it."

"Are you sure Colonel Molina will help?"

"It is not absolutely certain, but he is a man, he is proud of his honor. Hopefully, he will have compassion for you and help you."

"Me, and not Elena."

"He doesn't know this girl. You, he will know. Your concern for her will move him."

"I hope you are right."

"The important thing, my dear, is that you do not attack the system of which he is a part. Rather, we must make him aware of some excess and give him the opportunity to redress it."

"It strikes me as strange, Isabel, but I think I understand. Cleve has been giving me lessons in your ways in Honduras."

"Every society has its methods. To deal with you, I must know yours, no?" Isabel laughed good-naturedly, and Diana liked her all the more.

THE LIMOUSINE STOPPED on a major boulevard of the city, immediately in front of the entrance to a courtyard of elegant shops and boutiques. Isabel and Diana walked across the cobblestones and through the large iron and wood gate guarded by an attendant. "Francoise" was located in back, beyond a dribbling fountain made of stone, surrounded by lush flowering vines.

Francisca Ramos greeted them in a slate-gray tailored dress and pearls. Her carefully coiffed, gray-streaked hair and perfectly manicured nails were her statement. Diana knew that she would have to make a conscious effort *not* to address the woman as Francoise. Her demeanor almost commanded it.

After welcoming Isabel warmly, the woman turned to Diana, her smile polite but restrained. The introductions were made and Francisca immediately showed them to two ornate, antique French armchairs at the back of the small boutique.

"Señora Esparza described you perfectly," Francisca said to Diana in excellent, though heavily accented English. "You have a perfect model's figure, though a fuller bosom. Your height, however, may present a problem. Few of my customers are so tall as you."

"I'm sure we will find something, Francisca," Isabel said evenly. "After all, this is not a presidential inauguration, it is one of my little parties."

"Señora Esparza is unduly modest, *señorita*. Her parties are always the social event of the season." Her thin smile foretold her next comment. "And I am proud to say that my gowns form a majority of those present."

"That is because you are the only one in Tegucigalpa with taste," Isabel replied, "not to mention the fact that we know the same people."

"A point of honor, nonetheless." She smiled at the two women graciously. "May I offer you some coffee, *señoras*? The maid has prepared some in anticipation of your arrival."

"Thank you," Diana replied, "that would be nice."

Isabel shook her head. "Nothing for me, thank you."

Francisca Ramos went to a curtained door to the side and called out her instructions to a servant in the back room. Then she returned. "Now then, for the business at hand. What is your dress size, *señorita*?"

"Seven-eight."

"Yes, the American sizes. Hmm. But you are very tall...." She contemplated Diana. "A moment please." Francisca went into the back.

While she was gone, an older woman in a white uniform came from behind the curtain with a tray. She shuffled toward the women and placed an espresso cup and saucer on the small table between them. Isabel indicated in Spanish that the coffee was for Diana, and the maid slid it to her side of the table. Mumbling courtesies, she left the room.

A moment later Francisca returned with a shop girl carrying several dresses. The proprietor took them one by one and hung them on a rack nearby. Diana selected four dresses to try on.

The first was a black taffeta with a full skirt and low, square neck. The sleeves were puffy to the elbows, in a sort of Elizabethan look. It had a red sash. Diana looked into the mirror for a long time, and Isabel studied her, as well.

"You are very pretty in it," she volunteered at last.

"It's a lovely gown, but there's something about the look that bothers me. Too fussy, I think."

The dress was set aside, and Diana went into the dressing room with the second, a pale mauve, strapless gown with a slim skirt. It was classic, but didn't seem right, either. She stepped out briefly, just so Isabel could see, and retreated into the fitting room again.

The third was made of red satin. The look was very festive. It had a high neck, but it was backless and thus much sexier than Diana wanted.

"I think it's a bit obvious," Diana said to Isabel, "or as Cleve's housekeeper, Lupe, would say—'seen.'"

"Perhaps you are right. Again very pretty, but maybe it's just as well. Given our coloring in this country, a third of the dresses you'll see tomorrow night will be red. I don't plan to be among them myself."

Diana smiled.

"This then may please you," Francisca said, stepping to them with the fourth dress, a turquoise silk chiffon.

The color immediately caught Diana's imagination, and she eagerly took it back to the dressing room. The soft silk was gently folded into an off-one-shoulder classic Greek design. A rhinestone clasp on the shoulder held the gown in place. The image Diana saw in the mirror was simple and dramatic.

Isabel was enthusiastic. "I have some diamond earrings you can borrow that will be stunning with it, Diana!"

"It *is* nice," she said, spinning around in front of the mirror.

Francisca Ramos beamed approvingly.

They looked at shoes next, deciding finally on some delicate silver evening slippers. Isabel again admired Diana in the gown.

"Do you like it?" Diana asked, feeling very pretty indeed.

"I do. And what's more important, Cleve Emerson will, as well."

CHAPTER THIRTEEN

ON THE DRIVE BACK to the Esparza estate, Diana was quiet. She had her gown, was ready for the ball, but felt time was against her, much like Cinderella. As long as the party lasted she'd be okay, but when it ended the dream would end, too.

She thought of the terrible cruelty of her circumstances. There was simply nothing that could be done about them. Nothing. He would be leaving her life the next night . . . forever.

"You've traveled a great deal, Isabel," she said to her companion. "What do you think of a woman's life here, her role in marriage—as compared with Europe or the States, places like that?"

"Attitudes here are much more primitive, it's fair to say. But my personal case is unusual because of my education and because Alberto is a very enlightened man. My belief, though, is that people generally end up in the relationships they really want. Only when there is no freedom at all is this not so."

"Let me ask you this. If you think of marriage as a pie, would you rather be half the pie and your husband the other half, or would you prefer to be the filling and have him be the crust?"

"That's a curious question, isn't it?"

"A very wise person I know once described marriage that way."

"I see." Isabel studied Diana. "Filling, crust or a little of both. That's the choice, is it?"

"Something like that."

Isabel thought. "I'd have to say I'd like to be the filling, provided the crust is very enlightened and doesn't take his facade too seriously."

Diana laughed approvingly. "That's a very good answer."

"I am a very happy woman, Diana, because I *am* as I wish to be. Alberto's contribution is his wisdom to understand that."

The women looked at each other for a moment.

"Are you having trouble with the American philosophy of perfect equality?" Isabel asked.

"Freedom is not without its costs, is it?"

"The words are not necessarily those of a woman in love, but in your tone I hear it. I saw it in your eyes when you had on the dress. Is it Cleve?"

Diana nodded almost imperceptibly, turning her head to the window to mask her emotion.

Isabel Esparza patted Diana's hand sympathetically, then held it, not saying a word. After a few moments the emotion subsided, but neither of them spoke until they were at the gates of the estate.

ALBERTO ESPARZA AND CLEVE were in the salon having a drink when the women returned. They exchanged greetings, then Diana went upstairs to put her things away and freshen up. When she came down, Cleve was in the entry hall with his coat on and Diana's jacket in his hand.

"How about a little walk before dinner?"

She was pleased. "That would be nice."

Outside the front door Cleve took her arm. He turned her toward him. "I missed you."

Diana saw the emotion in his eyes and smiled bravely, not wanting to let it affect her the way Isabel's comment had in the car. "I missed you, too."

He held both of her arms, his body close to hers. She looked up at him, feeling heart-wrenching love as she never had. How could life be so unfair? Her only sin was traveling to Central America for the sake of a girl. The gods had given her Cleve, and now they were taking him away.

As he kissed her, Diana struggled for control, her insides a maelstrom of emotion. She wanted his love desperately. Pie, filling, crust—she wanted it all, but knew she could have none.

Cleve pulled back and, seeing a tear on her cheek, blotted it with his finger. "What's the matter?"

"The cool air, I guess. The car coming back was very warm."

He took her hands and they descended the steps, walking slowly across the grounds. It was nearly dusk, the sun long since having disappeared behind the mountain. They wandered toward the stables.

"Alberto and Isabel are going to a dinner party this evening," Cleve said, breaking the silence. "He invited us to join them, but I declined. I thought it would be better if we were alone tonight, just the two of us. I hope you don't mind."

"No, I'd much prefer being alone with you." Her voice was thin and brittle, but she was in control.

"We managed to get the tree on a stand and in the house. I thought maybe we could decorate it for Isabel. What do you think?"

"That would be fun. Just like Christmas at home."

Their aimless stroll had taken them around the stables and up the trail they had ridden along that morning. The valley floor ahead of them was covered by a thin mist, though the trees jutted into the crystal air. Above the dark side of the mountain, the sky was colored with the hues of the setting sun.

Diana stared up the trail, remembering the wild dash they had made on the galloping horses. She recalled how happy and free she had felt. Thinking about it—about her own frivolous innocence—saddened her.

Up there, where they had lain together, the marvelous, brilliant daylight had been swallowed by the night. That little patch of ground on which their bodies had intertwined in ecstasy was cold now, vacant, forgotten by the world.

They stopped on the trail, a hundred yards or so beyond the stables. There was no point in going farther. They were both drawn by the place, though neither had mentioned it, but the darkness stopped them. The world refused them their desire. It had given, but it had also taken away.

DIANA SAT in a chair with needle and thread in her hand. Cleve, at her feet, handed her a kernel of popcorn, which she lanced with the needle and pushed down the thread and into the basket on the floor beside her. While he dug into the bowl for the next piece, she looked up at the blazing fire. It seemed so warm, and with Cleve there it was just as their secret place in the mountains had been. She didn't want to leave it, ever.

Cleve kissed her knee, which was just inches from his face, then craned his neck to look into the basket. "Is it a popcorn string yet?"

"Enough for at least half the tree," she chided. "Cutting it down might have been easy enough, but decorating it will certainly put you to the test."

Cleve shook his head. "If I had known it'd be like this, I'd have packed my plastic tree."

"Now wouldn't that have looked silly in this big room?"

"Yankee practicality."

They finished the popcorn string and assembled the various baubles Isabel had supplied to use as ornaments. As they decorated the tree, they traded stories about other Christmases they had had, holidays spent in New England or Southeast Asia. The magic of snowy winter nights and the incongruity of Santas and steamy tropical jungles fascinated them.

Their childhood experiences were similar in ways, each of them having lost their fathers early. But as a young man Cleve had lost his mother, as well. Then there was his failed marriage and the years alone.

Diana had her mother still, but otherwise she had no one and, barring marriage, she would soon be no different than Cleve: entering the middle years of life without anyone to love and be loved by.

"What is it about the holidays that is so nostalgic?" Cleve asked as they settled on the couch, watching the fire.

"People carry more memories of that time of year than any other, I suppose."

He caressed her fingers in his hand. "I'll never forget this Christmas."

Diana stared into the fire, remembering that officer at the party in Washington who had looked at her so wondrously. "When you saw me that first time, did you ever in your wildest dreams think we might be together at Christmas?''

"I never thought specifically of that. But I knew I wanted to be with you." He pulled her tightly against him. "You know, it's strange, but in a way this is hardly more real than that was."

"Yes, I know what you mean. We've been pretending the past few days, trying to live a fairy tale."

"I wish it would go on forever."

"It can't, though."

"Hey," he said, smiling at her. "We weren't going to worry about tomorrow. Remember?"

Diana nodded and stared at the flames, not able to look at him just then. Sadness overwhelmed her. She bit her lip.

Cleve stroked her cheek with his fingers. Moisture filled her eyes and he kissed her.

In the midst of it all, teardrops spilled over and slipped down her cheeks. He tried to kiss them away, but they came too quickly. Diana didn't make a sound. She just looked at him until he pressed his forehead to hers.

"I love you, Diana. Even though we're from different worlds, I love you. I'll always love you."

She slipped her arms around his neck and let him hold her close. "I love you, too," she whispered, barely maintaining control. "I love you, too."

They stayed in each other's arms a long, long time, clinging to each other and to the minutes that were rapidly slipping away.

THE NIGHT for Diana was long and full of fitful dreams. In each one something terrible was impending. She awoke early, dressed and, taking the gift she had purchased for the Esparzas, went down for breakfast.

Alberto and Isabel were just sitting down when she arrived. Cleve had not yet come downstairs. They exchanged Christmas greetings, and Diana gave Isabel the present.

"I realize your big day to exchange gifts is January first, but I'll be gone by then, so I've followed the American custom."

"How thoughtful of you," Isabel said. "May I open it now?"

"Please do. I'm afraid it isn't much. The shopping in Comayagua was somewhat limited."

Isabel had removed the paper and held the leather box up for Alberto to see. "Isn't it lovely?"

"Very nice. And our guest is *muy simpática.*"

"Alberto, she's not only kind—Diana's lovely. Wait until you see her tonight in her gown. She'll be the most beautiful woman at our party."

"Do you suppose Cleve will let the other gentlemen even talk to her?"

"What's this?" Cleve asked, appearing at the door in a brown sport coat and open-necked shirt. *"¡Feliz Navidad!"* he said, coming to the table. "Am I being paranoid, or are you people discussing me?"

"I was saying how fortunate you were to have found Diana," Isabel replied. She smiled. "But it's apparent you're aware of that."

"You're very perceptive, Isabel," Cleve said, sitting down. "Sorry to be late."

Diana looked at him, knowing her face had to be full of anxious desperation. Cleve reached over and touched her hand. "Good morning, princess, and merry Christmas."

"Merry Christmas, Cleve." She didn't care that the Esparzas were there, she let her eyes hold fast to his. Already her heart was aching. It was their last day.

Diana listened as the others discussed the upcoming events of the day. She commented when it was called for, but spent most of the time watching Cleve, burning his image into her memory.

People would be dropping by all day, Isabel told them. Family members would be coming for a special lunch, and guests would begin arriving about seven for the party. Diana could see she would have little time with Cleve alone.

After breakfast they all went in to officially admire the tree Cleve and Diana had decorated. Christmas trees were not common in Latin cultures, but it was familiar to Isabel, and Alberto enjoyed the novelty of it.

"Between Isabel's dancers and your tree," he said, "my home will be very festive indeed."

Cleve put his arm around Diana. The servants had a fire burning to take off the morning chill. The room seemed homey and warm.

"What dancers?" Cleve asked.

"A few years ago, I had a group of Morenos come dance at my party," Isabel explained. "It was so popular that I've made it a tradition. It's as much a part of Christmas in this home as carols are in England or the States."

"What are Morenos?" Diana asked.

"They're the Black Caribs, an ethnic group from our north coast. The Morenos are the descendants of runaway African slaves who intermarried with the Carib Indians of Saint Vincent Island. Two hundred years ago they were deported by the British to the Bay Islands, and most of them moved on eventually to the mainland.

Their religion is part Catholic and part aboriginal. They
have some marvelous cultural traditions. The dances I
love in particular.''

"What are they like?''

"The *yancunu* is the dance they do on Christmas. It's
performed only by the men. It's just marvelous. More
like what you'd expect to find in Africa than the Caribbean. But you'll see for yourself tonight.''

"I can hardly wait,'' Diana enthused. "Sounds fascinating.''

"We have some wonderful and very diverse cultural
things in this country,'' Isabel said.

"Including those of my Spanish ancestors,'' Alberto
added dryly. "Fortunately for you Bay Islanders, my
dear Isabelina, the ladino heart is big enough to accept
even the most alien of cultures.''

Isabel turned to Diana and winked. "What do you
suppose a pie would be like *without* its crust?''

Diana laughed.

Cleve and Alberto looked at each other. The Honduran shook his head. "I haven't the foggiest, have you?''

"No, but I'm beginning to see a pattern. Must be some
sort of revival of an interest in baking.''

Both women laughed uproariously.

THE REST OF THE DAY was busy and full of people. Diana
helped Isabel where she could. Sometimes she just wandered around the big house when Cleve was off doing
something, but whenever possible, the two of them
gravitated toward each other, managing a few stolen
kisses.

After lunch Cleve took her aside. "Let's go out for a
walk, shall we?''

Diana eagerly agreed.

They strolled toward the fence surrounding the large pasture that spanned the valley. Cleve leaned against a post and Diana rested her arms and chin on a wooden rail, staring across the field at the horses grazing peacefully in the distance.

"I've racked my brain," he said after a while. "I can't think of a way to keep you here."

"There isn't a way, Cleve."

"I know there isn't. It's just not my nature to stand idly by and see you taken from me."

"Please don't . . ."

"Why couldn't you have been an army brat?" he continued, ignoring her plea.

"What if I was?" she interjected, feeling wounded more by the issue than by Cleve's suggestion. "We still couldn't be together!"

"There'd be hope."

"Don't hope, Cleve. There's no point in it. As long as we're the people we are, there is no hope."

"That's awfully pessimistic, isn't it?"

"I don't love you any less for the fact that our lives are incompatible. I just recognize that they are, that's all."

Cleve turned and stared across the field with Diana. "Better we were a couple of horses, like those out there."

"You'll forget me soon enough."

"No," he murmured wistfully, "I won't." And he knew he wouldn't. But Diana was right. There was no hope, not as long as they were the people they were.

Is this who I am? he wondered. *Is this who I really am?* He had never doubted his identity, his values, his life's plan before. He had devoted himself to becoming a general and now, with this woman, it was all in doubt.

"Maybe there's a compromise of some sort we're overlooking," he said with a glance at Diana.

"Not without one of us selling out. If one of us was to give in, there'd always be resentment. I wouldn't want a sacrifice from you under those terms, and you shouldn't want one from me."

Cleve gave a half laugh.

"What?"

"I'm supposed to be the strong one," he said, "and here you're being levelheaded and reasonable."

She touched his arm. "Men don't have a monopoly on common sense, you know. We've shared a wonderful dream, Cleve. It's been a fairy-tale life for a couple of weeks. Let's not spoil it by trying to stop the clock."

"Okay then, princess." He kissed her nose. "But I won't let you get away without something to remember me by." He pulled a small package from his pocket.

Diana held it in her hands, gazing at it for a moment. When she looked up at him, her eyes were like those of a gentle fawn. He could see she was touched.

"Go ahead, open it."

"Now?"

"It's Christmas."

She carefully removed the wrapping paper.

"It's not much, just a token," he said as she took the lid off the small cardboard box.

Cleve watched her lift the pair of handcrafted silver earrings from the tissue paper inside.

"Cleve, they're beautiful!"

"Something to put on occasionally and think of me."

She hugged him, then looked up into his soft brown eyes as his arms closed tightly around her. He rubbed his cheek against hers, savoring the velvety smoothness of her skin. Then he took her moist lips, caressing them, adoring the feel of them against his own.

"Oh, Cleve, every time I start to feel strong, like I can handle this, you kiss me."

"And?"

"I start to crumble. I can hardly bear it."

"Then I won't kiss you," he teased.

Shaking her head, she buried her face in the opening of his shirt, pressing herself against him. "Please hold me. Please."

CLEVE HAD THROWN his dress uniform in his bag when he had packed at Palmerola, figuring one of the Esparza's maids could press it for him. At six when he went up to dress, he found it hanging in the closet, beautifully pressed and ready to wear.

Though the party had yet to begin, Cleve felt wrung out. The day was one of the more emotional ones he had ever experienced. He decided to take a bath and try to relax.

Sitting in the old-fashioned tub, he thought of another day years before when he and Carolyn had decided to divorce. They both had known it was coming, but she had finally pushed the button—the day before he was to leave for Korea. It was funny, he thought, how the imperatives of military life precipitated personal decisions.

Cleve wondered whether the coming weeks would be like those first months in Korea. The night the divorce papers had arrived he had gone out on the town in Seoul with a couple of buddies. He had gotten drunk and then laid, though the details of that night had always been a blur in his memory. Somehow, though, he knew this would be different. He couldn't imagine one of the *señoritas* now. Not after Diana.

Twenty minutes later, Cleve descended the stairway. For some reason the dress uniform with bow tie, striped trousers and all, gave him a strong sense of being a soldier. He felt taller by several inches when he wore it, proud and "sharp," as his Uncle Paul used to say.

The servants were scurrying about, busy with last-minute preparations. Alberto, handsome in his tuxedo, was directing the activity, calmly standing in for Isabel, who was upstairs dressing.

"There you are, my friend!" he said in Spanish.

Two of the young maids looked with round eyes at the tall American officer before Alberto sent them on their way.

"Looks like you have your command well disciplined," Cleve said with a laugh.

"It's Isabel who's the disciplinarian. I merely provide the bravado."

Cleve grinned.

"How about a glass of sherry before the ladies come down?"

"Sounds good."

Señor Esparza had two sherries brought, and they stood near the fire, sipping their wine.

"Perhaps I'd better look in on the kitchen staff," Alberto said after a moment. "Isabel warned me to alert her if there were problems. Will you excuse me?"

"Certainly."

Cleve went nearer the cheerful blaze, enjoying its warmth as he leaned against the end of the mantel. While he sipped his sherry, Diana suddenly appeared on the stairs. Her floor-length turquoise gown, off one shoulder, was stunning. He watched in awe as she slowly descended.

Cleve felt himself straighten, feeling wonderment at the vision—different, yet so very much like the image she had presented that night in Washington. The diamonds at her ears caught the light. Her hair was up in a sleek chignon and, as she moved gracefully across the floor toward him, something in her dark tresses sparkled. She smiled and a wave of weakness washed over him.

"You look incredibly beautiful," he said, taking her hand.

She offered her cheek, squeezing his fingers firmly. "And you! It's no wonder half the women of Honduras are at your feet."

"What makes you think that?"

"I see it in their eyes, wherever we go."

He kissed her again, unable to resist.

A short time later, Isabel came down, looking beautiful in a low-cut black gown and opulent diamond necklace. She chatted with them for several minutes before being interrupted by the urgent question of a maid. Isabel was no sooner off with the girl when Alberto returned, full of praise for Diana's dress. He ordered her a drink from the barman, then Isabel returned and the guests began arriving. Cleve and Diana had no further time together alone.

Though he hated the separation, Cleve permitted Diana to be taken from him for introductions. It was the first time they had been in a social situation together, and Cleve soon saw that he was not the only man aware of Diana's charms. Despite an attempt to be polite to others, he found himself drifting away from conversations toward Diana, managing a few words with her before she was taken from him again.

When dinner was finally announced, Cleve found himself at the opposite end of the table from Diana. She was seated one place from the end, with Colonel Molina between her and Isabel. Molina was the man they planned to influence in order to help Elena, and Cleve knew it was important, yet he was resentful of the separation.

He engaged in polite conversation with those around him, ate without noticing the meal and looked repeatedly toward the other end of the table. Once or twice he caught Diana's eye, but mostly she spoke with Molina or the man on the other side of her. She smiled frequently, her conversation animated. She seemed happy, only the hint of sadness on her face when their eyes met told him otherwise.

Diana was powerfully aware of the man at the other end of the table, though her very purpose in coming to Honduras was on the line in the discussion occurring at her side. She focused her concentration as best she could, but occasionally, without willing it, her eyes turned to Cleve.

Often, their eyes locked. Once, his lips moved and she read the words, "I love you."

Blushing, she turned away, moved yet saddened by his gesture. She listened to Colonel Molina and ate, oblivious to the delicacies that had been put before her.

"As I understand thees situation, *señorita*, thees girl cannot pay her debt and so her employers are opposed to her leaving."

"Yes, that's the problem."

"But surely thees debt is not so great that it cannot be paid by her relatives and friends."

"But that's the problem, Colonel Molina, the proprietor of the cantina has set the price of...I mean has claimed the debt totals five thousand dollars."

"Five thousand!"

"In Honduras," Isabel interjected, "five thousand will feed a girl for many years and buy many, many lipsticks. Don't you think, Colonel?"

"Yes, it sounds to me excessive. And you say she has only been employed in thees place for a year?"

"That's correct."

Molina shook his head. "Are the local police aware of thees requirement of five thousand dollars by the proprietor?"

"I don't know, but they haven't shown a willingness to be cooperative."

"I see. Sometimes they become—how you say it?—too excited to protect the interest of the commercial people."

"They do seem zealous in that regard, yes."

"It seems to me, *señorita*, that you have discovered an irregularity, for which I am most grateful that you call thees to my attention. I am sorry that thees impression is given to you of my country."

"I have found many Hondurans who are sympathetic to Elena's situation. Unfortunately, none has been in a position to rectify the wrong."

"You understand, it is the job of the police to protect the commercial interests of the people of the towns. But it is not their job to protect unfair demands. Be assured, *señorita*, that I shall have a word with the captain of police in Comayagua about this matter."

Before she could thank the officer, Isabel addressed him in Spanish. They conversed for a minute or two, then Molina turned to Diana.

"Señora Esparza says to me that you are leaving our country in just two days and that it is your dream to see thees girl back in her village. For thees reason I will see to thees matter first thing in the morning. I will ask

Lieutenant Colonel Emerson to discuss arrangements for release of the girl with the captain of police, after I have had a word with him.''

"Oh, Colonel, I am so grateful. You are most kind.'' Diana looked up at Isabel, who nodded, then winked conspiratorially. Diana smiled, realizing that one of her burdens had been lifted.

CHAPTER FOURTEEN

WHILE THE GUESTS were dining, the servants had rolled back the carpet in the great salon, brought in extra chairs, which were arranged in a large semicircle, and built the fire up to a roaring blaze. Windows were opened, and the lights had been lowered when Isabel Esparza led her guests back into the room.

Diana found herself in a wing chair facing the fire. Cleve was seated on one side of her, Colonel Molina on the other. When everyone had found a seat, a couple of maids circulated among the guests with trays of after-dinner drinks. Then a hush fell over the room in anticipation of the dancers.

At the critical moment Alberto Esparza stepped before the group and made a little speech in Spanish. Diana assumed it to be a toast of sorts, because his manner was resplendent with polished gentility. She regretted all the more she wasn't able to speak the language.

The speech completed, Alberto took his seat. The lights were extinguished so that the only illumination was provided by the dancing flames, which sent long shadows throughout the room. Suddenly a door was thrown open, and a large black man in a native mask stood staring into the room. A gasp of surprise and excitement rippled through the gathering.

Diana looked at Cleve, who had been watching her with bemusement. The tender affection on his face quieted the excitement in her heart. He took her hand as the dancer led ten of his fellows, all masked and stripped to the waist, into the room. She turned back to the pageant, her hand still entrapped in Cleve's.

The small group of musicians that had accompanied the dancers began playing. The sound was reminiscent of the music of West Africa, where it undoubtedly had its origins. The dance, which was performed in a circle, was not so much African in nature as it was Indian, very much like that done by the inhabitants of the South American rain forests.

Diana sat transfixed as the spirited performers gradually built the rhythm to a frenetic pace. The dance was one of celebration and thanksgiving—incredibly, it seemed, in commemoration of the same event that inspired the tree in the corner and the carols being sung all across North America and Europe that night. The *yancunu* was something she'd never forget.

After a long time the mesmerizing rhythms abated, the music wound down, and the dancers and musicians made their exit to enthusiastic applause from the guests. Diana sat exhausted from the excitement, her cheeks red, her heart pounding. She turned to Cleve, beaming.

He leaned over to whisper in her ear amid the buzzing in the room. "I've never seen a more beautiful sight."

"They were magnificent, weren't they?"

"I was referring to you."

She squeezed his fingers tightly, wishing she could hold him in her arms.

The lights were turned up, and when the guests began circulating into other rooms, the staff started restoring the salon. Colonel Molina and Isabel were chatting, and Diana slipped away with Cleve.

They wandered into the conservatory where, amid the greenery, a baby grand piano had been set up and a pianist was playing festive pieces, mostly Latin music, but some American favorites like "White Christmas." They listened for a while, Diana acutely aware of Cleve's eyes upon her. She wanted him near, liked the feel of his hand on her elbow, but had trouble looking into his eyes, knowing well the emotions that would arouse. Despite the gaiety, Diana felt the minutes slipping through her fingers.

They listened awhile longer, then Diana saw Cleve look discreetly at his watch. Her stomach clinched. He leaned close to her. "I'm going to have to go upstairs and change," he said in a gentle voice.

Diana turned from the piano to face him, though her eyes were cast down on his fingers, which nervously fiddled with hers. "Shall I come upstairs with you?"

"No," he replied, giving a little laugh, "we may never come down again." He kissed her forehead. "I'll meet you in the foyer in about fifteen minutes. You can walk me out to the car." Cleve turned then and walked quickly from the room.

Diana stood at the piano for a minute longer, trying not to think about anything, trying to keep her mind clear. She turned around looking for a friendly face and saw Isabel standing in the doorway. Without hesitating, she went to her hostess, knowing the distress she felt was all over her face.

"Is Cleve changing?" Isabel asked simply.

Diana nodded.

"Come on, then. You and I will have a cognac."

Diana followed Isabel into the bar, and they each took a brandy snifter of French cognac.

"You did beautifully with Molina," Isabel said, touching Diana's glass.

"Thank you, but I did nothing. You orchestrated it wonderfully, Isabel. You had it figured out exactly."

"Perhaps I know my Honduran officials just as you know your American congressmen."

Diana was staring off into space. "All that—my job, my friends in Washington—seems so removed just now, almost as though it were a different lifetime."

"You've had a very emotional time during your short stay here."

Diana smiled, thinking what a colossal understatement that was. She sipped her cognac, liking its fiery warmth.

"I've been thinking about Elena," Isabel said. "It may prove difficult for her if she returns to her rural village. My organization sponsors a technical school that helps needy women learn skills that are in demand in the urban economy. To give her another option, I'd like to offer her a place there."

"I'm sure she'd be pleased, though I don't know what it will be like for her in the village or what her desires are."

"It may prove to be a viable option—after she's recovered from her ordeal. If you'd like, I'll see that she's made aware of the opportunity."

"I would appreciate that, Isabel. Thank you."

"Well," Colonel Molina said, approaching them. "Here are my dinner companions, the two most lovely ladies at the party."

Isabel laughed. "You flatter us, Colonel, so that we won't feel badly for having abused your generosity earlier."

The man grinned. "*Duramente, señoras*. Hardly abuse." He smiled at Diana benevolently. "I hope that the result of your visit to our country pleases you, *señorita*."

"Yes, most definitely, Colonel. As a matter of fact, Isabel and I were just discussing Elena's future. We hope to help her build a new life, offer her some job training."

"You are a most dedicated young woman, *señorita*. I admire you for thees."

Diana smiled, acknowledging the compliment.

Molina fell silent, thinking. He looked at both women. "You know, *señorita*, it occurs to me that it is most unfortunate that you will be unable to share the pleasure of thees young woman when she returns to her home. It is an experience that you deserve."

"It would be nice, but there are others who will look after Elena, including Isabel."

"Still, it would be good for you to see her again, I am sure. As I have promised you, I will speak to the police in Comayagua in the morning. I have been thinking also that it might be good for me to investigate the situation further. Perhaps a personal visit would be in order."

Diana and Isabel looked at each other.

"If I should make the arrangements for a brief visit to Palmerola, say the day after tomorrow in the morning, would you two ladies care to join me?" The girl might be brought from Comayagua to the air base. Perhaps, *señorita*, this will give the opportunity you deserve to see thees young woman."

Diana couldn't help the broad smile that broke across her face. She clasped Isabel's hands.

"I would certainly be happy to accompany you," the older woman said to Diana.

"Thank you, Colonel Molina," Diana enthused. "That's most generous of you! My flight home is not until the evening."

"Excellent! I still must speak with Lieutenant Colonel Emerson about this. Where is he?"

"Upstairs, changing for his return flight to Palmerola," Isabel replied. "He has an early morning meeting."

"I see. Could you tell him I would like a word?"

"He should be down any minute," Diana said. "I'm to meet him in the foyer. Would you care to join us?"

The three of them went to the entry, and Cleve came down almost immediately. Molina told the American officer of his plan, and Cleve looked at Diana, his sober expression changing instantly to a smile.

"Are you acquainted with the police captain in Comayagua, Colonel Emerson?"

"Yes, Colonel, his name is Lopez."

"Yes, yes, Humberto Lopez-Molina, a distant cousin I am sorry to say. He is a young man of energy, but sometimes he does it to the excess. I have told Señorita Hillyer I will speak with him in the morning. If you would be so kind, Colonel Emerson, to discuss with him tomorrow the debt of thees young lady, I am sure that an agreeable arrangement can be made.

"I would be happy to, Colonel."

"Excellent. Then until the day after tomorrow, Colonel..." Molina clicked his heels, bowed graciously to the ladies, turned and left just as Alberto Esparza arrived.

The two couples cheerfully discussed the success of the evening for a few minutes, then Cleve looked at his watch.

"I'm sorry, but I've got to get going."

Isabel had one of the maids fetch Diana a wrap, then she and Alberto bid Cleve farewell. With the shawl around her shoulders, Diana went with Cleve to the door and they stepped out into the cool night air. They embraced immediately, Cleve kissing her tenderly on the mouth.

"We've been given a reprieve," he whispered into her ear.

She nodded, clinging to him.

"I don't want you out in this cool air for long."

"I'm okay," she replied, looking up at him. "I'll walk you to the car."

They descended the steps, Cleve with his arm around her. "We may not have much time together when you come to Palmerola, so could I ask a favor of you now?"

"Yes. What?"

"When you get back to Washington, could you deliver a little present for Pam Dawson's baby for me?"

"Jack Dawson's wife?"

"Yes."

"I'd be glad to."

They had come to the limousine where the Esparza's chauffeur sat waiting. Cleve pulled a little package from his pocket and handed it to Diana. She clutched her wrap to her neck, the tiny package in her hand, her turquoise eyes on him.

"It's not goodbye, after all," he said simply.

"Not for two more days."

"Do you regret it?"

"No. I want to see Elena free. And knowing you'll be there, I couldn't possibly say no."

Cleve kissed her again, his lips lingering near, reluctant to leave. She opened her eyes when he broke away.

As he opened the car door, his fingers reached back a final time, grazing her cheek.

Through the window of the limousine she saw his eyes, frozen on her, unyielding. Then, in a blur of motion he was swept away.

Diana watched until the taillights had disappeared, then turned and walked slowly toward the house. She wanted so desperately to be with him that she would endure another final day.

THE DRONE of the helicopter engine seemed to change pitch as the large craft eased down onto the helipad at Palmerola Air Base. Diana squeezed Isabel's hand, and the two women exchanged excited looks. It was to be the culmination of her trip, and Diana was eager and pleased . . . and terribly anxious to see Cleve.

Colonel Molina unfastened his seat belt as the engine died, and the long blades of the prop slowly ground to a stop. His aide, a young major in a crisp uniform, stepped to the door as a crewman released the locks on the hatch. When the access ladder was securely in place, the major turned to his commander, addressing him with extreme deference and formality.

"We may descend now, ladies," Molina announced with aplomb. He led them to the door and went down the few steps to the ground. Turning, he helped Isabel and Diana.

A small welcoming party of officers, including the Honduran base commander, approached the craft. They saluted Molina ceremoniously, and he introduced them to Isabel and Diana. The base commander, a Lieutenant Colonel Luis Martinez, looked at Diana with curiosity, probably having heard about her stay on the American compound.

The group turned and began walking toward two staff cars waiting nearby, the breeze rippling the Honduran flags mounted on the fenders. Diana looked around, hoping to see Cleve, but he was nowhere in sight. She wondered if something had gone wrong.

Colonel Molina, Isabel and Diana were ushered into one of the staff cars, the rest of the party climbed into the second and they went in procession across the base. Everything that was said had been in Spanish, so Diana hadn't understood a word, though she had detected no obvious problem. She glanced at Isabel, who sat calmly between her and Molina, but saw no indication that there was anything amiss.

Diana sank back into the seat, wondering if in her anxiety to see Cleve she was imagining problems. Almost as though he were reading her thoughts, Molina leaned forward and addressed her.

"Lieutenant Colonel Emerson was unable to greet us because he is in Comayagua getting thees young woman, *señorita*. I am informed that he is expected to return very soon. We will go first to Lieutenant Colonel Martinez's house, where you ladies will be comfortable, while I have discussions with my officers about thees recent problems and thees mistakes that they make in Comayagua."

Colonel Martinez's villa was a comfortable but inauspicious dwelling. Diana and Isabel were taken inside, introduced to the base commander's wife and offered tea. Molina begged his leave to attend to his duties, and the women were left to wait.

Señora Martinez was a correct woman in her early forties, not nearly so refined as Isabel, though most hospitable. She spoke no English, which relieved Diana from the burden of socializing.

Sitting quietly while the other women chatted, Diana felt a great sense of frustration. She had made the triumphal return to Palmerola, only to have to sit drinking tea, unable to see either Cleve or Elena. It was nobody's fault really, she just had to be patient.

Isabel tried bringing Diana into the conversation, but she soon realized that her friend preferred to be alone with her thoughts.

Diana's mind turned to Cleve, and his involvement in this business that he had at first so adamantly tried to avoid. She wondered whether the incident might end up being a problem for him. He had been concerned about maintaining good relations with the Honduran authorities, and now here he was, dealing with the armed forces commander himself, trying to resolve the matter. She winced inwardly, hoping that in helping her and Elena, he hadn't messed things up for himself.

After more idle minutes of tea and conversation, an officer came to the villa to announce that Colonel Emerson was at his house with the young woman. Isabel and Diana were invited to join them. When Isabel had translated the message, Diana had all she could do to keep from jumping to her feet.

Moments later, they were in the staff car headed across the base. Near the American compound they saw a large U.S. Air Force transport plane unloading cargo as on the day Diana had secretly watched Cleve with his men. Her heart raced at the sight of the red berets.

As they approached Cleve's villa, Diana saw a jeep sitting in front. Her eyes searched the building anxiously. When the car finally stopped she looked out the window, clutching at the door handle. Then she saw him exiting the house.

Diana quickly climbed from the car. Cleve moved to her and they embraced, his strong arms wonderfully around her, his familiar musk enveloping her.

"Oh, Cleve, it's so good to see you!"

"Diana." He kissed her happily.

Isabel slid out of the car, and the couple turned to her, Cleve's arm still around Diana.

"Ah!" he exclaimed. "My favorite Bay Islander!"

"And the only one you know," Isabel replied, letting him kiss her on the cheek. "How are you, dear? Feeling better for our arrival, I expect."

"Much!" He looked at them both. "Come on in and see Elena."

They went to the house, and Cleve pulled open the door. Diana peered inside. Sitting on the couch with Lupe, her large, doleful eyes full of uncertainty, was the girl. A little smile touched her lips when she saw Diana. Elena rose to her feet as Diana stepped across the room. Immediately they embraced.

Diana stroked the young woman's head as she would a child, for she seemed hardly more than that. She felt Elena's thin little arms around her and held her tightly, trying, in one loving embrace, to make all that was wrong right, to erase a year of pain.

Elena was crying in her arms.

Diana looked back at Cleve, feeling her own tears running down her cheeks. His eyes, too, were filled, and so were Isabel's. Elena sobbed, her head against Diana's breast. But they were tears of relief. After all the sadness, the world was whole again.

THEY HAD ALL had a cup of tea, and Isabel was sitting on the couch chatting with Elena, telling her about the training institute. Lupe was bustling around the house like a mother hen, seeing that everyone was well taken care of, that all was in order.

"*Señorita*," she said, walking to where Diana and Cleve were standing, "why don't you take our colonel out of the house for a while? Thees es not the place for a man. It es a time for the women."

"Good idea, Lupe," Cleve said with a laugh. Then to Diana, "Let's go for a walk."

They left the villa and wandered off toward the row of trees where they had strolled once before.

"You've been wonderful with Elena," Diana said, taking his arm. "I hope your sacrifice won't create problems for you." She told him about Colonel Martinez's look.

"It's nothing to worry about. It was a minor breach of protocol, perhaps. I should have taken you over to meet them, but no major damage was done, I'm sure."

"What about Captain Lopez? Is he angry with you?"

"Not really. He managed to make himself look like a hero in the end."

"That doesn't surprise me. As I recall, he's rather adept at turning tables. What happened?"

"I got ahold of him yesterday morning and warned him that Molina would be calling about the situation in the cantina. That enabled Lopez to prepare his case, for which he was deeply grateful. Then, when I told him that Elena was being held for a ransom of five thousand dollars, he was duly horrified."

Diana chuckled. "He is rather slimy, isn't he?"

"Well, once the cards were on the table, he became very helpful, just like he was when I went to the jail to bail you out."

"He put pressure on the proprietor, I take it?"

Cleve nodded. "By the time I went to the cantina this morning, the old girl had decided that five hundred was all Elena owed."

"Well, quite an improvement."

"Yes, it was a 'gross misunderstanding.'"

"Who gave her the five hundred dollars?"

"I did."

"That's not your responsibility, Cleve. I'll pay you back."

"No, I won't accept your money. It's my little contribution to the cause. I want to do it, really."

"But it's not right."

He playfully rubbed her cheek with his knuckles. "Consider it a favor. Now you owe *me* a bottle of Spanish sherry."

Diana smiled and put her head on his shoulder, holding on to his arm tightly with both hands. "What do you think will happen to Elena?"

"Initially I'm sure she'll want to go back to the village. I called La Esperanza and left a message for Marta that I'd be bringing Elena back this afternoon. I don't think her prospects there are very good, long-term. Isabel's offer to help her get a start in Tegucigalpa seems her best bet."

"Yes, I was thinking that myself."

"What happened to her is a tragedy," Cleve said, "but, considering how it could have ended, she's lucky."

"Think of the other poor girls in the same situation."

"It's probably better you don't think about that, Diana. You've done enough already. Let Freedom International carry the ball for a while."

Diana grew quiet. "I don't want to bring up a sore subject at a time like this, but there's one thing that has hurt a great deal in this whole business."

"What's that?"

"The fact that the American troops are contributing to the problem. I understand that prostitution won't go away, but when innocent girls are made sex slaves and the soldiers use them—"

"I've already considered that. Yesterday I ordered all the more abusive cantinas off-limits to my troops. This morning Lopez and I discussed it. One of my officers will be working with him to determine which places should be avoided. I can't keep soldiers away from women, but I can keep them from spending money in the worst places, like My Glorious Night."

Diana turned and hugged him. "Cleve, that's wonderful!"

He kissed her hair.

They were standing under a large tree looking across the field. With no aircraft around, it was very quiet. Diana thought of that first day at Uncle Ernie's and the chickens.

"It's so peaceful," she said. "It's hard to accept that we can't just be here together." She glanced up at him, saw his jaw tighten and immediately regretted the comment. "I'm sorry to have come back and put you through this again. I should have just gone home."

"Don't be silly. Every minute with you is precious."

They stood holding each other around the waist. It seemed so natural to be in Cleve's arms. Diana couldn't imagine being without him, and yet they would soon be parted for good.

They heard a vehicle crossing the compound behind them and turned to see the staff car pulling up in front of the villa.

"Looks like they've come for you," Cleve said somberly.

"Yes, I suppose Colonel Molina has finished his meeting."

They began walking back toward the house. By the time they got there, Isabel was outside.

"Why don't you go on back to the helipad," Cleve said to her. "I want to see both of you off, so I'll drive Diana over in a few minutes."

"I'll go inside and say goodbye to Elena and Lupe," Diana added.

She made her farewell to Elena brief, hugging her a final time, acknowledging the girl's gratitude. Then she turned to Lupe. "You've been a wonderful friend," she said, clasping the woman's hands. "And I'll tell you a secret. You were right about Colonel Emerson. He *is* a true *caudillo*, and a wonderful man. You were right about something else, too. I love him." She smiled as bravely as she could. "Unfortunately, love is not always enough."

Lupe's eyes were filling with tears so she embraced Diana, not wanting to cry in front of her. "Write to him anyway, *señorita*. It will bring a little happiness to his life."

Diana nodded, kissed Lupe on the cheek and left the house. Cleve was in the jeep, his red beret tilted rakishly as always, his expression, though, a bit mournful. She remembered that afternoon at the police station in Comayagua when she had stomped out of the jeep, only to return to him. Diana climbed in beside him as she had that day. They exchanged looks. It seemed like a lifetime ago.

She could see the emotion in him, feeling the same things herself. But neither of them spoke. Everything had already been said.

Finally he reached over, took her chin in his hand, lifted her face and kissed her softly on the lips. Diana's heart ached. Ending the moment, Cleve turned away and started the vehicle.

A few minutes later they arrived at the helipad where the others were waiting. Cleve bid the rest of the party farewell but, when they turned toward the helicopter, he pulled Diana aside.

She looked up at him, unable to prevent the tears from welling in her eyes. Knowing the others were able to see them, Diana grasped Cleve's hand and shook it. "Thanks, Colonel Emerson," she said, smiling through her tears. "It's been a hell of a ride."

He smiled back, his own eyes misty. "I'll never forget you."

Diana turned to go, but Cleve wouldn't release her hand. She looked back at him anxiously, tears now running down her cheeks.

"How can I get ahold of you if I ever get to Washington?"

Diana swung her shoulder bag around, opened it, fumbled through the contents for a moment, then pulled out her business card and handed it to him. She looked at him a final time, then ran to the helicopter, where a crewman helped her aboard.

Diana fastened her seat belt and looked out the window. Cleve was still standing on the tarmac where she had left him. The powerful engine of the craft came to life and the prop began to spin, sending its wash across the tarmac, rippling the fabric of Cleve's uniform.

A few moments later the helicopter lifted from the ground. Cleve was still there, his booted feet firmly on the tarmac, his jungle fatigues fluttering in the wind. Diana had a last glimpse of his solemn face as the craft moved upward. His body was straight and motionless. Only his head moved, following the aircraft as it rose swiftly into the sky.

Diana leaned close to the window to keep him in sight. His figure was shrinking rapidly as they ascended. He hadn't moved yet, but as the distance between them widened, he gradually began blending into his surroundings. Soon he was just a speck on the vast intermontane plain, and then he disappeared, completely—expunged from her life as suddenly as he had entered it.

CHAPTER FIFTEEN

DIANA SAT at the back of the hearing room listening to the witness drone on through a long prepared speech. Among the congressmen on the subcommittee only the chairman seemed to be paying much attention, yet it was important that Diana know what those testifying against the bill said. The next day her side would have their say, and they wanted to be prepared.

The issues in contention were pretty straightforward, and they all revolved around money. Rarely anymore did it matter whether the legislative proposal was the right or wrong thing to do, only whether the government could afford it.

Only two of the committee members considered pivotal—Harkham from Connecticut and Barnes from Ohio—were there that morning, and Diana was sure that the arguments being advanced wouldn't bear on their decision one way or the other. The bill's fate would come down to whether the proponents could get the swing votes they needed by logrolling. It was that simple.

The amoral nature of the legislative process had always been one of the things Diana found hardest to deal with in her job. But ever since her return from Honduras three weeks earlier, she had seen Washington through different eyes. The scions of Capitol Hill—all the power brokers around the city for that matter—brought to mind the power elite in Honduras. Their styles differed and their values varied, but there was remarkable similarity in the political process the world over.

Diana had thought about that during the past few weeks, but Honduras mainly brought to mind the man she had left behind on the tarmac at Palmerola Air Base. Cleve Emerson was so firmly entrenched in her consciousness that without him the world seemed a wasteland, devoid of meaning.

Her life in Washington, once so full and significant, seemed strangely vacant. Men who at one time struck her as vital and interesting paled beside her memory of Cleve.

Countless times she had wondered whether leaving him had been the right thing to do. Yet, how could she have stayed? Even as his wife she couldn't have been with him in Honduras. Besides, Cleve had never spoken of marriage. He hadn't even hinted at it.

Except for taking her card, there hadn't been the slightest indication that he had even thought of seeing her again. Diana was sure that it hadn't been due to a lack of feeling for her—she knew Cleve loved her. It was simply that he recognized the futility of hope . . . better perhaps, than she.

That, more than anything, made things difficult. The matter was not even in her hands. Her life in Washington and her career were not all that was standing between them: *his* life and *his* dreams were between them, as well.

Diana looked up at the sound of the committee chairman rapping his gavel. People were climbing to their feet and moving toward the doors. She hadn't even heard enough to realize that the hearings had been recessed for the day.

Glancing at her watch, she was glad the tedium had ended. If the weather wasn't too bad, she would drive out to Chevy Chase and see Pam Dawson. Diana had told her on the phone that she would deliver the present Cleve had given her.

The task had been put off several times for one reason or another. Diana wanted it done, because she said she would do it and because it would close a chapter in her life, once and for all.

She went to a telephone and called her office, telling her secretary she wouldn't be in that afternoon. Several messages were passed on, and Diana asked the young woman to handle a couple of things for her. Feeling everything was in order, she left the House Office Building.

Outside, the snow was falling. Large moist flakes drifted down and coated the frozen ground. There was a sting to the air, and it seemed to cut right through the fur that Diana held tightly against her neck. She looked up and saw the great dome of the Capitol, nearly invisible in the leaden sky.

The snow was undoubtedly the leading edge of the storm that had been predicted. Before the night was through, a foot or more would fall, but at the moment, it was coming down lightly. Could she make it out to Chevy Chase and back?

Fortunately it was several hours before the evening rush would begin, and Diana's condo was fairly far out Connecticut Avenue in Northwest Washington. The drive back to her place from Pam's would be comparatively short and against the traffic. She decided to attempt the trip.

Diana elected to bypass the downtown area, which would probably be congested because of the flurries. She headed up North Capital Avenue to Massachusetts, which she followed to Du Pont Circle. Then she drove out Connecticut, past her building and on out to Chevy Chase.

By the time she reached the Maryland suburb, the snow was coming down pretty heavily and the streets were already thickly coated. Traffic was inching along, and Diana began wondering if she hadn't made a mistake.

Once she got to the Dawson's she couldn't stay long, that was certain. She'd just deliver the present, pass along Cleve's greetings and leave.

The street on which they lived sloped up slightly from the main road, and Diana felt her tires slipping on the slick pavement. She shuddered at the thought of getting stuck and regretted that she hadn't put off the visit. For some reason though, she had been anxious to meet Pam—probably because she represented a connection with Cleve Emerson. She would be the first person Diana had met who had known Cleve for any length of time, and the perspective she might offer intrigued her.

Diana anxiously peered through her windshield at the big houses on the street, checking the numbers against the notation she had made on a slip of paper. Finally she came to the house, a large brick colonial surrounded by barren trees and shrubs, their branches caked with ice.

She didn't attempt to enter the driveway. It seemed her best chance to avoid getting stuck was to leave her car in the street. Diana glanced at her watch. It was just after three.

She walked up the driveway through the fluffy powder, glad for her leather boots. At the walkway Diana stepped onto a narrow path that had been swept free of snow all the way to the front door. She rang the bell, brushing the flakes from her lashes and hair.

While she waited, Diana held the soft collar of her fur against her cheeks and ears, looking forward to the warmth of the house. After several moments, a pert woman with short brown hair answered the door. She had a pleasant smile.

"Pam?"

"You must be Diana," she said, stepping back and beckoning her inside. "I wasn't sure you'd brave the storm."

"I probably shouldn't have, but I've been putting off visiting you long enough." She smiled at Pam Dawson, who appeared to be in her early thirties. The happy, wholesome-looking woman shivered at the cold and pushed the door closed.

"Burrr. I think we're in for a storm." She took Diana's coat and hung it in the hall closet.

Diana glanced at Pam's figure that, though still showing signs of her recent pregnancy, was already fairly trim. She wore a white turtleneck and green wool slacks.

"So, when was the baby born?"

Pam returned from the closet. "December seventeenth."

"Oh, an early Christmas present."

"Yes, just early enough for me to recover for the holidays, but not so long ago that Jack has stopped pampering me." She rolled her eyes. "I was sure all along it'd be Christmas Day."

"Boy or girl?"

"Girl. Hilaire Elizabeth. Seven pounds, eight ounces."

"How nice. Your first?"

"Heavens no. Matthew will be five in May—you'll undoubtedly be meeting him soon. He doesn't nap anymore, so he'll be wanting to join us. My second, Sybil, is two. Hopefully, she'll stay down for a while, otherwise Mommy will be in for a rough evening. And 'Bleeper,' as Sybil calls the baby, will be hungry before long."

"Sounds like you have your hands full, Pam."

"Only a course in time management has saved me."
Diana laughed.

Pam shook her head. "I'm serious. I don't know how mothers without training in business administration do it." She led the way into the living room, where a fire was burning in the fireplace. She gestured for Diana to sit down.

Sinking into a comfortable overstuffed chair, Diana stared at the fire for a moment, memories of Christmas Eve night flickering at the edge of her thoughts.

"Nice on a winter afternoon, isn't it?" Pam said.

Diana looked up, collecting herself. "Pardon?"

"The fire. It's nice on a winter afternoon."

"Oh yes, I was just enjoying it."

"I love it, myself. I go through a fortune in firewood every winter, but it's worth every penny. Jack teases me about keeping the home fires burning."

Diana smiled. "Your husband seems like an awfully nice fellow. I met him a couple months ago at an open house at his offices. I went with friends."

"The one just before Thanksgiving?"

"Yes."

"I was there." Pam studied Diana's face. "You know you look familiar, but I don't believe we met, did we?"

"No, I don't think so."

"You'd probably have remembered. I looked like a circus tent at the time." Slowly Pam's eyes rounded. "Wait a minute, Cleve Emerson was there...but you weren't with..." She broke into a wide grin. "You were the one...the girl he saw and wanted to meet!"

"I did see Cleve that evening, but we didn't actually meet."

Pam looked confused. "But what were you doing in Honduras? You said on the phone you'd known Cleve in Central America."

Diana related the story of meeting Cleve Emerson in Comayagua and the time they spent together helping Elena.

When Diana had finished, Pam sank back in her chair. "My God, it must have blown Cleve's mind when you showed up down there. I think he fell in love with you at that party, right under my very nose."

"In love?"

"You should have seen him."

Diana blushed. "I did, actually. I think I noticed him that evening as much as he noticed me."

"It sounds like you finally connected in Honduras, though."

"Yes, we did."

"You must have seemed like manna from heaven to him." She looked at Diana quizzically. "But Cleve let you get away...that surprises me."

"We didn't really have any choice. I wasn't going to stay in Honduras, and he couldn't leave."

"Sounds like you became rather close, though."

Diana knew she had the option to be oblique, but somehow the situation seemed to call for candor. "To put it bluntly, Pam, Cleve and I had a love affair. I miss him very much."

The emotion Diana felt just saying the words was on her face. She turned to gaze into the fire. Pam obviously sensed the depth of her anguish. Her expression was sympathetic.

"It must have been rough leaving him."

Diana nodded.

"You poor thing."

"I'd be better off if I'd never met Cleve, I know, but I've never known a man like him, either." She turned from the fire to look at Pam, a little embarrassed. "Sorry. I didn't come over here to cry on your shoulder about Cleve."

"Oh, don't worry. Jack and I have always been close to him. I probably know him better than any other woman, apart from his ex."

"Yes, I know. Cleve told me how close you all were."

"Did he talk very much about Carolyn?"

"Yes, why?"

"That marriage—the breakup in particular—was a very traumatic experience for Cleve."

"Because he cared for her?"

"No. Because he got his fingers burnt. Cleve's military career was an issue between them, to be sure. But he blew everything out of proportion, jumped to all kinds of silly conclusions."

"Like what?"

"Cleve was convinced that a meaningful relationship and his chosen profession were incompatible. After Carolyn, he avoided anyone who he might come to care for. He didn't want to go through that kind of pain again, and he didn't see any reason why a new relationship should work out differently."

"There's something to be said for that. It's not an easy life."

"That's true, but the problems are not insurmountable."

"Perhaps, but I think your analysis of Cleve is an accurate one. He's convinced that the army and serious relationships don't go together."

"Did he say that to you?"

Diana thought. "You know, we never talked about it at length. It was just assumed. But I'm sure that's how he felt. He told me once that military life was hell on marriages. I took that to mean he had no intention of considering marriage again, certainly not with someone like me."

"I don't mean to pry, but did you two ever discuss getting married?"

"No, but I knew how he felt, and he knew how I felt. It was obvious to both of us it would never work out."

"Sounds like neither of you gave it a chance."

"We both were being realistic and honest."

"Well, if his career is really abhorrent to you, there probably wouldn't be much point in it."

"It's not his career per se that's the problem, it's the life-style. I'm a professional with a career of my own. I've got a home. And I don't intend to be a camp follower."

"Military life needn't be so dreary as all that. Besides, Cleve was just promoted to full colonel, and he could make general in a few years. Senior officials tend to pull better assignments, a lot of them right here in Washington."

"Cleve received a promotion?"

"Yes, Jack heard about it through mutual friends at the Pentagon. When Cleve was here in November he knew it was going to happen—it just wasn't official yet."

"He didn't say a thing to me."

Pam nodded knowingly. "That would be like Cleve. I imagine he gave you a rather selective impression of what his life is like."

"But why?"

"Carolyn. He probably didn't want a rerun, didn't want to talk you into something that wasn't right for you.

If you'd been an army brat—someone who really knew what it was like—he might not have been so negative. Of course that's just speculation on my part, but I'd bet a bunch of dollars on it.''

"It's true I didn't beat around the bush about the importance of my career and my home.''

"You see, he never got any favorable signs.''

"But I was being honest. I think we both were.''

"True, but it also sounds like a case of neither party being willing to take the first step.''

Diana looked at Pam thoughtfully. "You do know Cleve well, don't you?''

"Yes, but the issue is a familiar one, too. Don't forget, I was an army wife for a number of years myself.''

Somewhere in the house a baby cried.

"Oops! Somebody's hungry.'' Pam looked at her watch. "How about some coffee while I feed the baby?''

"I can't stay, Pam. With the snow, I'll never get home if I don't get going soon. Which reminds me, I have to give you the present—'' she reached for her purse "—since that's what I came here for.''

"At least stay for a cup of coffee. You'll need it if you're going to brave the storm.''

There was a more plaintive cry from the baby.

"I'll get Hilaire and your coffee,'' Pam said, rising. "Or would you prefer tea?''

"Actually, a cup of tea would be nice.''

"Black?''

"Yes, please.''

"Coming right up.''

"Can I help?'' Diana called after her.

"No thanks.''

While Pam was gone Diana watched the snow falling outside. It was coming down heavily now, and the wind had picked up, making the flakes swirl past the window. She worried about the drive home, but was glad to be inside and near the warmth of the fire.

Diana was enjoying her visit with Pam Dawson—though her comments about Cleve were a little unsettling, raising doubts about things she thought she understood. Pam seemed to be promoting the match, but heaven only knew what there was to promote at this stage. It was reminiscent of Lupe and her constant machinations to get them together. Everybody seemed to have the same thing in mind, but then *they* wouldn't have to live with the problems afterward.

Pam returned shortly with the baby and a cup of tea.

Diana rose and took the cup from her. "Look who's here," she said, peering into the receiving blanket. "Isn't she pretty!"

The baby grasped Diana's finger, momentarily distracted by the strange face hovering over her. Then she twisted her little mouth and began to cry.

"She's hungry," Pam said. "Come on, Hilaire, let's go see if your bottle's warm."

Diana sat down with her tea and listened to the sounds in the kitchen. A child's voice had joined Pam's and the baby's. Then a small boy with blond curly hair appeared in the doorway. He was wearing one shoe, and his shirttail was hanging out. He looked at Diana with curiosity for a moment, then retreated into the kitchen.

An instant later Pam appeared with the baby in her arms, the boy following behind. "Diana, this is Matthew, Hilaire's big brother."

"Hi, Matthew."

"Can you say hello to Miss Hillyer, Matthew?"

"Hello," the boy mumbled shyly.

"Have you been sleeping?" Diana asked.

He shook his head, his finger at the corner of his mouth.

Pam was seated, feeding the baby. "Did you see the snow outside?" she asked her son. "Maybe this weekend you and Daddy can make a snowman."

He beamed, then wandered toward the window.

The baby was sucking happily on her bottle. Pam smiled at Diana.

"Aren't you having anything to drink?" Diana asked.

"Oh! I poured myself a cup of coffee and left it in the kitchen." She started to get up.

"Let me get it for you." Diana rose and handed Cleve's gift to Pam. She went into the kitchen and returned with the coffee, which she set on the table.

Pam was looking at the neatly wrapped little package. "Cleve is really very sentimental," she said reflectively. "He's sent me something when each child was born. I think he's a frustrated father at heart."

Diana remembered how protective he'd been of *her* in Honduras. He was very tenderhearted.

"Have you heard from Cleve?" Pam asked.

"No."

"Have *you* written to *him*?"

"No."

"Sounds like a catatonic love affair to me."

"I think it's over. That's all."

Pam was wiping the corners of the baby's mouth with a cloth. "I think you ought to write."

"But why?"

"Just to tell him how you feel—assuming you still care for him, of course."

"I feel the same about him as when we were together. And I still don't see any point in it." She picked up her tea and took a sip.

"Maybe you can leave that part of it to Cleve. I would imagine knowing your feelings would make a great deal of difference to him."

"He knows that I love him. I told him that."

"Love's not enough, or at least it's not the issue. Not with the Cleve Emerson I know."

"If that's true, Pam, you'd think he would have said something about it—raised the issue, anyway."

"He might have been afraid of talking you into something."

Diana sipped her tea again, thinking.

Matthew wandered back from the window and leaned on the arm of his mother's chair.

"Would you like to help Mommy, Matthew? See this little package? Uncle Cleve sent it for Hilaire. Would you open it for me, please?"

The boy took the package and began pulling at the cord. After a concerted effort, he managed to unwrap it. "A spoon," he said, pulling it from the box with his stubby little fingers.

Pam took the spoon. "It's silver, Matthew. Isn't it pretty? Hilaire will enjoy eating with it when she's a little older. Do you remember the cup Cleve sent you from Korea?"

The boy shook his head.

"Remember the shiny one you let Sybil use now?"

"Oh." He nodded.

Pam looked up at Diana. "Sibling politics." She smiled. "Being a lobbyist, you'll probably handle yours beautifully." She shifted the baby in her arms. "Politicians and children have a lot in common."

Diana chuckled. "I can certainly agree with that."

Another small voice came from somewhere in the house.

"I believe Sybil's nap is over," Pam said stoically.

Diana's look was sympathetic. "I don't know how you do it."

"Time management."

"I'm sure a guest is the last thing you need now. I think I'd better get going. My car is probably already buried in snow."

"I hope you won't have any trouble."

"Fortunately I don't have far to go. I'm in Northwest Washington, on Connecticut."

"Oh, you are close. You'll have to come out again. Maybe sometime for dinner. The evenings are a little less hectic around here once we get the kids down."

"I'd enjoy that."

"We'll do it for sure the next time Cleve's in town."

Diana felt her heart skip a beat. "Do you expect him?"

"No, nothing specific, but he usually manages to stop in once or twice a year, though he has neglected us the past few times. To tell you the truth, I think Cleve is tired of Jack nagging him about resigning and becoming a partner in the firm."

Diana blinked. "Has Cleve been considering it?"

"To tell you the truth, I don't thing he wants anything to deter him from getting his star, but it has to be gnawing at the back of his mind. He may be avoiding Jack to avoid the temptation."

"He didn't say anything about that to me, either."

"You see! He didn't want to create false hope."

"Maybe he's decided against it."

"Perhaps. I guess the next time he's in town we'll just have to pin him down."

Diana got up, not really having considered the possibility of seeing Cleve again. Pam rose, too, and put the baby on the couch with a pillow next to her.

"When is Cleve's tour of duty in Honduras supposed to end?" Pam asked.

"I don't know exactly. We didn't talk about it. The future meant separation, no matter what. My impression was he'd be there quite a while, though."

"I'm not sure what kind of tour of duty is standard for Central America, but he's already been in Honduras more than a year. Between that and the promotion, I imagine he'll be reassigned before too long."

Diana had known that Cleve would be moving on eventually, but she hadn't considered what the implications might be. Her heart quickened. "Do you suppose he might be in Washington soon?"

"Who knows? Why don't you write to him?"

They had gone to the entry hall, and Pam handed Diana her coat.

The notion of making an overture to Cleve struck Diana as strange, though the suggestion was obvious enough. She had assumed all along that the affair was over, particularly after the yawning silence that had followed her return to Washington. But now, in light of what Pam had said, writing to him made sense. Maybe, if she was to encourage it, she might see Cleve again.

Her mind reeling a bit, Diana said goodbye to Pam and Matthew and promised to pay them a return visit. She stepped out into the blowing snow. Darkness had already begun to fall, and the landscape appeared hazy in the muted light. Three or four inches of snow covered the ground, and her car looked like a free-form ceramic sculpture, nothing but its broad outline visible.

After she had cleared off the windows, Diana got in and started the engine. It took several minutes for the heater to break the chill in the air, and she shivered, rubbing her numb hands together.

She turned her car around and started down the street toward the boulevard, thankful she was now going down the slope and not up. Without chains or snow tires, she was sure she never would have made it up the hill. The traffic on the main arterial was heavy and moving very slowly. Cars were slipping and sliding along. Some were off on the side of the road, either as a result of minor collisions or because they were stalled.

Diana crept along in the slow lane, moving like a turtle compared to those who were better prepared with chains. She passed several tow trucks and hoped desperately that she would make it home. With each passing minute, her doubts deepened.

Finally the traffic stopped on an uphill grade. When it moved again Diana's wheels spun. Before she knew what had happened, the car had slipped over into a drift and she was hopelessly stuck.

Diana put on her emergency blinkers and sighed. Undoubtedly, someone would be along soon to help, but she was definitely in for an annoying ordeal. She looked at the empty seat beside her and wished that she weren't alone.

Diana thought of Cleve Emerson then. Her memories of him were strangely comforting, and she would have given anything to be in his arms. At that moment, more than any other since she had left Honduras, being with him seemed right. She felt she *had* to see him again, to ask some questions and maybe say some things that hadn't been said.

CHAPTER SIXTEEN

OUTSIDE THE PENTAGON the March wind was blowing across the Potomac, but it had lost its bite. The fledgling days of spring had broken the grip of winter, leaves were budding on the trees and Colonel Cleve Emerson had come home.

He sat on the edge of the bare desk and looked around the office. The empty walls left no clues of the previous occupants—other than the nail holes where framed diplomas, citations and pictures undoubtedly had hung.

Cleve glanced through the venetian blinds at the next wing of the building as he waited for one of the white-coated porters to bring his boxes of possessions. The impersonality of the massive facility gave him an empty feeling.

"Good morning, sir. You must be Colonel Emerson."

Cleve turned to the open door to see a bald, heavyset man with a hand truck stacked with boxes. "Yes. And that must be my life savings you've got there."

"Don't know about that, sir, but these boxes got your name and office number on them."

"Let's assume they're mine then, shall we?" He got up and pointed at the desk. "Just stack them on here, would you, please?"

The porter quickly put the boxes on the desk and went to the door. "Hope you have a pleasant tour of duty with us, sir."

"Thank you." Cleve looked at the cartons, which promised to keep him busy for an hour or so. He took a pocketknife from his trousers and cut open the nearest one. Inside were some of his books. He carried the box over to the bookcase against one wall and put it on the floor. Then he returned to the desk and opened the next carton.

Inside he found personal files and items from his desk at Palmerola, including a small bundle of letters he had received during his tour of duty in Honduras. On top of the bundle, under a thick rubber band, was an envelope in Diana Hillyer's hand. He looked at the large yet feminine sweep of the characters for a moment, then slipped the envelope from the bundle.

Seeing her handwriting was a bit like seeing her, if only at a distance. A flutter went through Cleve's stomach as he pictured her face, her smile, the vivid turquoise of her eyes. He opened the envelope and pulled out the letter, which was dated January twenty-seventh. Though every line of it was seared into his brain, he read it again.

Dear Cleve,

I wanted you to know that I did my duty by you and delivered the present you sent for Pam Dawson. She was thrilled by your thoughtfulness and asked me to give you her thanks and love.

Pam is a lovely person, who I enjoyed very much, and I'm sure she will write to you herself, making this letter unnecessary. However, it seemed a chance for me to "talk" with you again, so I couldn't let it pass.

The truth is that Honduras and my memories of you are ever-present in my mind. After I left I hoped that they would be merciful and fade quickly, but my visit with Pam proved to me that I not only wanted to remember you, I wanted to see you again, as well. The sentiment is a traitorous one, I know, considering how final we both considered the parting to be. But it is one I feel compelled to share.

I left without discussing with you your plans for the future because I was convinced that I could never be a part of them. I realize now that was a mistake. Though it may make little or no difference to you, I want you to know that I relish the thought of seeing you again, whenever the opportunity might arise.

If this confession saddens or upsets you, please forgive me, for my intention is only to tell you what my heart contains. I know your life is a demanding one, and the last thing I wish to do is add to your burdens. So don't consider this letter to be a request for action or even a response from you. I simply want to tell you how I feel. Fate, I know, is the final arbiter of what will be, but just in case, I've laid away a bottle of Spanish sherry.

In the end, we'll both do what we must, but if nothing else, remember me and know that I love you.

                                        Diana

Cleve swallowed the lump in his throat that invariably formed when he read the letter. It had arrived on the heels of his glowing success with Operation Chaparral and a conversation he had had with General Holloway in Panama about taking a slot as the G-3, the head of operations, on his staff. The assignment would have been a real feather in Cleve's cap, considering it normally would have gone to a senior bird colonel, not a lieutenant colonel on the current promotion list.

Cleve had agonized for two days after Diana's letter had arrived and finally decided to call his uncle, Paul Emerson, in Washington to see if he could pull some strings to swing an assignment in the Pentagon. The timing was not the best from a career perspective, because he would be one of the most junior full colonels among the hundreds assigned there, but it meant being two miles from Diana instead of two thousand.

Her letter had freed him to do what he wanted most— to be with her—but Cleve couldn't tell her that, not until he knew with certainty where he'd been assigned. His first impulse had been to fire back a letter and tell her of his plans, but he didn't want to create false hope.

He had waited two weeks, then called Paul again, but the decision on his assignment was snarled in red tape, so Cleve had written to Diana, telling her that he loved her and that he would come to see her the first opportunity he had. Knowing the army, Cleve had thought, that might end up being after a couple of years in Germany or Alaska.

It wasn't until the beginning of March that his orders finally came through. Strategic logistics planning for the army chief of staff hardly seemed like an exciting way to pass a couple years, but it meant Washington, and Diana. With his reporting date only a week away, Cleve had decided to wait and tell her of his assignment in person.

After landing at Andrews the previous night, he had agonized over seeing Diana and ended up deciding to go to her office the next afternoon after reporting in at the Pentagon. The prospect left him feeling uneasy, because he wasn't absolutely sure how he'd be received.

After Tegucigalpa and her letter, he couldn't doubt her love. But he still wasn't sure where it all would lead. Only one barrier between them—physical separation—had been removed. Their disparate life-styles still stood in the way.

"Well, Colonel, does the new job feel as good as those birds on your shoulders?"

Cleve turned to the door. It was Paul Emerson with a broad grin across his face.

"Paul, I was going to come by your office and say hello—and thanks." The two men shook hands warmly.

The general dismissed the politeness. "When did you get in?"

"Last night, late. I stayed out at the base. Figured there was no point in calling in the middle of the night."

"Well, bring your things over to the house. Sarah will want you there until you've found a place. She needs to get in a dose of mothering from time to time, you know."

"How is Sarah?"

"Pleased as punch you'll be in Washington for a while. I think you were a fool to turn down Holloway on that job in Panama, but then you were due for a change of climate." He glanced around the office. "I tried to swing something for you a little more glamorous than logistics, but there just weren't any slots open. Fred Peery is a good man to work for, though. He'll give you a chance to shine, and that's what matters."

"I'll give it my best shot."

"I don't worry about your ability, Cleve. It's just that if you're going to get that star, duty like G-3 in Panama looks a hell of a lot better on your record."

Cleve looked at his uncle. "You know, Paul, you've wanted the same things for me that I've always wanted for myself, and I'm grateful for all that you've done, but I owe it to you to be honest."

The general's expression grew sober. "Yes . . ."

"One of the reasons I wanted to be assigned to the Pentagon is that I've been giving some serious thought to getting out."

"Resigning?"

"I'm a ways from any decision, but I intend to talk to Jack Dawson in the coming months. I want to be candid with you about that."

"Leave the army to become a consultant?"

"It's a possibility, but no decision has been made. There are also some personal reasons why I've considered it, but we can talk about that another time."

Paul Emerson looked at his nephew a little sadly. "I've known this could happen. It's always a possibility of course, but it hurts a little anyway."

"Hell, I might stay in till they roll me out of here in a wheelchair—that's possible too, Paul. It'll be a while—months or years, maybe—before I decide."

The general took a deep breath and exhaled. Then he smiled wanly, extending his hand to his nephew. "Thanks, son, for laying it out straight. I admire candor in a man."

"You'll be the first to know."

Paul Emerson nodded and stepped smartly to the door. Then he turned. "There's a three-star cooling his heels in a conference room up the hall. I'd better get going." He winked and left.

LATE THAT AFTERNOON, Cleve got out of a cab on K Street near Farragut Square, paid the driver and turned to look up the glass and steel facade of the office tower behind him. Seeing that the business card in his hand bore the same street number as the building, he went inside.

Cleve managed to maintain a calm visage, but his heart was pounding in his chest. He was terribly anxious to see Diana, but somewhere deep inside there was a spark of uncertainty—a fear of hurting her, of building up her hopes only to dash them, as he had in Honduras.

There was absolutely no way he could have turned down the opportunity to see her, though, even if this sudden appearance at her door was inconsiderate. He wanted to see her face when he told her he would be home for a long time. He wanted to read the reaction in her eyes.

During this whole business she had been brave—braver than he. Her letter had been an act of courage and it had been generous, but Cleve was still torn with doubt about whether it was right of him to walk back into her life.

The elevator stopped. Cleve stepped out and made his way to the suite where Diana's office was located. Inside, the receptionist, a middle-aged woman with dark, curly hair and a melodic voice, looked at him and his uniform inquisitively.

"May I help you, sir?"

"Yes, is Diana Hillyer in?"

"I'm afraid she's tied up in a meeting," the woman purred. "Did you have an appointment?"

"No, I just dropped by. I'm a friend of Diana's . . . Cleo," he said, noticing the woman's name plaque on her desk.

"I believe she'll be busy for quite a while, but you can wait. I'll try to get a message to her, if you like."

Cleve was glancing around the nicely appointed offices. "No, that's all right. I don't want to disturb—"

Just then the doors to a conference room opposite the reception area swung open, and Diana stepped out. Seeing him, she froze. Her mouth dropped.

Cleve's lips curled under his mustache at the sight of her. "Have time for a little Spanish sherry?"

Diana was stunned. Her heart rose to her throat. "Cleve!" She went to him, and his arms enveloped her. She looked up and he kissed her on the cheek. "What are you doing in Washington?"

"I told you I would come and see you as soon as I could."

"Why didn't you let me know?"

"I could get here faster than the mail, so I figured I might as well come."

She was looking at him with amazement. "It's so good to see you!"

Cleve's face was close to hers, his cologne caressed her, and his familiar, evocative scent brought Honduras cascading into her consciousness. His mouth touched her parted lips. She embraced him.

Diana glanced at Cleo, suddenly embarrassed. She had forgotten everyone and everything in her excitement.

"Can you get away soon?" he asked, his hands still at her waist.

Diana glanced at the open door to the conference room where voices could be heard. "I'm in the middle of a meeting—a strategy session with some people from the Hill."

"Shall I come by and pick you up after work?"

"No, I think it would be better to meet at my place. Say about six?"

"Okay."

"Do you know the address?"

"Connecticut Avenue, isn't it?"

"Yes. Let me write the number down."

She turned toward Cleo, who already had a slip of paper and a pencil in her hand and was extending them toward Diana, a wry smile on her lips.

"Your efficiency is remarkable, Cleo," Diana whispered as she bent over the desk, writing. She smiled at the woman and turned to Cleve with the paper.

DIANA MANAGED to get home a little before six. Her mind had been reeling ever since Cleve had walked into her office. It had been nearly three months since she had seen him, there had been just one letter, and boom—he suddenly appears out of nowhere.

He had swept into her office unannounced, took the slip of paper with her address and had swept out just as quickly. There hadn't been time to talk.

She had forgotten entirely about a dinner date she had that evening with Tom. But it would be later, and there would be time for her and Cleve to talk.

Diana paced the room anxiously, wondering what he was doing in Washington. He said he had come to see her as soon as he could, but what did that mean? Was he in town for just a few days? And where was he off to next?"

By the time the bell rang, Diana was a nervous wreck. She opened the door and there he was, tall and handsome in his green winter uniform. The incongruity of it all struck her. She couldn't help staring at him, incredulously.

"Are you going to invite me in?"

Diana blushed. "Sorry, I'm still not believing this." She stepped back. "Come on in."

Cleve slowly walked through the entry hall and into the cozy living room. The carpeting was chocolate brown, and two overstuffed white couches faced each other in front of the fireplace. He was glancing around as though he were on a voyage of discovery. Diana marveled that he was there.

Cleve looked for a moment at the fireplace, making her think about the Esparzas and the night they had decorated the Christmas tree. He turned to face her. Half the room separated them, but their eyes met and held.

"Will you have dinner with me, Diana?"

She sighed. "I'm afraid I have plans. I'm sorry. If I had known..." Her voice trailed off.

Cleve's gaze was unrelenting. They stared at each other for a long time in silence. Her heart was beating so heavily in her chest that she thought surely he could see her shaking. Finally she turned and went to the telephone. Taking off one of the silver earrings he had given her, she picked up the receiver and dialed. As she waited, she fondled the piece of jewelry, thinking.

"Hello, Tom. It's Diana. I'm afraid I have to cancel dinner tonight. Something's come up. I'm sorry.... Could you call me tomorrow? We'll have dinner sometime next week.... That would be fine. Sorry about tonight.... Okay. Goodbye." She turned to Cleve, trying to look casual as she replaced her earring.

He hadn't moved.

She stared at him, wondering if she was seeing the man she had known in Honduras, the man she had loved. "I do have some sherry, but to be honest the bottle's been opened."

"So I heard."

"Tom's just a friend." Diana felt his eyes on her. "Would you prefer a drink?"

"Yes, I think I would."

"Scotch, okay?"

Cleve smiled. "Sure. Why not?"

Diana went to the kitchen, feeling Cleve's presence in the apartment like a time bomb. She had no sooner poured their drinks when he was there, behind her.

She turned around, a glass in each hand. Cleve was inches from her, his closeness overpowering. He smiled slightly, took both drinks from her and set them down on the counter. Then he took her into his arms.

The feel of his lips, the taste of him, his strength, his tenderness, overwhelmed her immediately. She kissed him fiercely, her mind screaming his name.

When the kiss finally ended, Diana pressed her face against his neck, taking in his fine, masculine scent, liking the wall of his chest against her breasts. "I've probably dreamed this a hundred times," she murmured, "and here you are, in my arms."

He kissed her hair. "Diana, I love you so."

She raised her face to his. "How long will we have this time?"

He grinned. "How long do you want me?"

"Weeks, months, years . . . as long as I can have you." She searched his smiling face.

"I reported to the Pentagon this morning. It's a two-year assignment."

"Cleve!" Diana couldn't help shrieking with joy. "Two years! In Washington?"

He nodded, and she threw her arms around him.

"That's fabulous!"

Cleve lifted her chin. "I'm still a soldier, Diana. If something were to happen in the Middle East or Korea, I could be gone in a matter of days."

"But still, two years!" She looked into his soft brown eyes, seeing the question in them.

He was looking beyond Washington, into the future.

"What happens then? Another Honduras?"

"I don't know. Maybe. Or maybe I'll become a consultant with Jack Dawson. It's something I've considered, but I haven't decided. There's that star dangling out there in front of me, too."

Diana put her head against him again, holding him. She listened to the beat of his heart. After a while he again lifted her chin.

"You aren't sorry I came back?"

"No, of course not. I love you. It's just that there's so much all at once."

"I know," he said softly. "I wasn't sure what was going to happen, but I realize now I've been living the past three months for this day."

She kissed his chin. "And so have I."

"You know, after you left I used to lie in bed at night and listen to that empty, hollow world outside my room and wonder why you weren't there, beside me. I used to ask myself over and over...why? Why isn't she here with me where she belongs?"

Cleve touched his lips to hers, the warmth of his breath caressing her. His eyes filled with emotion, and they glistened. "Oh, Diana, I love you so much. So very much. I want you to be my wife."

Diana's heart was in her throat, her breathing at a standstill. Her lips trembled as she kissed him, holding him against her, loving the man in her arms.

"I want you to know," he whispered, "that whatever decisions are made, we'll make them together."

She felt tears of joy forming. "That's all I could ask for, Cleve. I want so much to be your wife."

"But is it enough just to be together? The only thing I'm halfway sure of is that'll we'll have a couple of years here in Washington."

"Yes, it's enough. The important thing is to be with you, and know that whatever we do, whatever we decide, the two of us will work it out."

Cleve picked her up, sweeping her into his arms. "I love you," he whispered.

Diana pressed her face against him as he carried her to the bedroom. Lovingly and gently he undressed her. And then they made love as though they had never parted.

Harlequin
Superromance

COMING NEXT MONTH

#226 CRIMSON RIVERS • Virginia Nielsen
Volcanologist Holly Ingram knows that it is her duty to
warn plantation owner Lorne Bryant when an eruption
is threatening Kapoiki. And she also knows that this
meeting will bring to a climax the rift that has alienated
them for eight long years....

#227 BEYOND FATE • Jackie Weger
Cleo Anderson thinks romance isn't for her—until she
encounters the charismatic Fletcher Fremont Maitland
at a summer camp in Georgia. Slowly love works its
magic, and the fate that first drew them together
becomes the catalyst for a lifetime.

#228 GIVE AND TAKE • Sharon Brondos
Performing a striptease for a group of women is
embarrassing for Kyle Chambers, but he'll "do
anything for charity." And no one is more aware of this
than Charity Miller. But the marriage and children he
wants to give her are more than she is willing to accept.

#229 MEETING PLACE • Bobby Hutchinson
When an arranged marriage brings the exotically
beautiful Yolanda Belan to a new life in the West, she
quickly discovers that exchanging vows is not enough to
win the heart of her husband, Alex Caine. But her
refreshing approach to life and her smoldering
sensuality soon have him behaving like a newlywed
should!

ATTRACTIVE, SPACE SAVING BOOK RACK

Display your most prized novels on this handsome and sturdy book rack. The hand-rubbed walnut finish will blend into your library decor with quiet elegance, providing a practical organizer for your favorite hard-or soft-covered books.

Only $9.95

Approximately 16" x 8" when assembled

Assembles in seconds!

To order, rush your name, address and zip code, along with a check or money order for $10.70 ($9.95 plus 75¢ postage and handling) (New York residents add appropriate sales tax), payable to *Harlequin Reader Service* to:

In the U.S.

Harlequin Reader Service
Book Rack Offer
901 Fuhrmann Blvd.
P.O. Box 1325
Buffalo, NY 14269-1325

Offer not available in Canada.

BKR–

Take 4 books
& a surprise gift
FREE

SPECIAL LIMITED-TIME OFFER

Mail to   **Harlequin Reader Service**®

In the U.S.   In Canada
901 Fuhrmann Blvd.   P.O. Box 609
P.O. Box 1394   Fort Erie, Ontario
Buffalo, N.Y. 14240-1394   L2A 9Z9

YES! Please send me 4 free Harlequin American Romance® novels and my free surprise gift. Then send me 4 brand-new novels as they come off the presses. Bill me at the low price of $2.25 each —a 11% saving off the retail price. There are no shipping, handling or other hidden costs. There is no minimum number of books I must purchase. I can always return a shipment and cancel at any time. Even if I never buy another book from Harlequin, the 4 free novels and the surprise gift are mine to keep forever.

Name _____ (PLEASE PRINT) _____

Address _____ Apt. No. _____

City _____ State/Prov. _____ Zip/Postal Code _____

This offer is limited to one order per household and not valid to present subscribers. Price is subject to change.

DOAR-SUB-1RR

Explore love with Harlequin in the Middle
Ages, the Renaissance, in the Regency, the
Victorian and other eras.

Relive within these books the endless ages of
romance, set against authentic historical
backgrounds. Two new historical love stories
published each month.

HIST-A-1